The Great Deception

The Great Deception

David Belbin

**FREIGHT
BOOKS**

First published 2015

Freight Books
49-53 Virginia Street
Glasgow, G1 1TS
www.freightbooks.co.uk

A CIP catalogue reference for this book is available from the British Library

ISBN 978-1-910449-47-9
eISBN 978-1-910449-48-6

Typeset by Freight in Plantin
Printed and bound by Bell and Bain Ltd, Glasgow

the publisher acknowledges investment from
Creative Scotland toward the publication of this book

For Dave and Gill Murray

After a while you believe the lies you tell
Mahendra Solanki, *The Lies We Tell*

New Year's Eve, 1998

Deborah brushed her hair, refreshed her lipstick and adjusted her basque. Tonight, more than ever, it was crucial that she looked the part.

Outside her flat, a taxi sounded its horn. This was the busiest night of the year and she was costing the driver money. A squirt of *Isse Miyake* and she was good to go. Deborah double-checked that she had the right purse. The one that held several cards showing her fake ID.

"Chantelle Brown" had been created several months earlier and embedded as a receptionist in a drug rehabilitation centre. Originally, Chantelle wore big glasses, an obvious but effective disguise, and dressed badly. When the centre closed down, her bosses, rather than "retiring" Chantelle, gave Deborah a new target: a former employee of the centre, suspected of large scale distribution. That was when she switched to coloured contacts and a push-up bra.

Deborah was twenty-four years old and meant to be an inspector by the time she was thirty. A superintendent at forty, if she stayed lucky and smart. That was why she'd gone in for undercover work: it put her on the fast track. Chantelle was a more street version of her true self, embellished with bits of girls she'd known at school in Leicester. Chantelle had A levels, rather than a degree. Preferred old school disco to House. Liked to smoke a bit of spliff, when the situation required it, but drew the line at anything stronger.

Deborah locked up, got into the car, and gave an address on the far side of Sherwood. The party was in a big house not far from the prison where her target, Nick Cane, had once been incarcerated. That was at the beginning of his eight-year sentence for drug dealing. Since Nick's release, three years early, he had kept his nose clean. If he was doing anything illegal, beyond smoking weed, Deborah had yet to spot it. But Nick had friends who were dodgy, and she needed to get closer to them. Which meant getting very close to Nick.

Normally, Nick wouldn't stand a chance with Deborah. She didn't date white guys, for a start. Also, for somebody his age, 37, with no proper career and a prison record, he was annoyingly sure of himself. He'd had a lot of girlfriends, including one who was now a Labour MP: Sarah Bone. The recent ones, however, were skanks. Nancy Tull, for instance: a teacher turned crack-head who became a prostitute not long after she finished with him.

And yet, Deborah had developed feelings for Nick. He had good hair, a square chin and warm, intelligent eyes. He'd kept in shape and was easy company, in every sense. He treated her like a queen. Deborah enjoyed playing the part of his flirtatious, initially hard to get, but increasingly enamoured young lover. There were times when she forgot that this was all an act.

It was a pity she had to dump him.

'Over here, please.'

This was the home of Nick's brother, Joe, who owned a taxi firm, and his wife Caroline, a school teacher. Deborah paid and got out of the car.

'Chantelle!'

Deborah turned to flash a smile at whoever was greeting her. And froze. There was no reason for this guy to be here tonight, with one hand behind his back. Unless...

The cab was gone. Nobody else on the street. In the party house, somebody turned up the music. Madonna had made it through the wilderness. The surrounding houses were quiet. He took a step towards her.

'I've been waiting for you.'

1

Two months earlier

'The right honourable member for Nottingham West.'

The setting changed over the years. In Sarah's twenties it was an exam hall. When she turned over the paper, the exam was one she hadn't revised for.

Sarah used to be terrified of making speeches. When she stood for the student union presidency, her then boyfriend, Nick, had to coach her. He'd done some acting, so was able to show Sarah how to breathe properly, deepen her voice a little. She learnt to emphasise at least one word in every sentence, and to vary her tone. Now and then she even used a theatrical pause.

Lately, the nightmare always took place in the parliamentary chamber. There, if you paused for a second, you were liable to be heckled. It was hard to make yourself heard over a rowdy house. The first time she stood to speak, Sarah found herself becoming shrill. It took a year to learn that the most effective technique was to lower her voice rather than raise it, wait calmly for quiet, the way a schoolteacher would.

The Commons presented a further problem. It was not acceptable for a backbencher to use notes. In the dream, Sarah was speaking in her first debate since stepping down as a junior minister. The speaker repeated her name. Sarah stood.

And dried. The speech was about an issue of great importance to her. Except Sarah could not remember what that was. It must be a burning issue that spoke to her principles as a socialist, an egalitarian. But what? She looked around. The chamber was nearly full. It surprised Sarah that her fellow MPs were not laughing yet, that she was not being barracked. Maybe they knew why Sarah had been away from the Commons for some time. She was looking after her mother, who had cancer. Felicity Bone was the daughter-in-law of the late Sir Hugh Bone, who had been a minister in two of Prime Minister Harold Wilson's cabinets. That was how Sarah would start the speech, with a reference to her grandfather. In her maiden speech, three years earlier, Sarah had not once referred to Grandad. She wanted to be seen as her own woman. It was time to put that error right.

She opened her mouth.

Still, no words came out. The laughter began. Sarah tried to make herself wake up. But no, she could see the smiling faces, the nudges and smirks. *Not good enough to be a minister,* they mocked. *Now she's lost her bottle altogether.*

Betty Boothroyd called the house to order. Sarah woke, momentarily surprised to find herself not at home in Nottingham, nor in her poky London flat. She was in her childhood bed, on a back road in Chesterfield, the town that her sainted grandfather had represented for twenty years. A single bed that could badly do with a new mattress. Sarah was not due to speak in the house for the foreseeable future, but if she didn't get back in the saddle soon, the nightmare would recur.

Downstairs, half an hour later, Mum sounded like her old self.

'How much longer do you plan to stay?' the invalid asked.

'Can't wait to get rid of me?' Sarah meant to tease but the words came out sounding closer to a whine. Mum had been through two operations in the last two months, and only been allowed home the day before. The doctors at Chesterfield Royal Infirmary weren't sure if they'd been able to blast all of the cancerous cells.

The present situation would be more tolerable if Mum were grateful for the attention. Felicity Bone, like her daughter, was stubbornly independent. She didn't like being looked after. Not by her husband, who had turned out to be bisexual and left when Sarah was a kid. Not by Sarah, who turned out to be a politician, like Mum's late father-in-law. Since Sarah's teens, mother and daughter had been at daggers drawn: stubborn egos clashing.

'Don't pretend you want to be here,' Mum chided, over her doctor-advised bowl of muesli. 'I'm not the real reason you resigned.'

'Most motives are mixed,' Sarah replied. 'But I told them that I stepped down to look after you, and you're not out of the woods yet. So let's hear no more about me going.'

'Don't tell me that if Tony Blair rang today, offering you a job in government, you'd not jump at it.'

'It'd depend on how good the job was. What do you fancy for dinner?'

The phone rang. Mum got to it before Sarah could. Lately, most calls were for Sarah, which annoyed Mum, especially as Sarah had a mobile. Sarah stood by the edge of the telephone table, expecting Mum to pass the handset. She could hear mandarin tones from the other end of the line. But she couldn't make out the man's words, only her mum's.

'I'll pass you… don't you want? … I see… yes, I have heard about that. They're going to say *what*? I don't… that's none of anybody's business, is it?' *Long pause.* 'I see. And there's nothing you can do to stop it? Isn't this a Labour government?' *Pause.* 'Thank you for warning me. I will. In my own time.'

'What was all that about?' Sarah asked, when Mum had hung up.

'I'll explain later,' Mum said, her face suddenly pale. 'I'm feeling very tired. I've been awake since five. Time for forty winks.'

She went upstairs. That was Mum all over, protecting whatever precious bit of gossip she had been given so that she could hold it over Sarah, create maximum suspense. There was no point in asking again. Mum would tell whatever there was to tell when she was good and ready.

The phone lived on a table in the hall, but had a lead long enough for it to be pulled into the small living room, where a conversation could be held in something approaching privacy. Sarah dragged the handset through and balanced it on the arm of the sofa. She pushed the door shut so that she wouldn't disturb Mum's kip, then dialled Eric Turnbull's work number.

'I was hoping I'd hear from you,' Nottinghamshire's chief constable said, in his usual, slightly nasal voice. 'How's the patient?'

'Grumpy as ever. She brings out the grump in me, too. But I've got to be in Nottingham at the weekend. I was hoping you'd take me to lunch.'

'It'd be my pleasure. Or we could make it dinner tonight if you're staying over.'

'Better not. It's the General Committee and I've hardly been seen in the city since September. I need to stay for a drink after.'

'Fair enough. What time tomorrow?'

'I should have finished my surgery by half past one.'

When she put the phone down, Sarah felt bad about turning down the dinner invitation. Eric, who was in his early fifties and separated from his wife, had made his intentions towards Sarah perfectly clear. On more than one occasion. She was attracted to him, even though he was fifteen years older than her and more conventional than most of the men she had dated.

They always found plenty to talk about. Sarah had been in the police force in her early twenties, while Eric's job these days wasn't far removed from that of a politician. Nevertheless, Sarah was taking the relationship slowly. They'd kissed and cuddled but she hadn't let him take things further. These days, however, she was conscious of feeling vulnerable. At the end of a pleasant evening, she might succumb to temptation. Lunch was safer.

Sarah had always preferred the company of men. At work, she used to see Steve Carter most weeks, but now he was Transport Minister, such catch-ups were harder to arrange. There was also the matter of her not being able to tell either Steve or Eric why she had resigned. Only one friend knew the truth behind that: her ex, Nick Cane. He was the man she would most like to unburden herself to. But she hadn't seen him for months, not since he'd moved house and not given her his new address.

2

1999, Nick Cane reckoned, was going to be the year his luck changed. His prison sentence was long behind him and he was in work. Of sorts. At the moment he had two sources of income: working the switch for his brother's taxi firm, and a handful of private tuition students. He lived in a spacious flat by the Arboretum, five minutes' walk from the city centre. And he had a beautiful, bright girlfriend, fourteen years his junior, whom he had been seeing for more than three months.

Chantelle often teased Nick about his age, which was nearer forty than thirty. They only saw each other a couple of times a week. Although she came over all independent, she still lived with her religious parents. He had yet to meet them, and she never spent the night at his. Nick was fine with taking things slowly. Since getting out of prison, he'd had two hurried, intense relationships. Neither had ended well. This time, he wanted to get it right.

Here Chantelle was on a Saturday afternoon. She'd come round for her lunch. They'd eaten well, homemade pea and mint soup, followed by a fruit cake from ASDA. Chantelle was yawning, but wouldn't stay for the siesta he suggested, perhaps for fear of where it might lead.

'Got to be on my way, I'm afraid.'

'What are you doing later, then?' he asked.

'Seeing friends.'

'I'm not invited?' he teased.

'You wouldn't like the crowd I'm talking about. They're church, you know?'

Chantelle wasn't particularly religious, or so she said. What she really meant was that her friends wouldn't approve of Nick.

His colour, age and criminal record would count against him. She didn't need to spell that out.

'It's fine,' Nick assured her. 'I have plans.'

'You seeing that friend of yours you were telling me about?' Chantelle asked. 'What was his name, Andy Saint?'

'The Saint prefers to be called Andrew these days,' Nick told her. 'I only see him when he has business in Nottingham. But he's always inviting me over to his place in Notting Hill. Perhaps you'd like to go with me?'

'Perhaps I would. A weekend in Notting Hill sounds cool.'

Nick's oldest friend was the city's biggest wholesaler of cannabis and cocaine, but Chantelle would never guess that if she met him. Andrew doubled as a high-class property dealer. A former cabinet minister fronted for him; a middle-aged Tory he was evidently screwing. Gill Temperley was a petite, fiftyish blonde. Nick had no idea what she was doing with Andrew. He only knew her from the media, where she often featured as the intelligent, acceptable face of Conservatism.

'Let me walk you into town,' he suggested to Chantelle.

'I was going to call a taxi.'

'It's a glorious afternoon. Won't you let me walk into the city with a beautiful woman on my arm?'

'When you put it like that,' she smiled, and planted a kiss on his lips.

He took her the long way. They walked through the Arboretum, past the aviary, bandstand and war memorial, Saturday the only day when this poor man's park was ever busy. Then they took the quiet route into town, down steep North Sherwood Street. When they reached Lower Parliament Street, the city's main thoroughfare, Nick stopped abruptly. In front of them, on King Street, a couple were leaving a restaurant. The grey haired bloke looked vaguely familiar. The woman, Nick knew very well indeed.

Eric and Sarah had lunch in Sarah's favourite Nottingham

restaurant, *French Living*, an intimate cellar on King Street. Eric ordered the *onglet* of beef, Sarah the pike. Eric, assiduous as ever when it came to topical conversation, brought up the big story that had broken earlier in the day. The former Chilean dictator, General Pinochet, had been arrested in London. A Spanish magistrate was using new international laws to extradite the general for human rights abuses, including torture and mass murder.

'It's a big test for your government's "ethical agenda",' Eric said.

'That's Foreign Office policy. The extradition order comes under the Home Office. In theory, it's nothing to do with ethics, but a judicial matter. Is the extradition order legal, or isn't it? I don't envy my old boss if he has to decide that it isn't. His name will be mud within the party.'

'If the Home Secretary lets Spain take Pinochet, it sets a huge precedent. Anyone suspected of war crimes will be wary of visiting an EC country.'

Sarah smiled. 'That sounds like a good thing, doesn't it?'

'Until you're the ones committing the crimes. You said you were going to make a speech in the Commons. About Pinochet?'

'I doubt we'll be allowed to discuss that. I haven't decided yet. Nothing too controversial, just a paragraph or two to remind my constituents that I exist. But while we're discussing ghosts from the past '

She told Eric about her mother's mysterious phone call.

'And she won't tell you what the call was about?' Eric asked.

'She says I'll find out soon enough because it'll be in the papers.'

'Not helpful.'

'The only thing I can come up with is that it's about my grandad.'

'The cabinet minister?' They had never discussed Hugh Bone before.

'Government papers from the year ending thirty years ago are released on New Year's Day. Which means the papers from 1968 are being prepared at the moment. Around this time of year, civil servants sift through the minutes, checking there's nothing that should remain secret. So I figure that there's something sensitive pertaining to my grandad or my dad.'

'That's a big leap.'

'Not really. The Hawthornden act in '67 decriminalised homosexuality. My dad was bisexual. There may be a connection in the timing. From the way Mum behaved when she got the call, my guess would be that there was some kind of a scandal. It could have been 1968 that Mum found out her husband preferred boys. She never talks about it.'

'Think she'll start now?'

'Only if she doesn't have long to live.' In saying this, Sarah was confessing a fear, but also preserving her cover. The reason she'd given for resigning from the government in the summer was that she needed to look after Felicity. But Mum had never been in mortal danger. Sarah's boss had told her to resign in order to pre-empt the exposure of a messy scandal: an affair she'd had with a married man who had been murdered. The ruse worked. Only a handful of people knew her secret: the Home Secretary, two or three London detectives. And Nick Cane. Not Eric.

The chief constable leant forward and squeezed her hand.

'I know how hard this is for you.'

'Either Mum will tell me or I'll read it in the paper on New Year's Day.'

'Does your mother really find homosexuality so difficult to discuss, in this day and age?'

Sarah shrugged. 'I'm not sure if she's homophobic or just Dad-phobic. We don't have those kind of conversations.'

Eric insisted on paying the bill. 'What are you going to do now?'

He was angling for an invite. Perhaps it was time to take things further. Sarah could get away with giving him a kiss on the narrow spiral stairway that led back up to the street. Or she could ask if he wanted to walk her home, then see how the mood took her. An afternoon in bed with a nice guy or straight home to her disgruntled, invalid mother. Ah, but, what would she be starting?

On the staircase, Sarah did not kiss Eric goodbye. Instead, she said, 'I was thinking...'

They stepped out into sunlight.

'Thinking what?' Eric said.

Before Sarah could reply, she saw them. Nick and a tall, shapely black woman with a tied-back Afro. "Chantelle", who used to be the receptionist at the Power Project, a drugs rehabilitation project that had been closed down four months ago. Nick had worked there too.

'Great to see you!' Nick said, with forced jollity. 'You're looking good. Remember Chantelle?'

'I do.' Sarah knew something about Chantelle that Nick didn't. 'What are you doing these days?' she asked her.

'Still dealing with people in pain. Dental receptionist.'

Sarah smiled. 'This is Eric.'

She didn't explain who Eric was. Chantelle would already know. He was, after all, her ultimate boss. Nick had a look on his face that said: *she can't be going out with him, can she?* He still shook Eric's hand.

'Sorry to rush,' Chantelle told them. 'I've got a bus to catch.'

'Nice to see you,' Nick told Sarah as they hurried on.

'Give me a ring,' Sarah called after him. 'Let me have your new number.'

'Will do,' Nick said.

They joined a bus queue farther down the road. Sarah glared at Eric. 'What is *she* doing with him?'

'Seems fairly obvious,' Eric said.

'You know what I mean.'

'I do, and I won't discuss it on the street.'

'We'd better go back to yours, then,' she said.

Eric flagged down a taxi before Sarah could decide if going to his was a good idea or not. Like her, Eric had a flat in The Park, the city's richest postal zone. The ride there was brief and silent. Eric's third-floor flat was in an anonymous new development near the site of the old General Hospital. It didn't look much lived in. Two framed prints on the wall: an over-familiar Dali, a second-rate Hockney. The only surprise was an upright piano, photos of his children on top of it. The boy was the spit of him.

'I didn't know you played.'

'I don't, much, but it relaxes me. Coffee, or something stronger?'

'Tea, if you've got it.'

While the kettle boiled, Sarah interrogated him.

'Is Chantelle there at your behest?'

'I don't get involved in operational matters.'

'But you've taken an interest in Nick Cane before.'

'Only because you asked me to. I got a driving charge against him dropped. That was the full extent of my involvement.'

'I appreciated your help. Since then, as far as I'm aware, there's no indication that he's gone back into drug dealing or manufacture.'

Nick had done time for growing cannabis on an industrial scale. But he was not, the way Sarah saw it, a real criminal. One of these days, cannabis would be legal and regulated.

Eric put tea bags into mugs, saying nothing.

'So why have an undercover policewoman going out with him?'

'Perhaps they like each other.'

'You mean perhaps he knows? So it'd be OK if, when he calls up with his new number I made a joke out of it. *Hey, Nick, I see you're going out with an undercover Drugs Squad officer, I'll bet you enjoy the irony!*'

'You mustn't do that.'

'You planted that girl in the Power Project in order to catch drug dealers. Nick hasn't dealt since leaving prison.'

Eric began to get testy. 'You were told of her role because you were on the board of the Power Project. Now the project's closed down, so why don't we talk about something more... amenable? You haven't seen Cane in months. You don't even know where he lives.'

Meaning that Eric *did* know.

Nick wouldn't go back to dealing. He'd told Sarah how he got into the trade in the first place. Pure happenstance. He had bought a flat in the Park, not far from here. It turned out to be built above an expanse of caves that had already been used for growing dope. It had felt like fate to him, but the real fate had been the five years he served of an eight year sentence.

Sarah tackled Eric again. 'If you wanted to find out if Nick was dealing, all you had to do was ask me to ask him. He wouldn't lie to me, because we're old friends. More than friends, actually.'

'I had worked out what went on between you and Cane,' Eric said, in measured tones, 'but it was a long time ago. You were both different people. For now, I can only advise you, as I've advised you before: steer clear of him. Sometimes it's best to leave the past behind.'

'That's what my mother thinks, too. You're both wrong.'

Eric poured milk into the mugs while the tea bags were still in. Sarah hated tea made what way. It always tasted wrong.

'Actually, forget the tea. I need to get back to my mum.'

'Let me drive you back to your flat.'

'No. You've had too much to drink. Thanks for lunch. Sorry it had to end on a sour note, but you can't blame me for looking out for a friend.'

Eric saw her to the door, not hiding how pained he felt. 'Is he only a friend? Or do you still carry a torch? Because the way you're acting, it's almost like you're jealous of the officer assigned to the operation.'

Sarah was tempted to slap him. '*Jealous?* It's not him sleeping with her I feel bad about, it's her sleeping with him. As part of her job. Do you know what that makes you?'

'I know nothing about their sex life. I'm not—'

'—in operational charge, I know. But I don't like it. And I don't believe that Nick's gone back to drug dealing. It's not in his character.'

'Characters change.'

'Weak ones do,' Sarah said, sharply. 'Thanks for lunch.'

Because of the intricate security system, he had to see her to the door, but did not attempt a kiss. Sarah tried to collect herself. Eric was only doing his job, she told herself. Undercover officers were a high risk but necessary strategy when investigating some serious crimes. She must not get involved.

'Don't worry,' she said, in a placatory tone, 'I won't tell him. Thanks again for lunch.'

She was back in Chesterfield by four.

'She was pretty friendly, that MP,' Chantelle said, as Nick waited in line with her.

'We go back aways,' Nick said. 'Did you recognise the guy she was with?'

'I didn't,' Chantelle said. 'But I can tell you one thing about him.'

'What?'

She leant over and whispered in his ear. 'He's way too old for her.'

Nick chuckled. 'You don't think they're...'

'You a little jealous? How well do you know your MP?'

'She's not my MP, actually. She's... an old friend.'

This wasn't the time to go into how close a friend. There was something else that Nick wanted to raise. 'Meant to tell you earlier. My brother's having a New Year's Eve party. I'm doing the music. You'll come, right?'

'I expect so. New Year's Eve isn't a big thing in our family. Just don't expect to see me over Christmas itself.'

'Let's do something cool beforehand then. How about a weekend away?'

Chantelle flashed him a big grin. 'I haven't been to London for ages.'

'I'll call Andrew, angle for that invite we talked about.'

The bus arrived and the queue shuffled forward. When Chantelle got to the front, Nick kissed her goodbye, then walked through the Market Square, his head full of Sarah and that old guy he had just seen her with. Was she really going out with him? He shouldn't feel jealous. But he did.

3

1982

Nick and Sarah left the M1 at Junction 29, the Chesterfield exit.

'Has Sir Hugh met any of your boyfriends before?' Nick asked, turning onto the A617. They were in Sarah's ten-year-old Mini. Both of them had passed their test in this car, which had been bought for Sarah by her grandfather.

'He used to have a big party here once a year. The last year, I did take a boy, but Grandad didn't show much interest in him. Neither did the boy, in me, for that matter. The parties stopped after Grandad left parliament.'

That had been three years ago, when the Tories came to power, just before Nick and Sarah met. Today, Nick was determined not to be daunted by Sir Hugh. Dads were meant to be the daunting ones. They didn't like it when some young lout started shagging their innocent daughter. And who could blame them? But Sarah's dad wasn't around, hadn't been for years. She barely mentioned him.

'Next left.'

They turned off the dual carriageway. Nick navigated country lanes on the outskirts of Chesterfield until Sarah told him to slow down and signal.

'Watch out, the entrance is quite narrow.'

Tall stone gateposts framed a long, cobbled driveway.

'Jesus,' Nick said. 'How big is this place?'

'It's hardly Chatsworth,' Sarah said. The drive twisted to the left, past a copse of oaks that turned out to conceal a substantial house, three storeys high, in yellowing York stone. It was grand yet provincial, the sort of pile you might find in the posher parts of Sheffield, where Nick grew up. Three stone steps led to the wide front door. One half of the dark oak door opened to reveal a grey haired man in a tweed sports jacket.

The retired politician was shorter than Nick had expected. Patrician rather than handsome. Square chin, a roman nose and the Bone ears, which were pointed. Since they started going out, Sarah had grown her hair long and thick in order to conceal hers. She kissed the old man.

'Grandad, I'd like you to meet Nick.'

A firm handshake.

'I've heard a lot about you. Boyfriend and campaign manager. I hope you're as talented in the first role as you proved to be in the second.'

'I'm working on it,' Nick said.

He and Sarah had been going out for the best part of a year. They'd met at a Labour party meeting where she had persuaded him not to resign from the party. He, in turn, persuaded her to run for Union president. Somewhere in between those two decisions, they had fallen for each other.

'Come in, come in. I'll show you around. Though I'm afraid half of the house is closed up.'

Sir Hugh's wife had died years ago. The house, he explained, was far too big for him, always had been.

'All the years I spent in parliament, I never got to properly enjoy my home. And I had to share it with Edith's helpers. Now that I'm retired I'm damned if I'm going to move into a bungalow. I can afford to run the place. I have a lot of friends who come and visit. And family, of course.'

There wasn't much family. Sarah's dad was an only child, as was she. After Labour legalised homosexuality, in 1967, Kevin Bone had ceased to be much of a father. Sir Hugh had, Sarah suggested, taken his place.

'No housekeeper these days,' Hugh said, as he filled the kettle. 'But your mother's going to help me cook this evening.'

He made a pot of tea, then, while it brewed, showed Nick around the house. Sarah went upstairs to unpack their shared bag. No question of their being given separate rooms. Nick was shown a massive hall and a dining room big enough to house a banquet, or a disco. Six bedrooms, including the attic that was Sarah's whenever she stayed. Sir Hugh had a cleaner, but there were parts of the house she didn't bother with. In the games room, the linoleum under foot was squeaky and dull.

Over tea, Hugh asked them about their degrees. Nick was waiting for his results. Sarah still had a year of university to go, because, as Union president, she'd been given a year's sabbatical from her degree. Union president was a cushy role. She was given a bigger grant than Nick, for hers was meant to cover a whole year, and a set amount of expenses, which allowed her to run the car.

'What's next?' Hugh asked Nick.

'A post-graduate teacher training course. English and Drama.'

Sir Hugh didn't seem terribly impressed.

'Country always needs teachers. If you're any good, you'll get a job, even in a recession. But you don't plan to teach forever, surely, bright young man like you? Sarah says you're very interested in politics.'

'Interested, yes. But I'm not sure I'd make a good politician. I'd be no good at toeing the party line. And the thought of making those endless, repetitive speeches...'

'Necessary evil. You become used to it. Though some people do come to love the sound of their own voices. That's what you have to watch out for.'

Sarah's mum, Felicity, turned up at six, after she'd finished work in Chesterfield Council's housing department. She was a little smaller than Sarah, with darker, shorter hair. She had a trim figure and intelligent, sceptical eyes. She cooked and Hugh helped serve. The old man didn't eat a lot. He preferred to talk, telling tales on his former parliamentary colleagues. The gossip was good, even if Nick couldn't place several of the politicians he referred to.

On their third bottle of Beaujolais, Nick asked Hugh about some of the scandals of the last twenty years. Profumo and that call girl, what was she called? The MP John Stonehouse, who had faked his own suicide and fled to Australia. The Liberal leader, Jeremy Thorpe, and what really happened when he was accused of attempted murder.

Hugh gave his guests juicy details that hadn't made it into the papers. Not just the famous cases, but several scandals that had yet to become public. The cabinet minister who was regularly photographed leaving brothels blackmailed by a madam who, by a convenient coincidence, met a sticky end. The pretty young Tory MP who slept with her predecessor in order to get his endorsement. On her arrival in the Commons it became apparent that he'd told most of his colleagues that she was easy. But she had turned this gossip to her advantage and was in the process of sleeping her way to the top.

'I forget her married name. Pretty lass.'

Nick wasn't much interested in sexual tittle-tattle. 'Have you read either of the spy books that have been in the papers lately? *Their Trade Is Treachery* one's called, and *The Climate Of Treason*? It's real John Le Carré stuff.'

'Why would I do that?' Hugh's smile had a trace of smugness.

'You already knew about the fourth man?'

'Anthony Blunt? Oh yes. Not when he was first found out, but long before it was made public. The government of the time let him keep his job, so he didn't defect. He ended up giving us an awful lot of intelligence, not just about Burgess and McLean.'

Nick tried to get the details straight in his head. Burgess and McLean were double agents who fled to Moscow when they were about to be exposed. Kim Philby, who warned them, later made his own escape. In 1979, the existence of the rumoured 'fourth man' had been publicly confirmed. Anthony Blunt was surveyor of the Queen's pictures. MI5 had kept his betrayal from everyone but the Queen, who had allowed him to keep his job.

'Stripping him of his knighthood doesn't seem much of a punishment,' Nick commented.

'It isn't. None of his London clubs have revoked his membership. That would have hurt him much more.'

'And the fifth man they've started talking about – do you think Roger Hollis was a spy?'

This was the most sensational claim that had emerged from both of the new books, that the former MI5 chief had been a Soviet spy all of his career. Sir Hugh hesitated.

'Hugh has signed the Official Secrets Act,' Felicity pointed out. 'Don't make him say anything he'll regret.'

'Are you suggesting I can't hold my drink?' Hugh teased Felicity. 'It's possible that Hollis was a spy. But probable? No. I believe Burke Trend is looking into it to see if he can give a definitive answer. So the truth may come out. It's a pity Hollis is long dead and can't defend himself.'

'One last question, then,' Nick said. 'Why did Harold Wilson resign? There were all sorts of rumours.'

'Excuse me a moment.' Sir Hugh hauled himself out of his chair. Felicity gave Nick a sharp glance, as if to say 'don't press him'. The politicians they'd been discussing were just names to Nick, people he read about in the papers, watched on TV, slagged off in the pub. Hard to remember that politicians were flesh and blood, with friends, families and debilitating illnesses. Wilson and his wife had stayed in this house at least once. The former Prime Minister had stepped down abruptly in 1976, just as Nick was starting to get interested in politics. There were all sorts of conspiracy theories about why he resigned so suddenly.

'Do you remember that day you took me to meet the Prime

Minister, Grandad?' Sarah asked, when Sir Hugh returned from the toilet. 'I'll never forget being taken to Number 10.'

'I remember. Harold was in good form that day. He's not in such good form now, I hear. He should have left the Commons when I did.'

'Do you stay in touch with him?' Sarah asked.

'Not as much as I ought to, given all he did for me. He's standing down at the next election, or so I hear. Maybe I'll see him then. There are things I'd like to talk over with him, when he has the time.'

4

1998

In the City Library's café, Nick phoned Andrew. He explained that he wanted him to meet Chantelle.

'You'll like her,' he told Andrew.

'Sounds more promising than the last two you were seeing. You never suggested bringing either of them over for the weekend. That Nancy sounded like a real goer, though. I rather wanted to meet her.'

'She'd have eaten you alive. This one's different. When's good for you?'

'My movements should be clearer later in the week. I'm going to be over your way, then. Why don't we meet for a pint?'

They arranged a time. Perhaps Chantelle would join them. Nick wondered how she and Andrew would get along. Andrew had a gruff charm that allowed him to play the part of the canny, successful businessman with impressive style. Nick would not so much as hint to Chantelle that Andrew's real business was less than legal. No more than he would tell her who the owner of his flat was. Even Sarah didn't know that stuff.

Sarah. When they met on King Street she'd asked for his new number, but Nick didn't have one. Only a mobile that he had already changed once. If she really needed to get in touch, there was always the cab office, though he hadn't mentioned to her that he was working on the switchboard, didn't want her to know that he had come down in the world. Again.

'Hi.' Jerry sat down opposite him. Her hair was cut short in a pageboy style that made her look younger. Her voice was starting to change too. Less Nottingham and more generic middle class.

That came from doing A-levels at college, mixing with a wider group of kids, many of whom were trying for uni. Nick got out his copy of *Othello*.

Jerry was bright. She would do well without these extra lessons. But she didn't have family to support her and she was his landlady. These one-to-ones were part of Nick's rent. Her past was a complicated story that neither of them chose to dwell on. Nick read out one of Iago's speeches, the one that ended.

> *For when my outward action doth demonstrate*
> *The native act and figure of my heart*
> *In compliment extern, 'tis not long after*
> *But I will wear my heart upon my sleeve*
> *For daws to peck at: I am not what I am.*

'What are the implications of that soliloquy?' he asked Jerry.

'He's a lying, using bastard and he's proud of it,' Jerry said. 'The world's full of blokes like that.'

Deborah made her weekly evening call to her liaison officer, Mike Lane. Turned out he already knew about her bumping into the Chief Constable the previous Saturday. Which meant that Eric Turnbull himself had become involved. Shit.

'That was unfortunate,' Mike said, understated as ever.

'It was hardly my fault.'

'Of course not, but it reminded the Chief of your existence. And the need for results.'

'The woman he was with, the MP, she doesn't know about me?'

She noted the momentary hesitation before Mike replied.

'The Chief wouldn't have worked out who you were if he hadn't been with her. She used to be on the board of the Power Project, right?'

'Right. And she used to go out with Nick Cane.'

'You're not suggesting she's...?'

'Dodgy? It's not impossible. She's friendly with Andrew Saint, too.'

Another hesitation, followed by a mumbled: 'Christ.'

'People say the Chief's getting divorced. Is Bone his new girlfriend?'

'That's not your concern. The MP isn't part of this investigation. The point is to find the nexus of the drugs cartels that supply the East Midlands. If you're right and Nick Cane isn't a big player, you need to find someone who is, quickly. Otherwise, you'll be pulled out and back on the bus to Leicester.'

'I need time. I think Nick's pal Andrew Saint is a big supplier. Nick and I are going to stay with him for a weekend. It's the breakthrough we've been...'

'Next weekend?' Mike interrupted.

'I can't press too hard, but very soon. I'm getting closer.'

'And how close are you to Nick Cane?'

Deborah's turn to hesitate. Mike didn't usually ask questions like that. This must come from the Chief. Turnbull wanted to know if Deborah was sleeping with someone who had slept with the woman he was sleeping with. This was a creepy feeling. For the Chief, too, probably.

'I've still got Nick hooked,' she said, carefully. 'I stick within guidelines, which give me operational discretion. Is that clear enough for you?'

'Crystal clear,' Mike said, and she wondered what, if anything, her minder had understood by what she'd just said: hand holding or blow jobs. It didn't matter. Mike was covering himself. The recording of this conversation would prove that he had, at least, asked the question.

'I need your help, Nick.'

Andrew and Nick sat in the dingy bar of the Vernon Arms, on the corner of Waverley Street and Forest Road East, up the hill from Nick's new flat. The city centre, with its multitude of pubs, was just down the hill, but here they could have a back room to themselves and not be overheard.

'You already asked me once. I thought it over and decided against.'

Andrew had offered Nick a lucrative job as his Nottingham number two. Nick had refused, for any number of reasons, the most immediate of which was that he couldn't live with the risk of going back to prison.

'That was me asking as a businessman. This is a different kind of help, and I'm asking as a friend.'

'Asking what?'

'I'm being investigated.' Andrew's bushy eyebrows furrowed.

'Surely it isn't the first time?'

'No. I expect the income tax and the VAT man to come after me every so often, but this is something else. Something new.'

'The police?'

'I don't think so. They've only looked into me seriously once. In '92.'

'Which is why you were out of the country when I was arrested.'

'I had to wait for things to blow over. Since then, I've always paid generously for police intelligence and I've never had any trouble. Until now.'

'Why do you need my help?'

'Whoever's investigating me, they're bound to come to you.'

'And I'll tell them precisely nothing. I've never told anyone about you. Who else have they been asking? Sarah?'

'I don't know. It would be awkward for me to ask her. She ducked out of meeting me for lunch last couple of times I suggested it. Said she spends most of her time in Chesterfield, looking after her mother.'

'That's true,' Nick said. 'But I think she has a new boyfriend, too.'

He described the middle-aged guy he'd seen her with in town.

'That's the only time you've run into her recently?'

'I've not exactly made it easy for her to stay in touch.'

'Do me a favour. Go for a drink with Sarah. Mention my name and see if she says anything.'

'I don't know,' Nick took a gulp of his pint. It was one thing to keep secrets from Sarah, another to set her up. 'What you're asking makes me uncomfortable.'

Andrew leant forward. 'You want to get back with her, don't you? You still pussyfoot around her in case, one day, you see your chance. That's why you turned me down. You thought it would do for your chances with Sarah.'

'That was part of my thinking, yes.' There was also a moral element to Nick's decision. He didn't like preying on people's weaknesses. Selling weed was one thing, but Andrew was about a lot more than weed. There was no point in telling Andrew this. He'd say Nick was being soft.

'I'd like to see Sarah,' Nick said, after a time. 'We're friends. I ought to find out how her mum is. When we meet, you usually get mentioned, so I'll tell her we had this drink and that you're still screwing Gill Temperley – you are, aren't you? – and if she volunteers anything re being questioned about you, obviously I'll pass it on. Will that do?'

'Appreciated.' Andrew got out a packet of panatelas and offered Nick one. He refused, preferring his roll-ups. 'Are you absolutely sure that nobody in Nottingham's been asking questions about me?'

'Only Chantelle, wanting to know if we're on for a visit.'

'You haven't told her any of our business, have you?'

'We don't have business any more, so there's nothing to tell.'

Sarah got to the chamber early. She'd hoped to catch up with Steve Carter before the debate, but he couldn't find time to meet her for a coffee. She remembered how busy she had been for the year she spent as Prisons minister. Now she was reduced to offering her services to support a bread and butter government motion about the New Deal for Jobs. She made sure that the deputy speaker had her down to speak. Then she waited. By the time she was due on, there were fewer than fifty members left in the house.

No need for great oratory on her part. Sarah was there to collect brownie points from the whips, who were being helpful about her frequent enforced absences, and to banish bad dreams. She'd spoken here a hundred times or more. Yet, when she was called, there was always fresh fear. Maybe she needed it to perform.

Today was no different. Worse, in fact. Her stomach tightened. Sarah was short of breath and felt her face begin to flush. Her brain, however, remained calm. Adrenaline would hit the moment she opened her mouth.

'I take pleasure in joining my honourable friend in congratulating the staff of the Employment Service who are working so hard to make the new deal a success. It is crucial to New Labour's mission that we help young and long-term unemployed people find meaningful, sustainable jobs. A radical culture change is being driven through the Employment Service. We appreciate the dedication of its staff and urge employers to work closely with the Employment Service to ensure that there is no repeat of the catastrophic unemployment we had under the Conservative administration in the 1980s. Under Labour, unemployed people will always be treated with dignity and respect.'

There was a 'hear, hear' from someone on her side, and Sarah sat down. She had said just enough, and had nothing else of interest to add. The biggest secret of public speaking, she and Nick had worked out, those seventeen years ago, was knowing when to shut up.

Chantelle arrived early. Her frizzy hair was loose, which made her look younger, more vulnerable. She gave Nick a big kiss, then said, 'must use the loo. I'm coming on.'

He tried to suppress his disappointment. When it came to making love, Chantelle always had a reason for putting him off. It was more than bad timing. She said she wasn't a virgin, but he had yet to find that out for himself. She wasn't comfortable in the bedroom, that much was certain. Chantelle's family were evangelical Christians and a certain prudishness had rubbed off on her. She hid it well in company, but not in bed.

When Chantelle returned, Nick opened a bottle of Sauvignon Blanc. Chantelle liked a drink. Very occasionally she would have a smoke, too.

'I'm so tired of being a receptionist, man. The number of tossers I have to deal with. You wouldn't believe the things people do to try and avoid paying. They pretend they're on benefits. Every day, at least two people try to sneak out while I'm on the phone...'

'There must be other things you could do. You've got A-levels, right?'

'Two Bs and a C.'

'That'd get you onto a lot of university courses.'

'What the hell would I want with a university course? All education does is separate you from people. Don't get me wrong, if you need it for a job, fine. But I'm not looking for a better job.'

'What are you looking for?'

'I'll let you know when I work it out.'

He went to the flat's small kitchen to get the starter.

'Did you go for a drink with that friend of yours, Andrew?' she asked, when he returned with pitta bread and taramasalata.

'Yes. He invited us over for a weekend, if you still fancy it.'

'Great. We don't have to meet his girlfriend, do we? That M.P.? I wouldn't know how to talk to somebody like that.'

'I think Gill Temperley spends the weekends with her husband.'

'What exactly does he do, this Andrew? For a living, I mean.'

Nick told Chantelle what Andrew put on his tax forms.

'Andrew's always bought and sold. He hasn't had a nine to five job since leaving university. Mainly property, but he does a certain amount of currency stuff too. Wherever he sees a big enough margin, he jumps in.'

'Have you ever worked with him?'

'What as?'

'Whatever. It just seems like you've got this wealthy friend who could easily help you out.'

'Sounds like a sure way to fuck up a friendship.' Actually, Andrew had given Nick some money when he came out. There was guilt attached, because of Andrew's being out of the country when Nick was arrested. 'Andrew employs builders to do up houses. He needs solicitors and accountants, not English Literature graduates. Anyway, what's wrong with what I'm doing now?'

Chantelle came over and plonked her big, beautiful bottom on his lap.

'There's nothing wrong, sweetheart. It's just that you're a very talented guy and I want to see you on top of the world, that's all.'

'I'd settle for being on top of you,' Nick told her and she gave a dirty, wicked laugh that held out promise for the future.

Sarah took Mum to Chesterfield Royal Infirmary on Friday morning. The latest test results were not as encouraging as the doctors had hoped. Mum needed a third operation, but there was at least a month's wait. The extra money that the new government was pumping into the NHS had yet to bring tangible results. Angry, Sarah managed to get the consultant on the phone. She asked whether there was any way she could pay for Mum to have the operation more quickly, as a private patient.

'I'm not one of those people who do private work,' the surgeon replied, testily. 'And if I were, this isn't the sort of operation that takes place outside the NHS. No profit in it. I understand your concern, but we'll give your mother a short course of chemo that will prevent the cancer spreading further. That will give the operation a much greater chance of success.'

For Mum, weeks of uncertainty stretched ahead, filled with strange aches, trouble in the toilet and bad sleep. And, perhaps most irritating of all, a daughter who had become a stranger yet insisted on hanging around, trying to get her to talk about stuff. The past, mostly.

Mum was on strong painkillers. When a new batch kicked in, she was at her most mellow, and expansive. Sarah had timed today's chat carefully, making a fresh pot of tea half an hour after Mum had her pills.

'I often wonder why Grandad joined the government so late. In '68, he was chairman of the public committee on national security. Why did he pack that in to become a junior minister?'

'He went into politics to get power. Being a committee chairman gave him prestige, he used to say, but being in government was the thing that really counted.'

'Why did Wilson leave it so long to promote Grandad?'

'You'd have to ask him.'

'That'd be difficult.' The former Prime Minister had died the week before Sarah entered the Commons, three years ago.

'Hugh should have had a job in '64, when Labour was first elected. It hit him hard when he was passed over. He thought about packing it in. But the next election came so quickly. He was definitely going to go in '71, then Wilson promoted him to the cabinet, and called an early election, so he couldn't resign.' She sighed. 'Are you going to tell me the real reason that you resigned, or do I have to keep guessing?'

Sarah found it hard to tell a direct lie to her mother. 'Did you read about that government policy advisor who was stabbed to death?'

'Yes. He was from Nottingham, wasn't he?'

'I was seeing him. He was meant to have left his wife, but he hadn't, so if our relationship came out, there would have been a scandal.'

'Like father, like daughter.'

'I don't remember Dad ever having his love life exposed in public.'

Mum didn't reply to this comment. She had fallen asleep.

Sarah tried to think of something to do. She had never been so on top of her constituency work. Her brief period as a minister had taught her to organise her work life more efficiently. The complete absence of a social life created space, too. It was Friday night. In Nottingham, she would have had invitations. In Chesterfield, it was read a book or watch TV. Sarah didn't feel like doing either. She found herself looking through the memorabilia that Mum kept on the shelves of an old oak display cabinet.

When Grandad died, and the house was sold, Sarah was a trainee police officer, living in temporary digs with no storage space. She'd been too busy to help with house clearance, or to get sentimental about mementos. She's asked Mum to hang on to the family photograph albums and any important papers. The rest of the contents had been sold, given away or destroyed. Her father hadn't come home for the funeral. He'd taken his share of the money though.

There wasn't much of it. Grandad had taken out a second mortgage on the enormous house. Not that Sarah would have wanted to live there. Too big. Sarah's grandmother, Edith, had been severely disabled for the last thirteen years of her life. Grandad bought the place because he wanted to give her the best of everything. Even though the cost crippled him. Sarah loved that house, too. Maybe that was why he kept it on after Gran died, when Sarah was ten.

Mum hadn't kept a lot of Grandad's stuff for herself. Why should she? He wasn't a blood relative. But now that Sarah had become an MP, she wished she'd looked through everything. She would have liked a better record of her political heritage. Mum had a few letters. There were Christmas cards from the Wilsons. Signed by Mary, rather than Harold, as far as Sarah could tell. The cards ran from 1968 onwards. Harold and Mary Wilson, running with their labrador at Grange Farm. Sarah remembered Grandad telling her how the PM liked the area around Chequers – the PM's country residence – so much that, when he was out of office, he bought a farm nearby. Another card showed Harold in a suit, while Mary leant over an armchair, wearing a smile that verged on smugness. Then the couple on the Scilly Isles, looking away from the camera. A later card showed the whole family, all grown up. Harold stood the centre of the group in their Grange Farm retreat. That was Christmas '73, a few months before he returned to office. There were two elections the following year and, in the second one, Labour managed a small, very fragile, overall majority. That made Wilson the only PM this century to win four general elections. Sarah couldn't see Tony Blair topping that.

There were also two cards from the Callaghans, who replaced the Wilsons at number ten. The couple had eschewed personal portraits, going for historic paintings and, oddly, a photo of the state dining room at number ten. Again, it was the wife who signed the cards. Why had Grandad kept these? Sunny Jim didn't give him a job. Or maybe it was Mum who hung onto them. She was, after all, Grandad's secretary during all that time, and, after his retirement, remained his frequent companion. So much so that locals occasionally made lewd jokes about the couple, though not when they thought Sarah could overhear.

What was due to be revealed in the 1968 cabinet papers? It must be embarrassing, or Mum wouldn't be keeping it to herself. She didn't understand why Mum felt a need to protect Grandad, who was long dead. More likely, Sarah decided, that Mum was trying to protect her from a story about her father, Kevin Bone. Of him, Sarah would believe anything.

5

1982

Nick was surprised when Sarah insisted on making breakfast. In Nottingham, she had little time for the kitchen. Nick did most of the cooking. In Derbyshire, she must want to impress her grandad. The smell of frying sausages wafted through into the vast dining room. Nick hoped she wouldn't burn them.

In the Sunday papers there was speculation that Argentina was about to surrender. Shortly after the Argentines had invaded the Falkland Islands, Nick and Sarah had been on demonstrations against a military solution to the conflict. At first, the protestors got plenty of support from the public. Then the government sent a huge naval task force across the Atlantic. Lives were at stake, and the mood changed. Hundreds of men had been killed, on both sides. Nick asked Sarah's grandfather if he had been against the military solution.

'Nobody votes for pacifists,' Sir Hugh said. 'The government sent clear signals that the Falklands were no longer a defence priority. That's why the Argies invaded. They knew how close we came to handing the islands over fourteen years ago.'

'What do you mean?' Nick asked. It was the first he'd heard of this.

'It was discussed in cabinet. We were having back channel talks with the Argentinian government. Harold wanted to give the islands back. There'd be a twenty year transition so that the older generation of islanders could die out. We thought the younger islanders were amenable. George Brown was Foreign Secretary then. He insisted that there be a referendum. We did soundings and it became clear the measure would never pass.

So we backed off.'

'Grandad, can you get Mum?' Sarah called from the kitchen.

Sir Hugh went to the hall and called Felicity down. Sarah's mother sat next to Nick at the long table, her hair wet from the shower. Felicity wore a towelling dressing gown and, when she leant forward to get a slice of toast, Nick got a flash of her right breast. It was as perfectly formed as her daughter's, with a similarly small, light-brown, inverted mushroom of nipple. Perhaps realising what she'd done, or might have done, Felicity adjusted her gown and tightened the belt around her waist. Sarah asked Nick to pass the toast.

'What have you two been talking about?' she asked Nick.

'The bloody invasion.'

'Only good thing this government's done,' Felicity said.

'You're kidding,' Sarah replied.

Felicity started to ask testing questions about why Nick and Sarah opposed the taskforce. Nick tried to join in, but Sarah gave as good as she got, so he and Sir Hugh stayed out of it. There was an odd dynamic between mother and daughter, Nick thought. Almost a rivalry. Felicity had a harder face than Sarah, and wasn't so swift to flaunt her opinions, but Nick was drawn to her. He liked strong, striking women. As did Sir Hugh, who piped up when the conversation moved on to the current Prime Minister.

'She knows how to keep those Tory public schoolboys in line,' Sir Hugh said. 'Secretly, most boys like being bossed about. You know, back in the 60s, when she was a new girl, I was quite taken by Margaret. Not many women to lust after in the Commons in those days. Not so many now, come to think of it. I chatted up the old girl more than once.'

Nick found this hard to take in. 'You had a crack at Margaret Thatcher?'

'I bought her a drink or two. She was a young mum with a very rich husband, but she enjoyed male company. She knew how to lead a man on, without taking it too far, if you know what I mean.'

'God, Grandad, you're an old devil sometimes,' Sarah said.

Felicity maintained a tactful silence, concentrating on the lumpy scrambled eggs. Wasn't Hugh's wife still alive in the 60s, albeit bedridden? It was odd, hearing the old boy admitting that he lusted after Margaret Thatcher. That said, Felicity was only a few years younger than Thatcher, and, if she weren't Sarah's mum, Nick might be interested. He'd never been with an older woman. Which was a thought he would most definitely keep to himself. He changed the subject, asking something that had not occurred to him before.

'Is Sarah's dad Labour?'

'Kevin hasn't got any politics,' Felicity said.

'Not even Gay Rights?' Nick asked. He wasn't sure if it was OK to discuss Kevin's homosexuality.

'Who you have sex with has nothing to do with politics,' Hugh said.

'But Dad was a Labour researcher,' Sarah pointed out.

'That was just a job,' Felicity said. 'One he did badly, like everything else.'

On Monday, Nick slept in. Hugh invited the couple to stay another night but Sarah had a late morning meeting. Her union presidency was nearly over. She was building up a network of contacts that would stand her in good stead when she looked for a job. Nick had a hangover but insisted on driving. Sarah seemed glad to have him to herself.

'Last night, Grandad had a go at me while you snuck out to smoke a joint. Don't think he didn't know what you were up to, by the way. Your pupils were really dilated when you came back. He gave me this funny smile.'

'A go about what?'

'My career. He offered to pull a few strings.'

On a good day, a trade union's research department was what she was aiming for. On her more cynical days, she talked about going into advertising. Today it was television.

'He knows people involved in Channel 4.' The country's fourth TV channel was about to launch. 'It's tempting. I could get a foot in the door as a researcher. Grandad knows people on *Weekend World* too.'

'I thought you'd ruled out journalism.'

'It's a way in. I figure the business side of TV might be interesting.'

'If you're going to sell out and go into business, you might as well go all the way and work in the markets,' Nick told her.

'I don't give a shit about making lots of money,' Sarah said. 'In fact, I've even been thinking about...'

'You can only say that because you come from money,' Nick interrupted. 'The size of that house!'

'It's way too big for him. I don't know why he stays there. He liked you, anyway. Told me I ought to hang onto you. But he thinks you ought to end up in politics, not teaching. What did you make of him?'

'I liked him well enough.' Nick was suspicious of all 60s politicians. As far as he was concerned, it was a given that any Labour politician who had been in government was a sell-out.

'Grandad was trying to impress you,' Sarah said. 'Perhaps he tried a bit too hard. All that gossip. I wouldn't take that stuff about coming on to Thatcher too seriously. He was devoted to my gran, never went near another woman, even though she was in a wheelchair all those years.'

'What about after she died?' Nick asked.

'He was already in his sixties when she died. I think he'd finished with all that.'

'That wasn't the impression he gave at breakfast. What about him and your mum? She was single by then.'

Nick always looked straight ahead when he was driving, so

didn't see the look on Sarah's face, but the noise she made was something like a retch.

'My mum and my grandad! That's... eeuurggh. They were company for each other, certainly, but he's nearly thirty years older than she is.'

'I guess. Has Felicity had other blokes, since the divorce?'

'Probably, but she never tells me. Mum likes to keep things close.'

And so did Sarah, sometimes. Nick decided it was time to change the subject.

'The Gang of Four are playing Rock City on Wednesday. Fancy going?'

'Which ones are they?'

'*At Home He Feels Like A Tourist.* Remember that?'

'Yeah. They're a bit too... angular for me. Can you persuade Andy to go with you?'

'Expect so.'

'You'll have a better time if you go with him.'

'Maybe,' Nick said, 'though he'll probably get me so shit faced that I won't be able to remember a single thing about the gig the next day.'

'You don't have to indulge if you don't want to.'

'Yeah, well,' Nick replied, signalling to turn off at junction 26. 'You're only young once.'

6

1998

'This place is kickin'!" Chantelle said, looking around the vast living room. Since Nick was last here, Andrew had hired an interior designer. His lover's influence, doubtless. There were wooden floors, expensive Indian rugs, Moroccan throws over symmetrically shaped sofas. A mill town scene by LS Lowry looked out of place, with its naïve figures and industrial setting. The painting, an original, portrayed Andrew's hometown. It had cost a pretty penny at auction. Andrew would never say how much.

They sat at a long, smoked-glass dining table. A laptop computer lay open in front of them, its modem lead trailing awkwardly to the wall. The top story on the BBC news site was the Truth and Reconciliation Committee's report in South Africa.

'A pleasure to meet you properly,' Andrew told Chantelle.

'Do you mind if I freshen up? Travelling in London always makes me feel grubby.'

'That's because this city is grubby.' Andrew directed her to their bedroom's en-suite bathroom. Once she'd gone, he offered Nick a cigar.

'Let's stand on the balcony', he suggested. 'We wouldn't want to cover the delicious Chantelle with cigar smoke when she returns.'

The house was large but the garden was small. Patio doors opened onto a raised, covered area warmed by an antique calor gas heater. Huge waste of heat, Nick thought, disappearing into the open air like that, but it took the chill off and Andrew could afford whatever he wanted. Where they were stood, Andrew could see Chantelle coming from twenty yards away. This would give them time to change the topic of conversation when she returned.

'What happened to the last girl you were seeing?' Andrew asked.

'Nancy dumped me for an ex-boyfriend who liked to smoke crack with her. I saw her old boss a couple of months ago, Eve. She used to be my boss, too. Eve was trying to track her down. Seems Nancy stopped showing up for work, got herself sacked. But I didn't know where she'd gone.'

'Crack takes people that way.'

'I'm well rid. It was Chantelle who told me that Nancy was on the pipe. She doesn't miss much.' Nick had promised Eve that he would keep an eye out for Nancy. But, so far, not a dicky-bird. Andrew changed the subject.

'Have you spoken to Sarah?'

'I'm sorry, no. I left a message at her place. When she didn't call me back, I rang her office at the Commons. Her secretary said she was on leave, looking after her mother, wouldn't say more.'

'Have you heard anything at all?'

Nick shook his head. 'You could be getting paranoid. Have there been any developments?'

'A couple of times I thought I was being followed. My solicitor tells me that some of my registration documents have been accessed at Company House. He has a friendly clerk there.'

'What does that mean, *documents accessed*?'

'A tax investigation is the most likely explanation, he says, but I don't agree. I struggle to find taxable income to justify my standard of living, so why would they investigate me – for over-paying?'

'Tax was how they got Al Capone,' Nick said.

'I'm not Al Fucking Capone. If the government taxed what I do then I'd be happy to pay it. In our lifetime, they will. You know that, don't you?'

'Is that what Gill Temperley thinks?'

'Gill's been a naughty girl in her time. She knows I don't tell her everything. It turns her on.'

'I'll bet it does.' Nick puffed on the Cohiba, inhaling just a tiny amount. Good cigars made him feel more alert. 'What plans do you have for us?'

'Theatre, restaurant, galleries, the usual shit you do to impress girls.' Andrew glanced back into the house. 'Chantelle's taking her time.'

'Women like you to wait. Sometimes it's the only power they have.'

'Hark at my feminist friend. She's sharp. I like her. I'll bet she goes like a train. What I don't get is why she works as a dental receptionist, when she could clearly do a lot better.'

'Not everybody wants a career,' Nick said.

'Does that include you?'

Before he could think of a reply, Chantelle returned, wearing a dark knitted top and a long skirt that accentuated her bum. 'Where are you two handsome men taking me tonight?'

'A show, followed by a late supper at Rules,' Andrew said. 'Does that suit, Madam?'

'Sounds like the life I'd like to be accustomed to,' Chantelle said. 'But hurry up and finish those cigars. It's cold out here.'

The hospital had a cancellation. Sarah wasn't sure if this was down to luck, the pressure she'd put on the consultant, or some administrator realising that she was the mother of a local MP. Whatever the reason, Mum's op had been slotted in on Friday afternoon, after a wait of only ten days. Mum was still unconscious from the anaesthetic, so there was no point in Sarah visiting until the next day. All the doctors would tell her was that the operation appeared to have been a success. Sarah drove back to her childhood home. Tempting to return to Nottingham, but she had to be back in the morning and couldn't justify an extra hour spent in the car. Even so, she felt trapped in Chesterfield, where she knew nobody. Her school friends had all fled the town for university. Like her, they had not returned.

Sarah didn't much care for the past. She barely remembered the surnames of the people she'd been at school with twenty years ago. In a supermarket the other day, a woman said 'hello'. They had attended primary school together, the woman insisted. Sarah pretended to remember her, though the name and face meant nothing. Suppose Sarah were to move back here, succeed Tony Benn as MP? She'd run into such people all the time.

The phone rang. The Public Records Office, wanting to speak to her mother.

'She's in hospital,' Sarah explained. 'She's just had a major operation and hasn't regained consciousness yet. I've no idea when she'll be home.'

'I see,' the official said. 'Well, I'm sure your mother has told you about the situation I want to discuss. It does affect you, after all.'

Sarah thought quickly. Which was likely to elicit the most information – the truth or a lie? Lying nearly always worked better.

'The thirty year old matter, yes. But she hasn't been at her most coherent lately, for obvious reasons, so I'm glad you've called.'

'Right. The story is somewhat sensitive.'

'What, exactly, is my grandfather accused of doing?' Sarah asked. Could it be bad enough to affect Sarah, given that she shared his surname?

The official hesitated. 'The issue is more to do with your father. How much has your mother explained?'

'Very little. As I said, she's been very ill, and is recovering from a major operation.'

'I urge you to speak to her as soon as she's able, then perhaps we could meet in Whitehall before a final decision is taken. I'll tell my secretary to give any appointment with you the highest priority in my diary.'

7

Nick was surprised when Andrew took them to the National Theatre, not the West End. Chantelle wasn't a theatre-goer. He feared she'd find the play elitist, or, worse, incomprehensible. He needn't have worried. It was a comedy about Sid James and Barbara Windsor having an affair while making the *Carry On!* films. Chantelle seemed as familiar with these bawdy farces as Nick was. It featured an actress who Nick had always fancied, Gina Bellman, playing Imogen Hassel, star of *Carry On Loving.*

'She was the only good thing in Dennis Potter's *Blackeyes.* I used to watch anything Potter wrote, mind, good or bad. What's he done lately?'

'Died, mate.'

'Oh.' Eighteen months out and Nick could still be stopped short by something he'd missed during the five years he'd spent inside.

'That's the best Friday night I've had in ages, but I'm knackered,' Chantelle announced when they got back. 'Mind if I turn in early?'

It wasn't yet midnight. After they'd said their goodnights, Andrew got out the malt whisky and Nick rolled a spliff.

'Don't normally have the stuff in the house,' Andrew said, when Nick passed the smoke to him. 'You can't be too careful.'

'Still worried about being watched?'

'No more than before. Listen, I don't want to press you about Sarah, but...'

'Tell you what,' Nick interrupted, 'my brother's having this party on New Year's Eve, said I could invite a few people. Sarah will probably be in Nottingham by then, so I'll ring and invite her. Mention you while I'm at it.'

'Wouldn't it be odd, having Chantelle and Sarah in the same place?'

'No,' Nick insisted. 'They know about each other. Life moves on.'

Andrew took a long hit of the joint. 'Do I get an invite to this party?'

'You'd come to Nottingham on New Year's Eve for a party full of ex-footballers and schoolteachers?'

'Depends if I get a better offer.'

On Sunday morning, when Andrew and Nick stumbled downstairs, Chantelle was already up and about. Andrew offered to take them to a cafe for breakfast, but Chantelle insisted on cooking.

'You've got loads of stuff in, be a shame to waste it.'

Andrew, still in his red, silk dressing gown, looked at the frying pan. 'I don't remember buying those big tomatoes.'

'I picked them up when I went to church. Didn't you hear me go out?'

'Ah, no. I was dead to the world. We were so wrecked that I managed to make Nick listen to an entire side of Captain Beefheart's *Trout Mask Replica*,' Andrew boasted. 'Still couldn't persuade him it's a masterpiece.'

Nick had replaced the album with John Martyn after two tracks, but Andrew had been too stoned to notice. He'd had some exquisite, Peruvian hash delivered by courier after Chantelle went to bed. In London, you could get anything, any time, provided you were minted.

'What were you two smoking?' Chantelle asked, with a wicked laugh.

'You'll find out. I'm making Nick take it home with him. He's a corrupting influence, your boyfriend.'

Later, when Chantelle was in the bathroom, Andrew was as good as his word. He gave Nick the lump of hash.

'Can I ask you another favour?' Andrew asked.

'Sure.' Andrew had no need to be subtle about seeking a quid pro quo. They knew each other too well for that.

'There's somebody I've been working with in Nottingham. He's gone off the map. I might need you to track him down before he disappears altogether.'

'Just track him down?'

'And give him a message. Nothing that can land you in trouble.'

They could hear Chantelle returning.

'OK,' Nick said, head still fuzzy from the previous night. 'If it's just a message.'

'I like Andrew,' Deborah told Nick on the train back to Nottingham. 'He's a good laugh.' That morning, she had tried, and failed, to get into their host's PC. It was password protected. He had a laptop, too, but she'd found nothing interesting on it. From a police point of view, she'd had a wasted journey. The only incriminating thing in the house was the dope the two men had smoked.

'I'm glad,' Nick said. 'I think he likes you, too.'

'It's cool to see you with somebody you've known for a long time. The way you are together, it makes you *younger* somehow. He's got a really wicked side though. Bet he led you astray a few times when you were younger.'

'We led *each other* astray,' Nick told her, but didn't offer any details. 'I've invited him to that party I was telling you about. I was thinking of inviting another old friend too, Sarah. Would you be cool with that?'

'The MP? Sure.' She tickled him under the chin, a habit of hers that he seemed to like. 'Long as you weren't thinking of getting back with her.'

'Last thing on my mind.'

8

Despite her secretary's best efforts, Sarah's in-tray was overflowing, but she had to take a break to go to Home Office questions. The new Prisons Minister was making her first appearance. Sarah wanted to see how her successor performed, and show her support. Ally Blythe was one of the 1997 intake. A few months ago, Sarah had found her naively idealistic. Today, however, she made a reasonable fist of her answers, and managed to slip in some praise for Sarah's year-long tenure in the post.

After questions, in the Tea Room, at least a dozen members came over to ask after Sarah's mother. Even Ted Heath, the former Conservative PM, managed a shy word. He had never spoken to her before.

'I met your mother once or twice. Lovely woman. Give her my best.'

'Thanks,' Sarah said, then struggled for something to add. 'You must have known my grandfather. He always spoke well of you.' It was nearly true. Hugh Bone respected Heath's getting the UK to join the EC, but always ridiculed his failed attempt to take on the miners.

'Ah, Hugh. Interesting man. I never quite knew what to make of him. But let's not speak ill of the dead, eh?' Having exhibited his well-known clumsiness, the father of the house waddled off.

Ex-prime ministers were often lonely figures at the Commons. Thatcher was rarely seen these days, although her successor, John Major, seemed cheerful enough whenever Sarah saw him. But then, he had had a wretched time in office, so being out of it was likely to be a relief. Heath, the longest serving MP in the Commons, had long outlasted Harold Wilson, who had been Grandad's boss. Wilson had beaten Heath in three out of four elections, but – according to those who were around in the late 70s and early 80s – he had the saddest parliamentary afterlife of all. Abandoned by his former allies and acolytes, he was usually left to sit alone.

'Seeing him like that made me feel guilty,' Grandad told Sarah once, 'and I joined him when I could. But I stood down at the next election, while he hung around for another four years. Rotten way to go, but politics is a cruel trade. I'd stay out of it if I were you.'

Back then, Sarah had no intention of becoming an MP. Her vocation came later, when Sir Hugh was on his deathbed. She had never discussed the matter with him. Grandad had already given her the lessons she needed to make up her mind. Or so she thought, at the time.

Back in her office, Sarah asked for her latest phone messages.

'There was a personal call from someone called Nick.'

'Nick Cane? Did he say what he wanted?'

'Actually, no, and that's the second time he's called. First was about ten days ago but I didn't put it in your immediate 'to do' list as that one didn't sound urgent either.'

There was a mobile number, Sarah saw. He'd given her his number at last. She was embarrassed by how good this made her feel. Nevertheless, she waited until her secretary had finished for the day before she called.

He answered on the third ring.

'Nick, how are you?'

'I'm very well. But never mind me, how's your mum?'

She told him.

'Remember me to her. The reason I was ringing, I wondered whether you were in Nottingham much, wanted to go for a drink.'

'I'd love to, Nick, but I'm pretty tied up until after Christmas.'

'Best tell you about the other thing, then. There's this party...'

It was a do at his brother's on New Year's Eve. Sarah couldn't remember the last time she'd been to a New Year Eve party.

'I'll come if I can. Are you doing the music?'

'I certainly am.'

'It's years since I last had a good dance. Will anybody I know be there?'

'You've met Chantelle. There's Joe, of course. And Andy might come – Andrew, as we have to call him these days – you come across him lately?'

'No. I owe him lunch. It would be good to catch up with him, too.'

'I don't know if he's bringing his fragrant girlfriend, the Tory MP.'

This meant Gill *was* screwing Andrew, as Sarah had long suspected. 'You know about her, do you?' she said, using her *amused* voice.

'I gather that you introduced them.'

'I never expected anything like that to happen. Gill used to be seen around with tall, young researchers who had floppy blonde hair and public school accents.'

'People's tastes change.'

'Do they?'

There was a knock on her door. Steve Carter came in. She'd forgotten that they'd arranged to grab a quick meal. She interrupted Nick.

'I've got to go, sorry. If I can't make that party, I'll meet you for a drink soon after, I promise.'

She hung up. 'New haircut,' she observed to Steve. 'Very stylish.'

He'd had his hair curled a little. And was it dyed, too?

'Thanks. Cost a bomb. I'm sorry, but I only have time for a quick coffee, not lunch.'

'Better have it in here, then,' Sarah said. 'Or we'll keep getting interrupted. I'll put the kettle on.'

'New bloke on the phone?' Rob asked, as she hunted down clean mugs.

'Old bloke, one I used to sleep with.'

'And might again?'

'Dream on. He's going out with someone ten years younger than me.'

And ten times as dangerous, Sarah thought. If Sarah did go to that party, got a few drinks down her, she'd have to be very careful not to let on that she was aware what Chantelle was and had been in on the deception from the start.

Nick had an hour between a GCSE tutorial and his evening session on the switch, so he phoned Andrew to tell him about Sarah's phone call.

'She might come to the party. I told her you'd probably be there. She didn't make any funny comments, only wanted to know if you were still seeing Gill Temperley. I don't think anyone's been onto her about you.'

'Have you had time to do me that other favour we talked about?'

'Not yet.' The favour Andrew was asking might not risk landing Nick back inside. It was still dubious. Yes, they were mates, so Andrew did Nick a good turn whenever he could. But Andrew's world was full of heavy people. The heavies scared Nick, who knew how to deal with that world. They would terrify Chantelle, and he had no intention of letting her go anywhere near them.

Half an hour after the phone call, Nick cycled to the cab office in Sherwood, freewheeling down steep Mount Hooton Road, where the council were talking about putting in a tram line, then turned right onto wide Gregory Boulevard, alongside the Forest School. He turned onto Premier Road, on the off chance that the person he needed to see would be home.

Premier Road was lined with tall, multi-bedroomed semis

that rose up a steep hill. Some of the houses still belonged to families. Others were broken up into flats or shared student houses. This one's status was less clear. Nick knocked on a heavy door, which was painted black and had a small eye-hole.

'Whatcha want?' A gruff, anonymous voice.

'I'm here with a message for Terence.'

'Who from?'

'Tell him our friend in the south sent me.'

A minute later, the door opened.

'Wait in there.'

To Nick's left was an office, though he'd hesitate to call it that. The room had a desk as well as a couple of chairs. In one corner, a portable TV was propped on top of a small fridge which itself stood on a tea chest. The walls were painted in a murky off-white that was beginning to flake. The room's bay windows were covered in sheets from tabloid newspapers, to give the impression that the place was abandoned, when it was anything but. Nick sat in one of the chairs. To his right was a blind, where no blind should be, for the wall was shared between two houses. Nick resisted the temptation to open it.

A short, heavily-built black guy came in. He looked a bit younger than Nick and spoke with a Jamaican accent.

'You come with a message for me.'

Nick nodded. 'Your mobile stopped working. My friend is concerned.'

Terence nodded his head twice, a terse, military nod. 'I had a... security issue, but it is sorted now. However, I lost some numbers.'

This was not convincing. Nick spoke carefully. 'Is our friend's security compromised? Ought he to be changing the number he contacts you with?'

'I think not.'

Think isn't good enough, Nick thought, but didn't say. 'Perhaps you could give me the new number you want to use for communication with him.'

'Fine. Or I can call him now if you tell me which number to use.'

'It doesn't work that way.'

'Of course.'

Terence wrote down the number. 'When will he be in touch?'

'Very soon, I think. Do you have any other messages for him?'

'No, but let me do something for you. For your trouble.'

Terence stood suddenly and pulled the cord at the side of the blind. The black material whizzed up. Nick half rose from his chair, momentarily threatened. The window that had been concealed by the blind was a metre square and gave off a red glow.

'You know what kind of place this is?'

Nick looked through the window. 'I had an inkling.'

'The two houses are knocked together. There's a door between them on each floor. This window provides extra security and allows privileged guests to choose without being observed. Please, select any of these girls and I'll have her brought to our best room, for as long as you like, at no cost.'

Nick looked into the room. It was the same size as the one he was in, with two large sofas, a wide armchair and a gas fire. Little else, except for the women in their underwear, draped over the furniture.

'The girls can only see a mirror, so take your time, have a good look. Which do you like?'

There were four girls, two white, one Asian, one black. All had good figures, expensive looking hair.

'I don't...'

'These are good girls, the best at what they do. And clean. Men pay a hundred pounds a half hour, but they must still use a condom.'

A woman returned to the room. Nick leant closer to the window.

'Ah, she's your type, I can tell. No surprise. She's our most popular girl. Would you like her? Or would you perhaps like more than one? That could be arranged, too. Here, let the girls do their party trick.'

Terence rapped on the window, a sharp, rhythmical beat. Immediately, all of the girls stood up, whipped off their bras, and approached the window. They posed, topless, in front of him. The one in the middle was unmistakeable now, despite the weight she'd lost and the heavy make-up, which made her look artificial, a parody of her old self. Nick took a deep breath and collected himself before speaking.

'Thanks for the floor show, but I have to go and call our friend. Maybe I'll take you up on your offer another time.'

He unlocked his bike and cycled through Forest Fields, images from the brothel recurring so strongly that he paid no attention to where he was going. Only when he reached quiet Hedley Square did he stop, prop up his bike against the railings of the small playground and turn on his mobile. He was meant to call Andrew as soon as he found something out. Instead he rang Eve, the deputy headmistress who had once been his boss and, for a few months eight years ago, his lover.

'It's Nick,' he said, as soon as she picked up. 'I've found Nancy.'

9

Nick had never met Eve's husband, Geoff. But he knew that Geoff knew that she and Nick were involved when he started seeing Eve. This overlap meant that Nick's visiting her at home might prove awkward. But it was also awkward for Nick to come to Stoneywood School. This redbrick comp, serving a working class catchment area, was where he'd worked for the best part of a decade. The pupils he'd taught were all gone, but teachers from his time were still around. They were unlikely to have forgotten a colleague who had been sent down for eight years. Or what he had been sent down for.

This was a rite of passage, Nick told himself, as he cycled through the car park. I served my sentence. I can look these demons in the eye. Let them look down on me if they want, but would they have had the balls, the initiative, to do what I did? If Nick hadn't been betrayed, he might still have a job here. He used to enjoy teaching, and doing it part-time was a good cover for his main source of income.

This was the first time he'd been in a school since leaving prison. He'd heard that, since the Dunblane massacre, which he'd read about while he was inside, all schools had tightened up their security. True here. Nick didn't recognise the secretary who slid open the glass window of the school office.

'I have an appointment. Nick Cane.'

At the sound of his name, an older woman behind a computer terminal looked up, gave him a good once over. He didn't remember her, but she clearly remembered him, or, at least, knew his name.

'The deputy head will come and collect you,' Nick was told.

He recognised Eve's footsteps before she came into view: brisk yet delicate, even rhythmical, like a composer tapping out the right number of notes to every bar.

It was only a few months since he'd last seen Eve. Then, she was in school holiday casual, trying to track down an errant colleague who she suspected of a drugs meltdown. Today, she was in deputy head mode, wearing a grey, tailored tweed suit, black tights and kitten heels. Her hair was up, and impeccably styled into a bun. She looked older, yet more alluring. Funny how, in Eve, the suggestion of power turned Nick on, whereas when he saw Sarah dressed this way it had the opposite effect.

'You're glowing.' She handed him a tissue. 'You must have cycled. Thanks for coming here. Geoff and I are having... difficulties at the moment. Your showing up at the house wouldn't have helped.'

'It's a little weird,' Nick said. 'I never expected to see the inside of this place again.'

'Things haven't changed much. Do you miss school teaching?'

'There's no point in missing what you can't have.'

'You always were practical. What's the practical thing to do about Nancy? You said she'd deteriorated. Are you absolutely sure it was her?'

'Positive.' Nancy's eyes were large and a little too close together. There was also the small pimple below the nipple on her left breast, which he didn't mention.

'The question is, what can we do for her? Things have gone too far for there to be any chance of her returning to work. Her contract was terminated. The dismissal letter was returned to the city council, addressee's whereabouts unknown. But I want to help her.'

'I don't know if she wants to be rescued,' Nick said.

'Tell me about the place where you found her.'

Nick told her what little he knew, including the rate she went for. 'They make the men wear condoms. They ensure that the girls stay healthy, which is good news – kind of – where Nancy's concerned.'

'Yes, I suppose it is.' Eve was too canny to ask Nick how he had come across the brothel where Nancy was working. She knew him well enough to know that he would never be a client there. At least, he hoped she did.

'I don't know if the old boyfriend, Carl, is still around. I doubt it.'

'Is she living at this… brothel all the time?'

'No idea. There's bound to be a way to get to her. Question is, what to say when you do talk to her?'

'Offer her a way out.'

'She may not want one,' Nick said. 'Crack's a very seductive drug.'

'There are places that help people clean up.'

'There are, but the effective ones are very expensive, and still fail more than half the time.'

'Let me look into it, at least.'

'Sure. And I'll see what I can find out about her movements.'

They arranged to meet for an early evening drink on Tuesday, which was the next night that Nick had off.

'That's when Geoff plays squash. You're sure Chantelle won't mind?'

'We're not in each other's pockets. I mostly see her weekends.'

'I sometimes think two nights a week is enough for any relationship.'

'I'm the wrong person to ask,' Nick said, 'but seems to me, if you're with the wrong person, two nights a week is still too much.'

10

'That's a pretty scuzzy set-up your friend Terence has,' Nick told Andrew on the phone. 'Were you aware he runs a brothel?'

'Drugs and girls are always connected.'

'They weren't for us,' Nick argued.

'We never paid for it, but I got lucky more often than the average short, pudgy guy. Can't have hurt you, either. Think back to the early 90s. Coke was rare as hen's teeth, and you always had some. How many girls slept with you because you had a line for them?'

Hardly any, was the answer. Nick had been seeing Eve at that time and, anyway, Nancy excepted, he'd never been drawn to women who did drugs. Andrew did have a point, however. Until recently, Jerry, Nick's student and landlady, had lived in a hostel for girls in care. Most of the girls there had pimps. First, the guys got them high. Then they became their boyfriends. Once the girls were completely dependent on them, the boyfriends put them on the game. Then the cycle started again, with a new girl.

'This woman I used to see, Nancy. She's working for him.'

'Jesus, you can pick them.'

'I know. Thing is, I feel partly responsible.'

'Because she got into crack while you were going out with her?'

'Back into it. She'd been using before.'

'But you still want her and you hate knowing that she'll let anyone with the money stick his dick where you used to stick yours.'

'I've got no desire to get back with her, but I still feel a bit responsible.'

'You really need to kick that irrational catholic guilt thing. So why are you telling me this?'

'Because I'm going to need to go back to the brothel. I thought you ought to know, seeing as how Terence thinks of me as connected to you.'

'No problem,' Andrew said. 'When you see him, tell him his communication still leaves a lot to be desired.'

'That's just the point, I'll try to avoid seeing him, but if I do, I don't want him thinking that my presence has anything to do with you.'

'So tell him that. What are you going to do with the girl?'

'Try to get her out of the life.'

'Why? What she's doing is a legitimate choice.'

'One driven by addiction.'

'It's not your call. You know more about this stuff than I do, but the way I understand it, the desire to give up has got to come from the user themself.'

He was right, and there was no point in continuing the conversation.

A text had arrived while he and Andrew were speaking. Chantelle, cancelling their date that evening. No explanation, just a brief apology. *Sorry, lover.* Nick wasn't her lover, which saddened him. He liked the person he was when he was with Chantelle. She made him feel younger, more in touch with himself. But there was something else going on: a constant, low level hum of judgement. Nick must be some kind of masochist, because he liked that, too. Chantelle rarely directly criticised him, but it was clear that she didn't think the sun shone out of his behind. She did not automatically take Nick at his own valuation of himself, as a girlfriend normally would. That kept him on his toes.

Chantelle motivated him to get his life back on track. He had to push the relationship onto the next stage. This meant reducing the influence of her family and religious friends. It wouldn't surprise him if she'd like to reduce the influence of his family and friends, too. Which might not be a bad thing.

Most of all, he wanted to get into her knickers. Five years inside had given him his fill of abstinence. They'd waited long enough.

Since Mum's first operation, Sarah rang Chesterfield every day, either from home or, if she was working late, from the Commons. Mum never bothered to ring her. Today's call, therefore, was a surprise.

'A letter for you came here. It looked important, so I opened it.'

'Important, how?' Sarah asked, irritated. She was thirty-six years old. Her mother should not be opening her mail for her.

'It's from the Spanish authorities. Looks like a bill. Or a threatening letter.'

'You'd better send it to me.'

'It seems to have a deadline. The end of this week.'

'Seriously? Let me think… do you know anyone with a fax machine?'

'The stationery shop has one. They charge by the page.'

'OK, I'm going to give you a number.'

When the call was over, Sarah turned to her secretary.

'I need to find somebody who can read Spanish. Any ideas?'

'It's a common language. You must know an MP who speaks it.'

'Not that I can think of. Look up the members of the All Party Parliamentary Group for Spain.'

He got the list on screen. One of the members on it had an office nearby. When the fax had finished printing, Sarah took it to Gill Temperley.

'Hello, stranger. How's your mother?'

'They operated again last Friday. She seems to be recovering well.'

'Glad to hear it. Is this a social visit?'

Sarah held up the fax. 'I'm after a favour. That is, if you can read Spanish.'

'I lived in Madrid for two years before I became an MP. Best two years of my life. Then I came home, found a seat, got married. Do you know, I haven't been back since. What's this about?'

Sarah explained. Gill read the three page document.

'The house has been abandoned,' she translated. 'There are taxes owing and the state's threatening to repossess the place. Is it yours?'

Sarah shrugged. 'In theory, but my dad's boyfriend had the right to live in it for as long as he wanted, and as he's only a few years older than me...'

'Maybe he moved without telling you. Or died. We need to sort you out a lawyer in Spain, get them to stop the repossession.'

'I could be looking at a fortune in fees here,' Sarah said. 'Maybe it would be best to let the state have the place, forget all about it.'

Gill frowned. 'I can't imagine the fees would be substantial compared to the value of a house. Unless it's a wreck...'

'I wouldn't know. It's got three bedrooms. A pool.'

'You own a place like that and you just let it go?'

'I don't think of myself as owning it, I think of it as Sergio's.' Sarah nearly said that she didn't want to be one of those Labour MPs who has three homes, then remembered that Gill and her husband owned at least four places. 'Also, the villa has some bad associations for me.'

'Then sell it, after you've paid your taxes. I've got a friend who works for a law firm in Madrid. Would you like me to call him?'

'That would be great. The only thing is, the deadline...'

'I'll catch him at home.'

Gill looked up the number and rang it. Her Spanish sounded fluent. She read from the document and made a few notes, then thanked her friend.

'He'll get the deadline shifted. You'll have to establish legal ownership and he'll appeal against the back taxes for you. But you'll have to make good the property.'

Sarah swore. 'I haven't the time to go over there and sort that out.'

'I'll bet Andrew would know somebody he could subcontract it to.'

'That's a good idea.' Sarah tended to think of Andrew as a property dealer in the abstract. Yet he must have to pay people to look after and fix up the buildings he bought and sold.

'You're a lifesaver, Gill. Can I buy you lunch as a thank you?'

'Deal. Why don't you join me for a drink now as a down payment? John's in Brussels and I get so fed up of going home to an empty house.'

'Tell me about it.' Sarah looked at her watch. Nearly eight. 'Let's do that. I'll just tell my secretary to go home.'

'He's a nice looking young man,' Gill commented, with a sly smile. 'Very dedicated. I hope you reward him well for his extra efforts.'

'He plays for the other team,' Sarah fibbed, for no good reason, 'which is a good way of avoiding temptation.'

'Pity,' Gill said. 'Giving in to temptation can be so much fun, can't it?'

Deborah didn't like working at the dentist's. It was busier than her old job and the clients were needier. Now and then, she pulled a sickie. But that pissed off the dentist, Mr Copping. It was a small practice, and things tended to go to hell when the hygienist or dental assistant had to cover reception. The other part-time receptionist, Marlene, had kids at home so couldn't come in at short notice.

The reception work was part of her assumed identity, but Nick hadn't once called Deborah at work, or turned up at the practice. It would have been easy to quit the job and string him along, but that was not the way CID did undercover work, and Deborah respected procedure. She also respected that she had to pay all of her dental salary back to the force, minus her expenses, which were minimal. Deborah didn't own a property, so the flat she rented in Chantelle's name was her only home. Now and then she returned to Leicester to see friends, stayed at her mum and dad's. The two cities were less than half an hour apart on the train, but felt like different planets, whose orbits rarely overlapped. Leicester had the biggest proportion of ethnic minority citizens of anywhere in the UK. Mostly Asian. Leicester residents were far more prone to visit Birmingham than their neighbouring city. The same went for people from Nottingham. Not so much local rivalry as mutual disdain.

The practice closed for forty-five minutes at lunch. Deborah headed for Arnold library, where she returned a graphic novel that she'd read at Nick's suggestion. Even her library loans had to be in character. She hadn't minded the story, which had interesting theories about the real nature of Jack the Ripper, and she liked the art a lot. She took out a racy romance she had no intention of reading, but which Chantelle would enjoy, then thought 'fuck it' and borrowed *Beloved* by Toni Morrison, which she'd been meaning to read for years. It wasn't like Nick ever came to her flat, or got to see her library records. Even if he did, she could argue that she'd made a mistake and borrowed the book on the basis of its title.

Deborah was in the queue at the issue desk when somebody tapped her on the shoulder and said, in a voice loud enough for the whole library to hear.

'Debbie! What are you doing in Arnold?'

She spun round, in her hand the library card with 'C. Brown' scrawled across it. She hadn't seen the woman with frizzy red hair for the best part of eight years, but recognised her at once.

'Tracey. Hi. Long story. I didn't know you lived round here.'

'I got transferred to Arnold ASDA. Assistant warehouse manager.'

'That's brilliant. Congratulations.'

Deborah had been at school with Tracey. She'd stayed on to do A-levels, while Tracey left after GCSEs. They hadn't seen each other since, so at least that meant she didn't know...

'I heard you joined the police!' Tracey said.

Shit. Deborah left the queue before someone clocked her, pulling Tracey away from the busy desk. There was a procedure for this situation. She leant forward to create a conversational huddle, then stumbled to get her lies in the right order.

'Hated it,' she told Tracey. 'I only lasted a few months.'

'Oh. Right. What do you do now?'

'I'm looking for work in finance. Got a part time clerking job to tide me over. Due back in a few minutes. But we ought to get together, catch up. Give me your number?'

Tracey had a mobile. Deborah pretended that she didn't and wrote down the number, then gave Tracey a non-existent landline number. Her former friend didn't ask where she was working. When Deborah got back to the dentist's, she checked the records: Tracey wasn't a client, which was something. But from now on, she'd have to stop using the library.

Later, at the flat, Deborah called Mike Lane. She explained what had happened.

'Something like that was inevitable,' he said. 'But no harm done. You'll get your life back after Christmas.'

'I'm so close.'

'Top brass don't see it that way, and you're on their radar since you bumped into the Chief Constable. Do you know how expensive an operation like this is? Your original job was to monitor the Power Project, not Nick Cane. It's been more than three months and you have nothing.'

'Andrew Saint is a major target.'

'I'm sure the Met will be very pleased with whatever you're able to find out about him. But there's no evidence of Saint doing anything illegal in Nottingham, and it's us who pay your wages.'

'Saint spends time here. Nick did some kind of errand for him recently.'

'It's not enough. If we're to keep you in place, you'd need to get closer, much closer.'

'There's this New Year's Eve party. Andrew Saint will be there.'

'I'll ask about that. But prepare a solid story to explain your rapid departure. You might be gone by the end of next week.'

'OK,' Deborah conceded. 'Please tell my mum that, either way, I'll be home for Christmas. Nick knows I won't be around.'

'I'll tell her. And, whatever happens, you've done a good job here. There's no shame in bailing out.'

11

Early evening. Peak period for punters, surely? But this was the second time Nick had cycled round to the house on Premier Road and found nobody home. The only response to his knocks was a window opening across the street.

'They're not there any more, you dirty bogger!'

'Who's not there?' Nick shouted back.

'I know what you're after, but you can piss off. They've been gone since Tuesday. Tell your friends 'n' all. Stop coming round disturbing decent people.'

Nick got back on his bike. No point in asking where the brothel had gone. But there was one person who could easily find out.

Caroline answered the door. It was a Friday night and his sister-in-law looked knackered.

'Come round to scrounge some dinner? You're out of luck. Joe's getting fish and chips.'

'I need a word with him. Though now you come to mention it, I am hungry.'

Caroline picked up the phone and used speed-dial. 'Been served yet? Your brother's here. Get another cod.'

She put the phone back in its cradle. 'How are you?'

'Not bad. Sorry I haven't been round for a couple of weeks.'

'I expect your new girlfriend keeps you busy. When are you going to introduce us to her?'

'She says she'll come to the New Year's Eve party.'

'Not good enough. You never get to talk to people properly at your own parties.'

'We'll do something beforehand, then. But it won't be Sunday dinner. Chantelle's religious, does stuff with her family on Sundays.'

'That's a first. But Saturday and Sunday are the only times I'm up to socialising, and the last time you brought a woman round on a Saturday night, I had a horrible evening.'

'I'm sorry about that.' Nick apologised, not for the first time. That was Nancy. His ex had got herself, Nick and Joe coked up. Caroline, who didn't indulge, felt excluded, and went to bed early. Nick hadn't done coke since. Not that anyone had offered him any.

'Have you looked into that jobshare you were talking about?' he asked. Caroline had been complaining about being overworked since she went back to school full time.

'We've put it off for now,' she said. 'I suppose you'll want tea?'

You always had a mug of tea with fish and chips, to cut through the grease. It was a Northern thing, perhaps a Sheffield thing. The Cane brothers rarely returned to the city where they grew up, but retained ancestral habits.

'Please.'

Caroline put the kettle on and they talked about her family, who were from Lancashire, although she had long ago eradicated whatever accent she used to have. Joe returned with three fish, a huge bag of chips and a large portion of mushy peas. There was little conversation until they were each down to scraggy chips and bits of batter.

'Not working the board tonight?' Joe asked his brother.

'Don't you do the rotas?' Caroline asked.

'Do them, yes. Remember them, no.'

'I'm on tomorrow,' Nick said. 'There was something I needed to ask. Thing is, when I was driving, we used to know where the brothels were.'

Nick expected Joe or Caroline to make a joke, but neither did.

'You can usually work it out, yeah. Some of the Asian drivers moan about taking blokes but, you know, a fare's a fare.'

'There used to be one on Premier Road, in Forest Fields.'

'There did, but it was never going to last. Getting very middle class round there. Social workers and teachers, even more so than round here.'

'It closed down a week or so ago. I need to know where it moved to.'

Now Caroline couldn't resist chipping in. 'Was there a particular girl who knew how to push all your buttons?'

'There's a girl working there who I promised to try and get out. Nancy.'

'Bloody hell,' Joe said.

'I'm sorry I joked about it,' Caroline told him. 'That's awful. She was teaching when she came here. How did she…?'

'Crack,' Nick said, and filled them in on the rest of the story.

'I'll ask around,' Joe said, when he was done. 'If a new place opened as soon as the old one closed down, some of the lads are bound to have spotted it by now. What do you plan to do if you find her?'

'I've got no idea,' Nick said.

12

'Did you track her down yet?' Andrew asked, phoning from Notting Hill.

'No. Don't suppose you've got a new location for Terence?'

'Only a mobile number. We don't meet up at his place of work. I could ask, if you like, pretend I'm interested in sampling the goods.'

'I might need you to do that,' Nick said, reluctantly.

'I've been thinking. If Nancy does want to kick, there's a rehab place I can get her into.'

'In London or Nottingham?'

'In rural Kent, where it's not so easy to score if you lose your resolve. I'll make a call, see if they have spaces.'

'What sort of fees do they charge?'

'Let me worry about that.'

'You're a mate.'

The doorbell rang. Chantelle had come straight from the dentist's and still wore her long, black, surgery slacks. Not for the first time, he thought about offering her a key, wondered if she'd take it.

'You told me you weren't working,' she said, 'so I thought I'd surprise you. Mind if I use the shower?'

'Be my guest.' Perhaps Nick should ask if she wanted to keep some spare clothes here. Was that what he wanted? Or was he hoping that, if he showed more commitment, so would she? Sometimes, things felt great between them. Others, it was like something was off, not quite real. Perhaps this relationship was only an experiment for Chantelle, a walk on the wild side. No strings, no need to dwell on the culture gap or age difference.

He joined her in the shower, which was very nice. Afterwards, they dried each other off and she gave him a blow job. She took her time to make it as nice as possible, asked what he liked, then stroked his balls the way he requested. He went down on her and she got very excited. Yet, when he gestured towards a packet of condoms, she shook her head, whispered 'not yet'. She finished him off with her hand. In bed, snuggled up to him, she said.

'I appreciated you being so... patient. I know I talk a good game, but I've not had a lot of experience with men. It's a big deal for me, what we're doing.'

'I can be very patient,' Nick said. 'I'll wait as long as I have to.'

'Not too long now, maybe.'

She went to the loo and didn't come back. He found her in the living room, stood at the window, looking at the city spread beyond.

'This is a really nice location. It must cost you a bomb.'

'Not as much as you might think.' Nick had spent some of his savings doing the flat up. He now had a decent TV and a compact disc player. He meant to get himself a computer in the sales after Christmas. It was about time he was on the internet, like half the people he knew. The phone rang.

'I've got an address for you,' Joe said.

Nick wrote it down. A street in Hyson Green, on the other side of the main road from the ASDA hypermarket, not far from a Methodist church.

'It's a cul-de-sac,' Joe said. 'Couple of boarded up houses, mainly rental. One of our pick-ups reckons the residents have been told the police are in the owners' pocket. If anyone makes a complaint, they'll know who it is and make sure their life isn't worth living.'

'What was that about?' Chantelle asked, when he was done.

Nick told her, leaving out the bit about how he had come across Nancy because he was chasing a payment for Andrew. He ought to phone Andrew, but that could wait until he'd spoken to Eve, planned what to do next.

'So you spotted this woman, how?' Chantelle didn't miss much. She wasn't accusing him of using a brothel, not exactly. His presence there did need an explanation, so he used the same lame story he'd had ready for Eve.

'I happened to be passing when I saw her go in. I asked around, talked it over with Eve and went back to the place to try and speak to her, but the brothel had moved on.'

'That Eve, she's the one who helped you move in here, isn't she? Was that why she came round to see you then?'

'To see if I knew where Nancy was, yes.'

Chantelle rolled her eyes. 'You sure can pick them, your girlfriends. The one before that went out with a murderer, didn't she?'

It was worse than that, but Nick didn't let on what he knew about Polly. 'We all make mistakes,' he said.

'Why are you so keen to help this, what's she called, Eve? I know she used to be your boss, but... you weren't an item with her, too, were you?'

'Ummm...'

'Bloody hell, you were! How much older than you is she?'

'About the same difference as between me and you.'

Chantelle shook her head and smirked. 'Touché. When was this?'

'Long time ago. Ten years, nearly.'

Chantelle put the kettle on, then got dressed. 'I suppose if I go out with a guy your age he's bound to have history,' she said, her back to him. 'So you're going to go round there. Do you want me to come?'

Nick considered. 'Not sure how to do it. On my bike, in a one-way street, I'll be conspicuous. Even more conspicuous if I'm with you. I was going to call Eve, get her to come over in her car.'

'You and Eve, there's not something still going on, is there?'

'God, no!' Nick over-emphasised the *no*.

'I'm not stupid. She's good for her age. But I warn you, I might not put out, but I don't share.'

'Neither do I, I promise.'

'All right, then, you can call her. Only I'm coming too.'

This proposal was not what Nick had planned, or expected. But he couldn't think of a reason to say no. He phoned Eve. Geoff was out playing squash. She said she'd be right over. Nick felt ill at ease. This was happening too quickly. He needed time to think the situation through.

Twenty minutes later, Eve collected Deborah and Nick from the flat. Eve Shipton was older than Deborah's mum and, in her blue North Face anorak, she looked it. Deborah found it creepy, knowing Nick had slept with her. She knew him well enough to tell when he was being evasive, and this was one of those times. There was something else going on here.

'What's the game plan?' she asked, when they turned onto Radford Road. 'We can hardly park on a cul-de-sac and spy on them. They'll spot what we're up to in no time.'

It was seven in the evening. The streets had been dark for hours. It was clear to Deborah that Nick didn't have a strategy, but she could hardly brief him on police surveillance methods.

'First, we need to establish which house it is,' Eve said. 'After that, we're going to send Nick in. I brought some money.'

She pulled five crisp twenty pound notes from her wallet and handed them to Nick. 'You said a hundred pounds was what she charged?'

'That's what I was told,' Nick said.

Deborah decided that she ought to sound outraged, so put on a huffy voice. 'You're going to pay him to sleep with her!'

'To get in the same room as her,' Eve said. 'Do you know how these things work, Nick? Do you have to pay someone else before you get to go in?'

'No idea,' Nick said. 'In films, you always pay the girl.'

'What if she tells you to fuck off?' Deborah said. 'What if she says, *I like my crack and I don't care what I have to do to get it.* Will you try and kidnap her?'

'All I can do is make it clear that she's got options.'

'What options?'

'I'll give her a couple of numbers. A friend of mine helps fund a rehab place. He said he'd get her a place there.'

Deborah's ears pricked up. 'Do you mean Andrew?'

This could be significant intelligence.

'A friend who prefers to be anonymous,' Nick said.

He did mean Andrew Saint. This was gold. The first official connection between the Saint and the drugs business. Enough to keep her on the case.

13

Eve's Volvo turned onto a short road of dilapidated 1920s semis that culminated in a school playing field. The security fence was as high as a prison's.

Nick wasn't sure what to say if he saw Terence. The guy would assume that Nick was here on Andrew's business. That could be to Nick's advantage, but it was dangerous territory. He would play it by ear.

An unfamiliar guy answered the door. White, tracksuit, thirtyish.

'Yeah?'

'I'm looking for business.'

'Through here.'

Inside, the set-up was similar to that on Premier Road: two halves of a semi knocked together. A curtain in the office, behind which – he presumed – would be the one-way mirrored window.

'Been here before?'

'Only to the old place.'

The guy ran through a list of prices. Full sex, including oral, for half an hour, with any girl, was a hundred quid.

'Tip the girl if you want extras. Anal or unprotected, whether she does them and what she charges, that's up to her. Understood?'

'Understood. I just need to know if the girl I like is here.'

'Which one is it?'

Nick didn't know what name Nancy was going under, though he would bet it wasn't her real one.

'I'm crap with names. Black hair, pointy chin, small bum, really dark nipples. Know the one I mean?'

The guy smiled. 'Miss Pops. You might have to wait a few

minutes.'

'OK.'

'Or you can take a look and see if there's somebody you fancy more. We've got a couple of new ones. Very young. Want me to open the curtain?'

'Can't hurt.' It would look odd if he didn't.

The brickwork around the window frame was unplastered, indicating that the room had been knocked through in a hurry. Only one of the long sofas from Premier Road fitted in the room. There were three girls on it. One was plump and close to Nick's age. The waif next to her was young enough to be her daughter. The third girl was in her twenties. She was heavily made-up to disguise her crack pallor and had straggly hair but a good body, shown off in a see-through negligee.

'That's Rosie,' the guy in the tracksuit said. 'A lot of the guys who like Miss Pops like her too.'

There must be a subspecies of John who liked to screw drugged-up women. Nick wondered what the appeal was.

'I'll wait for Miss Pops, if you don't mind.'

'It's up to you.'

He closed the curtain.

Minutes passed. Nick found himself thinking about the first time he saw Nancy, a nervous student on her first day of teaching practice at the secondary school where – until his arrest – he had taught English. She had too much make-up on and wore a trouser suit that was far too old and conservative for her. Compensating for being just a little older than the teens she was about to teach. She had been enthusiastically grateful for every scrap of help Nick could give, and it soon became apparent that she had a crush on him. A crush that he was honourable enough not to exploit.

Nancy was the only person from his teaching days who wrote to him while he was inside. When they got together, eleven months ago, it seemed inevitable. He'd thought they had a future.

Turned out they were both on a nostalgia trip. The lust was still there, but the person he used to know wasn't. Nancy was harder, more self-centred, and deeper into drugs than he had ever been. He, too, had changed. He was only now beginning to realise how much.

Tracksuit man opened the curtain.

'She's ready for you.'

Nancy sat at the furthest point from the window, as though willing herself not to be chosen. She wore a short leather skirt and a see-through top.

'Money.'

Nick handed over Eve's crisp notes. The guy pressed a button on the intercom and spoke softly into it. 'Miss Pops, room three for thirty.'

The transaction was as mundane as Nick taking a taxi booking.

'Go up the stairs, second left.'

Before the guy could close the curtain, Nick glanced at the room beyond. Nancy stood slowly. She looked beaten, worn down. Even at this distance, he could see how much make-up she wore. She had once been extraordinary, but the young teacher he used to fantasise about in prison was long gone. He dreaded the encounter that was about to take place.

'He's taking his time,' Deborah said.

'Maybe Nancy was already with someone.'

'I guess that must be it,' Deborah replied.

'You can't be worried that he'd...'

'Hardly. I mean, he already has. It was me that told him she was on that stuff. You know, the crack.' She'd spotted Nancy smoking in a scummy after-hours club where she'd been sent on a reconnaissance job. 'Nick can be quite – what's the word – *naïve* for somebody who spent so long in prison. He has a tendency to see the best in people,' Deborah added, aware that this wasn't how Chantelle normally talked. Still, Eve hardly knew Chantelle, and we all become different people depending who we're talking to.

'Naivety's not necessarily a bad quality in a person,' Eve said.

'I suppose not,' Deborah said, annoyed by Eve's condescending tone. In the house adjoining the one where Nick had gone, a door opened. A middle-aged guy came out. He wore a cloth cap, as so many men over a certain age still did in this city. Head down, he walked rapidly towards the street. When he passed Eve's car, Deborah got a glimpse of his face: ordinary, gaunt, possibly quite distinguished if he didn't have that haunted look. The mac he wore looked expensive. Deborah glanced in the mirror, watched the guy cross Radford Road.

'He's left his car in the ASDA car park,' she told Eve, 'He'll probably pick up some chocolates for his wife before he drives home.'

When Eve didn't reply, Deborah turned and saw that she was crying.

'What's wrong?'

Then she worked out what it must be and breathed in deeply. 'He's...'

Eve gulped before she spoke. 'He does bring home chocolates sometimes. Or a bottle of wine. Has a shower when he gets in because the ones at the leisure centre are always too busy, he says.'

She began to cry again. Deborah found her a tissue. When she was done, Eve turned on the interior light and patiently repaired her make-up.

'Don't tell Nick,' she said when she was finished.

'Did you suspect?' Deborah asked. 'Is that the real reason why we're here?'

'What do you think?'

At first, Nancy acted like she didn't recognise him. She rolled off her tights.

'I don't do unprotected or anal, so don't ask.'

'I'm not here to have sex.'

Nancy looked up. She had begun to take off her top but, recognising him, she pulled it down again, then hunched her shoulders so that her breasts no longer poked forward. She frowned. 'You paid your money, didn't you? What else are you here for? To talk old times?'

'I... want to help.'

'You help by paying for what I used to give you free.'

'Don't talk like that,' Nick said, gently. 'I thought we had something.'

'Sex is never equal,' Nancy replied, in the voice of the sharp school-teacher whose lessons he used to observe. 'There's always one person who wants it more than the other. There's always a bargain to be made.'

'Wasn't how it felt at the time.'

'Then you were deluding yourself.'

'I can't believe you're happy doing this.'

'It's a lot easier than what I did before. Do I enjoy it? Not often, but I like the money, and what it buys me.'

'You like the sort of guys you have to deal with?'

Nancy pouted. 'You're not the only person from my old life who comes here. You'd be surprised. Word gets around.' She paused and gave him a significant look. He wondered who she meant. Joe? His brother used to fancy Nancy something rotten.

'How much crack are you smoking?'

'What's that got to do with you?'

'Nothing, except I accidentally supplied you with some.'

A grand's worth of crack had been planted in Nick's old flat by an enemy who wanted him back in prison. Nancy had witnessed the plant, and moved the stash before the police got there. Then, when Nick wasn't around, she'd smoked her way through the lot of it.

'You think I wasn't into it before I started seeing you? Did you ever find out where that shit came from?'

'I've got a pretty good idea. The guy's dead now.'

'Did you kill him?'

'I'm not that kind of person.'

'No,' Nancy said, relaxing the scowl she had worn since the beginning of their conversation. 'You're not. Listen, if you're not going to screw me, let's have a smoke. I'm gasping.'

She tossed him a Silk Cut.

'How long have you been doing this?' he asked, after lighting her up.

'Since I split up with Carl. I got evicted from the flat and lived with a guy called Beany for a few weeks.'

'I've met Beany. I know what he's about.' Beany was a dealer and a pimp.

Nancy nodded. 'He wanted to run me but I asked around, heard about this place. There's a chain of them. The locations change all the time. Most girls are freelance. Some of them even pay tax, can you believe that?'

'Where are you living when you don't live here?'

'I have a flat. I've got a nice TV, a view.'

'You can't live like this forever,' Nick argued. 'I've got a friend who's well off. He offered to pay for a rehab place, a really good one – remote, luxurious. If you ever want to escape, all you have to do is give me a ring.' Nick wrote down his mobile number on the back of a Cane Cars card. 'I'm not making judgements, Nance, just trying to help.'

'I thought you'd stopped working for the drugs project place.'

'Doesn't mean I stopped believing in the message.'

'What were you doing talking to Terence the other week, then?'

Nick was taken aback. 'How do you know that I was there?'

'The punters are told it's a one-way mirror, but it's just tinted glass. We like to get a look at who comes in. Helps to know what's coming.'

'Did you tell him you knew me?'

'Never tell anyone stuff they don't need to know.'

Nick laughed awkwardly and still didn't answer her question.

Nancy joined the laughter. 'We all have our little secrets, eh? Give me a kiss for old time's sake.'

He kissed her on the lips, then handed her the card with his number.

'Now fuck off,' she said.

14

Nick returned to the car thirty minutes after he had left it. Eve began to drive the moment he had fastened his seat belt.

'How did it go?' Deborah asked.

'I'm not sure what I was doing there,' Nick said. 'I paid a hundred quid to give her my phone number, but I don't think she'll be calling.'

'How did she look?' Eve asked.

'More face-paint than she used to wear. Hair a bit longer. But basically the same. She reckoned she liked what she was doing more than teaching. Hinted that she even serviced some guys from her old life.'

'She didn't say who?' Deborah asked.

'No. She gave me this look, though. It made me wonder.'

Eve said nothing. She drove up seedy, run-down Radford Road, then cut across Forest Road and took a back road shortcut to Waverley Street.

'Will you come in?' Nick asked Eve. 'Talk things over.'

'There's not much to say. You found her. You gave her the number. Did you mention me?'

'No. There didn't seem to be any point.'

'At least we can say we tried. Thanks, Nick.' She leant over and kissed him on the cheek. Deborah looked at her watch. If she went into Nick's now, she would not get away until late and she needed to talk to her cover officer.

'Actually, Eve. I need to get home. Could you drop me at the bus stop on the Mansfield Road?'

'Of course,' Eve said.

Nick looked disappointed. Two women had just refused his company. He didn't argue, though, only leant back to kiss his girlfriend goodnight.

'It's been a weird evening,' he said. 'But I'll see you soon, yeah?'

'Very soon,' Deborah promised.

Eve set off again, doing a rapid U-turn to take them back up steep Waverley Street. 'Where do you live?' she asked.

'Far side of Arnold.'

'That's not much out of my way. I'll take you.'

'There's no need, honest.'

'I'm in no rush to get home,' Eve said. 'Let Geoff stew, wonder where I am. Give me directions when we get near.'

Deborah had never given Nick her address, despite having a legend that involved living with her parents. The beauty of the mobile phone was that you could be anywhere, any time, and nobody knew any better. If push came to shove, and he discovered that she lived alone, she would think of another story. What should she tell Eve? Lies multiplied, but, after tonight, there was no reason for Deborah to see Eve again. It didn't matter if Eve found out where Chantelle lived.

'Will you confront him?' Deborah asked. She couldn't stop herself. Chantelle would not be so upfront, so prying, but Deborah wanted to know.

'Do you think I should?'

'You seem like the sort of woman who'd be too proud not to.'

Eve kept her eyes on the road ahead. 'Some people wouldn't describe it as infidelity. Just a natural release. "Better that than an affair", they'd say. We've been married nearly seven years and I'm going through the change.'

'If he's hard up he can buy dirty DVDs or a wank mag.'

'You'd dump him, if it were you?'

'It's not for me to say. I've never been married, never had a relationship that lasted more than a few months. But if it were me, I think I would, yes.'

'At your age, I'd have said exactly the same.'

They didn't speak again until it was time to give directions. Deborah told Eve where to drop her. Preoccupied, Eve asked no questions about her home situation, but parked where she was told.

'Thanks for tonight. It was good to have another woman there. You're good for Nick. He's not a bad lad. I always had a lot of time for him.'

'It's early days between us. Can I ask you something?' It was the question she'd asked before, and not had answered. 'Tonight, was that about helping Nancy, or did you suspect that your husband would be there?'

'Both,' Eve said. 'I was suspicious about what he did on Tuesday nights, yet I hoped not to find him there, and I hoped that Nick would persuade Nancy to leave. But I got what I expected. Was I using Nick?'

'We all use each other', Deborah said, opening the car door. 'I wouldn't let it worry you.'

As soon as she was back in her flat, Deborah rang Mike. He wasn't interested in the brothel.

'A place in a back street slum: so what? We have enough trouble sorting out massage parlours in middle class neighbourhoods, even if they're using illegal, underage girls. We gave up the war on prostitution before it started. The war on drugs is all that matters. Have you got anything new for me?'

'He's seeing Andrew Saint again soon,' Deborah said.

'Saint's not a primary focus of interest. He hasn't got a Nottingham residence. Have you laid the ground for a rapid exit? Talked about travelling or mentioned a job somewhere on the other side of the country?'

'Not yet. It's coming up to Christmas, nobody makes those kind of decisions at this time of year. You've got to give me until the new year.'

'You've got until the first Monday of January. After that, you're back in uniform. Don't see this as a failure. You can start studying for your sergeant's exams in the new year. Onwards and upwards.'

He was right, Deborah decided when she had put down the phone. She rolled herself a small joint with some of the grass that Nick had given her. The stuff helped her to think and it helped her to sleep. Lots of other coppers used it, she'd discovered during training, though they kept it to themselves until you got to know them really well. Sometimes, she felt like a hypocrite, trying to bring down a guy whose only crime was to be good at growing the stuff. But it was all a game. Nick would respect that, the day she busted him.

The two women polished off a bottle of Chablis between them.

'Are you still seeing a lot of Andrew?' Sarah asked Gill.

'He's a very persistent chap. And he insists on paying me rather well, even though the work I do for him is negligible. Introductions mainly. Did he help you with those Spanish property repairs?'

'He said he'd get someone to look into it. Did you come up with a new name for his company?'

'Not yet. He suggested *Andrew Saint Securities*. Good acronym.'

Sarah smiled. 'That sounds like the Andy I knew as a student.'

'What was he like?'

'He was an operator, even then...' Sarah was circumspect, because she still wasn't sure of the ground. Apart from his riches – and Gill wasn't short of a bob or two – Andrew was hardly what Sarah would call a catch. Was Gill really sleeping with him? Sarah couldn't ask directly. Her phone rang and she checked the caller display. Eric.

'Aren't you going to answer that?'

'The Chief Constable I've told you about. He's been pressing me about my Christmas plans. He'd like to whisk me to the Caribbean or somewhere equally expensive, take our relationship to the next stage.'

'But you can't leave your mother?'

'It's not so much that. I like him. We're good together, only he's a bit old for me and I never feel that – I don't know what to call it – erotic rush – when he comes on to me.'

'Men his age can be very patient,' Gill advised. 'And surprisingly vulnerable. You say his divorce hasn't come through yet?'

'They've barely been separated for a year.'

'There are advantages to having an older guy who understands the pressures you're under, who can give you counsel as well as company.'

Gill's husband, a Euro MP, was more than a decade her senior.

'Older men can be very understanding. Worldly, too. When I was in Spain, I had a boyfriend five years younger than me. He broke my heart. Only time I let it happen. For a while after that, I was a bit of a floozy, always falling into bed with older blokes who offered to look after me. Married, most of them. I'm not saying my behaviour made sense. By the time I got into parliament, I had a bit of a reputation. Then Peter rescued me, and I really was safe. He's very understanding.'

Sarah understood what was meant by 'understanding'. However, she didn't want a licence to cheat on her boyfriend, and wasn't sure that Eric would be as 'understanding' as Gill's husband if she chose to do so.

'Still,' Gill went on, 'it sounds as though you aren't terribly tempted in the bedroom department, or you'd have sampled the goods by now.'

Sarah replied to this home truth with a wry smile. Gill went on.

'You're too young to marry for security and company. Hold out for your dream man. You won't have trouble finding someone to keep your bed warm while you're waiting.'

Sarah wasn't so sure about that, but nodded anyway. She thought of something she'd been meaning to ask.

'I can't remember if you got in in '74 or '79. Did you overlap my grandad in the Commons?'

''74. I was the second youngest woman in the house. Your grandad was still in the cabinet, then, so I didn't run into him much. He spoke to me once, can't have been long before he retired. Asked how I was getting on. I asked him if he was looking forward to retirement. He said *no, but it's your turn now.* Then he offered me some advice that I've never forgotten.'

She stared into the middle distance, then drained her glass.

'Are you going to tell me what it was?' Sarah asked.

'I'm not sure if I should. I was quite insulted at the time. He said, *keep your legs together and your mind open. Then you might go far.*'

Sarah gave an awkward laugh. 'I hope you slapped him.'

'I should have done, but I probably giggled. He was an old charmer, Sir Hugh. I've never trusted blokes like him. That generation of men, too young for the First World War and too old for the next, they sometimes acted like they didn't trust themselves. I'm sorry. He was your grandfather.'

'I don't mind,' Sarah said. 'I loved him, but he was an enigma to me. I know what you mean about his generation. They always held something back.'

'It's the British way,' Gill agreed. 'There's a lot to be said for reticence. What did your grandad do in the war?'

'I'm not entirely sure,' Sarah said. 'Something to do with national security. He never talked about it.'

15

1968

There was a current vogue for boasting about your IQ, or intelligence quotient. Over 160 and you qualified for Mensa, a club of the super-bright. Hugh Bone went to secondary school during the First World War, long before the advent of intelligence tests. He had no idea what his IQ was. Nevertheless he had learned to determine when men were cleverer than him. There weren't many of them.

It was how you used knowledge that counted. Most men used what little intellect they had to cover up how little they really knew. And most politicians lived their lives in fear of being found out. But not Harold. The more Hugh got to know the PM, the sharper he found him. That was why he regarded tonight's appointment with some trepidation. Harold was the sort of man who could persuade you to do something that you didn't want to.

The PM's character was avuncular, charismatic and, most of all, consistent. Successful politicians designed a mask to wear in public. The mask, in time, moulded the face beneath, until mask and face became indistinguishable, even to those who knew the wearer best. Hugh Bone had worked this out soon after he became an MP. There was, however, a difference between learning something and acting on what you'd learnt.

When did the mask become the face? Hugh was badgered by the fear that he had, long ago, picked the wrong image, and now it was too late to change. Edith would have been able to tell him, had she not had a stroke within months of Hugh first taking up his seat. He had returned from Parliament one Thursday evening to find her prone on the kitchen floor. The doctors at the Royal Infirmary said that she had been in that state for at least twenty-four hours. Another night without help and she would have been dead. Which would have been kinder to all concerned.

Hugh dealt with his guilt at leaving his wife alone by buying a house that was far too big, but fully kitted out for her disability, complete with room for staff and guests. Bone Mansion – as Hugh came to call it – cost a fortune and was mortgaged to the hilt. On top of this, there was the live-in home help to pay for. Not easy, when he was on a backbench MP's salary, but Hugh always found the money. Somehow.

In '64, when Labour returned to power for the first time in thirteen years, Hugh found himself several years older than the new Prime Minister. Which rankled. However, Wilson had become an MP fourteen years earlier than he had, and experience was what counted. Most of Hugh's old pals in Five and Six hated the new PM. It was the PM's intellect, rather than his politics, that they resented. Lefties they quite liked. The secret services were riddled with old communists. Wilson wasn't one. Perhaps that was why he got so much hatred from both left and right. The PM wasn't left wing enough.

Harold and Hugh had never been close. Until recently, they had circled each other cautiously. Hugh was too junior to get into the shadow cabinet during his first parliament. When Harold didn't offer him a ministerial job in '64, Hugh made a name for himself as a backbencher. He was soon chairman of a powerful committee. In '67, when Harold offered him a junior ministerial post, Hugh nearly decided it was beneath him. Hubris, of course, but what he told friends was true: he had far more power as chairman of the committee on state security. This unpaid post offered him regular meetings with the Home Secretary and, occasionally, the PM himself. But ambition got the better of him. That, and the much needed increase in pay.

He joined the government.

Hugh and the PM were educated men who had each chosen to play the bluff, professional Northerner. Their relationship could have gone either way, but they had decided to get on. The Wilson family had visited Chesterfield, stayed overnight. That was six months ago. Today, there was a reshuffle in the air, and Hugh had been called in, midevening, for a private chat.

Everyone knew that the government was in trouble. Four years ago, when they first got in, Labour had seen the extent of the economic mess left behind by the Tories. They should have devalued the pound at once, when they could credibly blame the action on the previous government's policies. Except that would have looked like an admission of defeat. Their majority was tiny. Rather than risk losing a vote of no confidence, they struggled on. Won a world cup. Got re-elected with a decent majority. Autumn 1966 would have been a good time to devalue the pound. But no. Harold waited until he had no choice. No surprise, then, that the public were taking a crap on Labour in the opinion polls and local elections. No surprise that Harold felt forced to make changes.

Why come for Hugh? Not for his economic know-how, which was negligible, or he wouldn't be so badly in debt. For his security contacts, then?

Hugh rang home to explain to Edith that he wouldn't be able to make it back until Friday morning. Joan, his wife's home help, held the phone to her ear while he spoke, but Edith did not respond.

'Goodbye, dear,' he concluded the one-sided conversation. He was about to ring his secretary, who was also his daughter-in-law, when the office door burst open. The man who came in without knocking was two inches taller than Hugh, with ten times as much hair, but only half the brains.

'Hi, Dad. Going back to Chesterfield tonight?'

'No, change of plan. I have a meeting.'

'Ah, right. Perhaps I could use your train ticket.'

MPs got a warrant to travel first class between London and their constituency. Tickets had to be booked in advance and collected from the warrant office. Hugh hadn't collected his yet, and now he'd be changing it.

'I don't think so,' he said. 'You'd get us both into trouble.'

'Worth a try,' Kevin gave his irritating grin. 'I might stick round here anyhow. Lots happening this weekend.'

'I'm sure that Felicity and Sarah will be very disappointed if you do,' Hugh told his son. In Felicity's case, at least, this was far from true. Hugh had no intention of bribing Kevin to travel home with him for the weekend. His son stood in the doorway, flaunting his ludicrous, bright pink bell-bottoms.

'You'd never get away with dressing like that if you were still working for me,' Hugh told him. 'Doesn't Tom mind?'

'Tom wouldn't mind if I wore a dress.'

Thirty years old and still trying to shock his father. Hugh gestured at the papers festooned across his desk.

'I have an important meeting to prepare for. Was there a particular reason you dropped by?'

'Felicity wants to invite you and Mum to Sunday dinner. Can you come?'

'We'd love to,' Hugh said, with fake bonhomie. 'I'll see you then.'

'You may do.'

His son saw himself out. Hugh fumed for thirty seconds, then returned to worrying about what the Prime Minister wanted. He decided to walk to Downing Street. It would give him time to think.

At a newsagents, he picked up a copy of the new *Private Eye* and scanned the political gossip. There was yet another piece strongly hinting that Harold was having an affair with his secretary, Marcia Williams, and she was pregnant with his child. The *Eye* was ill informed. Marcia was pregnant, true. However the father was not Harold, but one of their own: a journalist. Marcia kept the relationship quiet because the guy was married. The *Eye*'s hatred of Harold blinded them to the obvious: Wilson was an uxorious man. He adored his wife, the poet, and was far more interested in power than he was in chasing skirt.

Hugh was shown to a sparsely furnished private room on the third floor of Number Ten. He was surprised to find the PM waiting for him.

'Prime Minister, how are you?'

Harold had bags under his wise owl eyes.

'No need to *Prime Minister* me when it's just us. I'm getting by. You're looking too well, old friend. We can't be working you hard enough.'

'I've nothing to complain about. Not been in this room before. Always surprises me, how much Macmillan managed to expand this place.'

'A botched job, half of it. We're already getting dry rot in some of the bigger rooms. Not enough ventilation. Too many corners cut.'

He gestured for Hugh to sit down in the armchair next to his.

'How's that son of yours?'

'Keeping out of trouble. I hope.'

'And the little girl? What was her name?'

Hugh tried not to give Harold a suspicious look. The PM was known for taking an interest in family matters. A deep interest. Most families had secrets that not all of their members shared. Hugh wanted to know what Harold knew.

'Sarah's bright as a button. She gets prettier every time I see her.'

'Edith?'

'No change. Mary and the boys well?'

'They're fine.' The PM took a puff of his cigar. 'To business. I want you in the cabinet.'

'I'm flattered. Which job?'

'A new one. Minister Without Portfolio.'

'Meaning?'

'It means whatever I want it to mean. *Special projects* is the public version. Privately: watching my back. Taking care of the Cabinet is the easy bit. I'm also worried about the Security Services. Still got friends there?'

'Friends is perhaps too strong a word. Contacts, certainly.'

'Start turning the contacts into friends, then. Find out what they're thinking. But don't let them know where your loyalties lie.'

'They'll assume I'm your man, unless I dissemble from the start.'

'Dissembling's what you're good at. Keep them guessing, that's what I always try to do. Never let them be sure what you're really thinking.'

'I'm a politician, Harold. Even I don't know what I really think.'

'So I said to him, *I'm a politician, Prime Minister. Most of the time, even I don't know what I really think.*'

'And how did he respond to that?' Felicity asked.

She took the hotpot out of the oven and put it on the kitchen table to cool.

'Guess.'

'He either said, *me too* or *you'll think what I tell you to think.*

Hugh laughed. 'Neither. He gave one of those inscrutable smiles, then we shook hands.'

'When will it be announced?'

'Monday.'

'Grandad!' Sarah charged into the kitchen and jumped onto his lap. She wore a tartan skirt and a purple jumper that clashed horribly. Her lips tasted of Angel Delight. It never ceased to amaze Hugh, how much she resembled his late mother. He had seen pictures of his mam as a child, and the resemblance was remarkable. He tickled Sarah under the chin.

'Are you staying for dinner?' the six-year-old asked.

'I haven't been asked yet,' Hugh told her, 'but I can see that you've already had yours.'

'I went to Sally's for supper.'

Hugh wiped a little pink gunge from the corner of her mouth. Sarah squirmed as he did this, then looked thoughtful.

'What is it?' Hugh asked her.

'When are you going to let Daddy come home?'

'What do you mean?'

'Mummy says that Daddy works so hard for you in London, he can't come home every weekend.'

'Ah, I see.' Hugh exchanged glances with Felicity, who swivelled her eyes. He hated it when she did that. Hard to explain to a six-year-old that her father spent his weekends in London because he liked being buggered by men he met in toilets. Hugh hated lying to Sarah, so he told her a version of the truth, and damn Felicity if it didn't quite tie in with what she had told her beloved daughter.

'The thing is, my little munchkin, your daddy doesn't work for me any more. He's got a job with another MP, Mr Driberg. And Mr Driberg makes him work very hard indeed.'

Sarah considered this. 'I don't *like* Mr Driberg!' she announced.

'Neither do I,' said Felicity. 'But it's nearly your bedtime. Kiss Grandad goodnight.'

Sarah did as she was told.

'I'm sorry, Flic, but please don't make me the bad guy,' Hugh said when the child had left the room.

'How... dare... you?' Felicity struggled to keep her voice low. He saw that he had made a bad mistake. 'Sarah likes to know her dad's working for her grandad. He might not be here, but she feels safe with that story. Now you've introduce Driberg, I'm going to be pestered with questions about him.'

'Tell the truth.'

'What, that her father's been given a better job because his new boss has sex with him? I don't think so!'

She had begun to raise her voice. Hugh, worried that Sarah would hear, shushed her. More was required, so he got up, put one arm around Felicity. With his left hand, he stroked her hair, then used his most soothing voice.

'I'll have a word with Kevin, get him to come here more.'

Felicity pulled away. 'I don't want him here. You should see how resentful he is when he does make an appearance.'

'He's fond of Sarah.'

'For half an hour at a time! I don't want him to come any more! I want a divorce. I want...'

She began to cry, and this time she let Hugh hold her, buried her head in his shoulder. The phone rang, and he knew who it would be. His wife's helper, warning him that her shift ended in half an hour, which was when his would begin.

'One of us had better answer that,' he said, releasing his hold on Felicity.

'I'll put your dinner on the table,' Felicity said. 'Or you'll have to bolt it down.'

'Thanks.' Hugh picked up the phone. The caller wasn't the home help. 'How are you, you old bugger?'

'I'm very well,' Hugh replied. He didn't use Peter's name, because the old boy had a justifiable paranoia about phones being bugged, and he shouldn't be talking to Hugh on this phone. He had made contact the night before, off channel. 'Clever of you to track me down here.'

Peter laughed. 'It wasn't difficult. Your message said something about inviting me to Chesterfield for the weekend. I'm intrigued. Long time since I've seen the old place.'

'Then come and find out how much it's changed.'

'I'm not sure I want my childhood memories sullied. Are you

sure we can't meet at my club?'

'In future, maybe, but I want our meetings to look like what they are, two old friends who enjoy each other's company. You must bring the wife.'

'I'll see if I can persuade her. I'm sure she'd like to meet Edith.'

Peter knew that Edith could barely communicate.

'Ring me when you know what train you're on. I'll collect you.'

'Who was that?' Felicity asked, when Hugh sat down to eat his hotpot.

'An old work colleague who I invited over for the weekend. I know I said I'd bring Edith to Sunday dinner but, if Kevin doesn't show up, would you mind awfully cooking for us at Bone Mansion?'

Felicity turned to little Sarah. 'Would you like to have Sunday dinner at Grandad's this week?'

'Yes please!'

Felicity gave Hugh a tired nod. 'Does he have a name, this old friend of yours?'

'Peter. His name's Peter Wright.'

16

1998

Christmas recess was a week away. In the Commons, Tony Blair made a statement about the Americans bombing Iraq. The attack had been billed as a joint Anglo-American initiative but Sarah knew that was bullshit. The bombing was a show of machismo by the US president.

Bill Clinton was about to be impeached. His crime? Lying about sex. Everyone knew men lied about sex. The public accepted politicians lying to their spouses. They did it themselves. Clinton, however, had lied to the American people. *I did not have sex with that woman,* he'd said on TV. A blowsy intern had given him a few blow jobs. In the US, apparently, fellatio was not legally classified as sex. If he were female, Big Willy might get away with that argument, but for a man to claim that fellatio wasn't sex was an insult to every woman who had ever choked on a penis.

At least the Commons wasn't required to vote on the bombing of Iraq. Sarah wanted to get back into government one day, and she wouldn't succeed if she rebelled on this issue again. She wondered how many children had died because the president couldn't resist a star-struck intern.

Her mobile rang. Eric. He was the same age as Clinton. Those men were from a different generation, she reminded herself. They came of age before feminism had made any impact on the male psyche. They thought of sex as a right that came with success. Sarah could understand their mind-set. Didn't mean she had to put out for them.

'When are you coming home for Christmas?' Eric asked. He

had given up on the holiday idea.

'I'm not. I'm staying at my mum's.' And Eric wasn't invited.

'Then what are you doing on New Year's Eve?' Eric asked.

'There's a thing at an old friend's. I said I'd probably go.'

She wasn't going to let on who the 'old friend' was.

'Pity. I was hoping to take you to the do at my golf club. I was sorry to miss it last year. Good music, great food, decent company.'

'I'm not a golf club kind of girl, Eric. Invite someone else.'

'There's nobody. You're condemning me to a quiet night in.'

'Don't make me feel guilty, Eric. We're not in a relationship. And I can't invite you to the thing I'm going to.'

'Because you're going with someone else, I understand.'

This was the moment, Sarah realised, the gentle let-down. All she had to say was 'yes' and he would withdraw gracefully. But she liked him too much to lie to him. There wasn't anybody else for her to lie about.

'We'd both be a lot older than most of the people there. You wouldn't be comfortable, and your not being comfortable would make me uncomfortable. Do you understand?'

'Of course.'

'Go to your golf club dance. Take your ex-wife. That'll show everybody, including her, how civilised you are.'

Eric paused. 'That's not a bad idea. You *are* a politician, aren't you?'

Sarah laughed.

'So, when shall I see you?'

Sarah agreed to lunch. As soon as she put the phone down, it rang again. Andrew Saint. Also wanting to meet, but her days in London were limited.

'I'll be seeing you in Nottingham, won't I? Nick said that he'd invited you to the New Year's Eve party at Joe's.'

'You're going to that, are you?'

'I don't see any reason why not.'

'Indeed, no. Well, if you're going to be there, I shall do my very best to be there too. Have you met Nick's new paramour, the lovely Chantelle?'

'I have. He's introduced her to you, has he?'

'Brought her over for the weekend, yes.'

Nick must be getting serious about her. Shit.

'I don't suppose you'll be escorting the fragrant Mrs Temperley.'

Andrew gave a forced chuckle. 'No such luck, which does give me more time for the pleasure of your company.'

'You old flirt, you.'

'The food won't be up to much at Joe's. Let me take you out for dinner beforehand. I can update you on all the repair work that your Spanish villa is about to undergo.'

'Thanks for your help with that. I'd love to, but it would need to be something light. I always eat far too much over Christmas. Chinese?'

'Done.'

Sarah put the phone down, feeling more positive about herself than she had earlier in the day. Two men fighting for your company will do that, even if you haven't got a romantic interest in either of them.

Nick was preparing to make party tapes. These days you could buy a CD recorder and burn your own discs, but the blanks were expensive. Cassettes still worked for Nick.

His five-year absence made it tricky to get the party mix-tape right. He'd asked Chantelle if she had any favourite sounds. She claimed not to buy music. He might have known that, had he ever been round to hers, but visiting Chantelle's home was still a no-go. From the reluctance with which she answered his question, he figured she was ashamed of what music she did have. In Nick's experience, women rarely took music as seriously as men, but didn't like the shallowness of their interest to be exposed.

The doorbell. Andrew. The drag about having a top floor flat was walking down three flights of stairs to let visitors in. Nick took the needle off the song that was playing, stopped the tape, picked up his coat and keys, then locked up behind him. No point in Andrew coming all the way up when they were just heading straight out again.

His friend had a new leather jacket. Hugo Boss. Nick stroked the soft animal skin.

'Very nice.'

'Early Christmas present from Gill.'

'I hope you got her something equally extravagant.'

'Tricky, giving gifts to a married woman. I settled for a fancy phone she can tell hubby was a business expense. Not romantic enough?'

'You're asking the wrong guy,' Nick said. 'Thought I'd get Chantelle jewellery. Dunno what. Every gift has a hidden message, doesn't it?'

'Mine says, *call me*. Gill's been a bit hard to get hold of lately.'

They got into his 4x4. 'Appreciate your taking me there,' Andrew said. 'You don't have to come in. Useful to know that you're outside, where Terence can see you.'

This situation implicated Nick more than he intended. He'd only meant to show Andrew where the brothel was.

'Terence probably won't be there,' he told Andrew. 'It wasn't him I spoke to when I went to see Nancy.'

'Ah, yes, Nancy. I take it you couldn't persuade her to leave?'

'She said she was suited to the work. Go right here.'

They turned off Gregory Boulevard onto narrow, busy Radford Road. 'How are they going to fit a tram line on here?' Andrew asked.

'Close it to traffic, I suppose.'

'If the tram's approved, house prices will collapse while the work's going on, then rocket afterwards. You should buy a few, rent them out. Lots of money to be made.'

'What with?'

'My offer still stands. I could advance you the mortgage deposits.'

'Next left. You know why I can't be involved. I shouldn't have gone to see Terence in the first place. I'm not sure about staying here now.'

'Understood. If anyone asks, you took me here because I'm a punter. You stay in the car until I'm sorted, then you clear off. Either I'm back within five minutes or I ring to tell you to go. How does that sound?'

'Fine. It's over there on the right.'

'And the office is that front bay window?' Andrew parked in a spot where, should Terence look through the window, he would be able to see Nick in the passenger seat. Maybe Andrew would tell Terence that Nick was armed. Nick used to have prison muscles. They had softened, but that wasn't obvious from a distance: he was still built, and over six foot tall. Most people would think twice before crossing him.

'If you get out, push that plastic knob down, car locks itself,' Andrew said. 'And I'll take you for a thank-you pint later.'

Nick watched Andrew go into the brothel. Two minutes later, his phone rang. 'Everything's copacetic. I'm going to stay here a while, so take yourself off. I'll see you for a pint in the Vernon at eight.'

Andrew was already in the pub when Nick arrived. Had a couple of pints waiting. They sat at a table in the corner farthest from the bar, where nobody could overhear.

'I take it Terence was there?' Nick said.

'Oh yes.'

'Did you get sorted out?'

'In a manner of speaking. He has to go up the chain for approval but we reached an accommodation: lower rate, bigger bulk, more profit all round. In future, he'll be paying in advance.'

'They trust you that much?'

'More than I trust them, anyway. It's a profitable sideline he has there.'

'You took a look through the window, did you?'

'The one-way mirror, yes.'

Nick hadn't got round to telling him the truth about the 'mirror' and now wasn't the time. He could see where this was going.

'You didn't..?'

'Gill and I are hardly "exclusive", for obvious reasons. And Terence didn't lie when he said that your friend gives the best blow job on the planet.'

'You screwed Nancy?'

Andrew gave the guiltily satisfied smile of the child who has eaten all the cake.

'Some things are very hard to resist, old friend.'

'You bastard.' Nick said, not masking his sense of disbelief. Andrew had crossed a line. Nick wasn't sure he could articulate what the line was. Sleeping with a friend's recent ex was dodgy enough, even if Nancy weren't in need of help. But Andrew was exploiting her. Andrew, of course, would have another way of looking at it.

'Don't say you wouldn't have taken up the freebie if you weren't fully occupied with the luscious Chantelle,' Andrew said.

Nick wasn't going to tell Andrew that Chantelle had never had full sex with him. Nor could he pretend that he no longer fancied Nancy. But he hadn't been remotely tempted to have sex with her, even though he'd paid for it, even though he hadn't had full sex since they finished, best part of a year ago.

'I didn't pay, of course,' Andrew went on, when Nick didn't reply. 'Which isn't to say I'm always against paying for it, on principle. Terence offered me a freebie and it was the only way I could get to talk to the girl. You still want to get her out of there, don't you?'

'Yes,' Nick said. 'I guess I do.'

'Your way failed. So let's try mine.'

'Which is?'

'Wait and see. She is a fantastic fuck, isn't she? I can see why you were upset when she dumped you. Or should I say, chose crack over you.'

Nick didn't trust himself not to insult Andrew, so kept silent.

'Sorry, touchy subject. But you're with the fantastic Chantelle now.'

Men did not kiss and tell about their sex lives, not after the age of sixteen. At least, that was how Nick saw it. Andrew, by contrast, had always been inclined to boast about his triumphs. Maybe because, when they first knew each other, there were so few of them. A short, badly groomed, bearded bloke with acne was never going to do well at university. Fifteen years later, a rich, well groomed guy with lifts in his heels had a rather better chance, but still couldn't believe his luck when women as classy as Gill Temperley or Nancy Tull slept with him. For whatever reason.

'Chantelle's great,' Nick agreed. 'Does Nancy know that you're connected to me?'

'Of course not. And let's keep it that way.'

Which implied, Nick realised at once, that Andrew was planning to sleep with her again. He changed the subject.

'Seen Sarah recently?'

'Talked to her on the phone. We're having dinner together before your New Year's Eve party.'

'You're definitely coming, then?'

'Oh, yes.' Andrew's phone buzzed, indicating a text, which he checked. 'Gotta go. It's been a pleasure.'

He left his pint unfinished. Nick guessed that he was off to meet his Nottingham number two. This was the lucrative position that he kept offering to Nick, a job that Nick was sometimes tempted to take.

At the bar, a white guy with a shaved head glanced at Nick, then followed Andrew out, his drink still on the bar, untouched. Nick drained his pint in two gulps before following him. Andrew's 4x4 had been parked a little down Waverley Street. He was already doing a U-turn. Nick stood in the shadow of the pub door, watching his old friend leave. Less than ten seconds later, a grey Audi-80 came out of a side street and shot uphill in the same direction as Andrew, catching him up at the lights. Both cars turned right. The Audi driver was the guy from the bar at the Vernon. Probably a coincidence. Nick made a note of the car's registration anyway.

17

The weekend before Christmas, Deborah gave in her resignation at the dentist's.

'I don't understand, Chantelle,' her boss said. 'I thought you liked it here.'

'Sorry, I got a better offer.' Deborah avoided eye contact to indicate that she would not be saying what this 'offer' was.

'It'll be very hard to recruit someone new over the holiday period. Can't you hold on for another couple of weeks?'

'I wish I could, really.'

This was true, but Mike had given her clear instructions. She had to be back in uniform by the first week of the new year. She'd tried to argue her way around it, even offered to carry on seeing Nick in her spare time. That way, it wouldn't cost the force anything to continue building intelligence.

'We don't work like that. You're not getting emotionally attached to this guy, are you? That would be dangerous.' When she didn't reply, Mike added. 'You need to cut off communication at once if things are getting messy.'

'I want a clean exit in case I need to return to the cover in future.'

'That's unlikely. You've established that Nick Cane isn't a dealer.'

'I still think Andrew Saint is a big, big distributor and Nick knows more than he's told me so far.'

'Then prepare a report for us to pass on to the Nottingham Drug Squad. But don't use it to argue for continuing the operation. Word is, the Chief Constable himself has ordered this to be finished.'

Fuck him. Fuck everything. Before Mike had even rung off,

Deborah decided: there was no point denying herself any longer.

Tonight, she'd sleep with Nick.

This time, when the Public Records office rang, Mum refused to take the call.

'Tell them I'm too ill to come to the phone.'

'But you're feeling better. At least, that's what you keep telling me. You just ate a big lunch.'

Mum had spent the last couple of days insisting that it was fine for Sarah to move out. She was perfectly happy to spend Christmas alone.

'I don't want to talk to them.'

'Well, I do.' Sarah returned to the phone and asked if she could deal with the matter. Her mum wasn't up to it.

'We'd need some kind of written authorisation, I'm afraid.'

'I'm on to it.'

Sarah hung up and confronted her mother. 'Are you going to tell me what's in the 1968 Cabinet Papers before I go to the Public Records office?'

'You're being a bully,' Mum complained.

'I wonder where I get it from. Not my dad, that's for sure. The story's about him, isn't it?'

'Yes. People are going to find out that he was homosexual.'

'He wasn't homosexual. He was bisexual. Otherwise he wouldn't have been able to father me. But I don't understand. Why has Dad's sexuality got anything to do with cabinet papers?'

'Because of what it led him to do.'

'Which was?'

Mum stopped doing the dishes, and sat down opposite Sarah at the kitchen table. 'You were only five when your father finished working for your grandfather as a research assistant. So you won't remember.'

'Remember what?'

'Hugh was chairman of the National Security Select

Committee.'

'Until he became a minister, yes.'

'There was a leak.'

'What kind of leak? Who by? Dad or Grandad? Are you trying to tell me that one of them was a spy?'

For a moment, Mum looked like she was about to slap her. 'Don't ever say something like that about your grandfather. He had more integrity than any other man I've known.'

'But my dad...'

'I've said all I've got to say. It'll be in the cabinet papers.'

'I could see Dad stealing secrets for money.' Sarah thought aloud. 'But, by '68, Grandad was in government. He'd stopped chairing the state security committee.' Shit. She realised it was true. 'After which Dad no longer had access to secret documents. Which was why he went to work for Tom Driberg.'

'Homosexuality had just been decriminalised, but it happened too late to make much difference to Kevin. The Russians had him. And he got caught.'

'Then why didn't the police arrest Dad? Or did they?'

'They didn't. For the same reason they didn't arrest Anthony Blunt. It would be embarrassing for the government, and your father was very cooperative. Eventually, Hugh parcelled him off to Spain.'

'Why Spain? Somewhere with lots of handsome boys?'

'It had more to do with extradition laws.'

'And you haven't told me this earlier because...?'

Mum scrunched her eyelids as if she were able to hide behind them. 'It's embarrassing.'

'Far more embarrassing for me than it is for you. I want to get back into government. A story like this will set me back.'

Mum, for once in her life, was apologetic. 'I tried to persuade them to withhold it. They said there were some grounds on which they might be able to. But, I'm sorry, with all the time in hospital, I lost track.'

She wrote a letter authorising Sarah to deal with the matter.

18

Something changed. And in a good way. The week before Christmas, Chantelle came round when Nick was still sleeping off a night shift. He'd given her a key so that she could let herself in. He woke to find her naked beside him, stroking his cock.

'I think you've waited long enough,' she said.

He thought the first time might be awkward, but she was already moist and ready for him. She'd told him that she wasn't a virgin, but it was easy to tell that she wasn't very experienced either. She'd never been with a good lover before, one who was patient and willing to put her desires before his. Nick found this very, very exciting.

And so did she.

Deborah had been on a course about going undercover. Thirty people on it, all but four of them blokes. In the ladies' loos, she had discussed sex with two of the other female officers – one married, the other living with a boyfriend – and the range of excuses you could use.

The women agreed that a hand-job was as far as they'd go, and even then they wouldn't dream of telling the blokes they went home to. One advised Deborah to go on the pill, just in case. Which she had. The other reckoned that, in Russia, the KGB used to train women agents in love-making techniques, so that they could act as honey traps for foreign spies and diplomats. The Russians had no moral hang-ups about their spies screwing their targets, but Deborah would bet that the Russian women who prostituted themselves never got promoted to senior positions.

Deborah didn't have a bloke to go home to. But she had

needs. They didn't discuss them on the training courses. Now Nick was in the clear, and the operation was all but over, she could justify doing whatever she wanted without it affecting her career. And it was strange, how much she enjoyed the sex. She had no illusions about Nick. There was no danger of her falling for him. But the act was much better than it was with the two guys she had been with before – one when she was nineteen, the other a couple of years ago. She had slept with each of them because she thought they were in love. Naïve not to remember how some guys swore *love* when all they really meant was lust.

With Nick, by contrast, she was the one in lust. The part she was playing didn't distract from that. It added to the excitement. As did Nick's being an experienced, patient lover. Older guys had their advantages.

She thought kindly of Nick, yes. But not lovingly. How could you love somebody who didn't know your real name?

The time had come to draw conclusions. The Chief Constable had ended the operation. Too quickly for Deborah's liking. It could be a conspiracy. Eric Turnbull was screwing Sarah Bone. The MP was in league with Nick Cane. Both were protecting Andrew Saint from the police. But where was Deborah's evidence? How did Nick afford a flat opposite the Arboretum? He said it was rented, but she had looked into the records, and it had been bought earlier this year, for sixty grand, and was held in a complicated trust. Even more suspiciously, the previous owner was Frank Davis, who was awaiting trial for drug dealing on a massive scale. There had never been any evidence to link Davis to Nick, but at least one witness had connected Davis to Andrew Saint. Was it too far-fetched for Nick, the MP and the Chief Constable to be in league with Andrew Saint? Yes, it was.

She rang her mum. 'Sorry, I won't be able to come home for so long at Christmas. Work. I hope you'll understand. That's the bad news. The good news is I'm being transferred back to Leicester in the New Year.'

The best cover story, the manuals said, was a version of the truth. It was true that her parents were religious and that she lived with them. This was one reason why her experience with men was quite limited. It was also why she'd been happy to get a flat of her own when she was working undercover, first at the Power Project, then at the dentist's. But she did miss her parents. When Dad came on the phone she promised that she'd make it home for church on Christmas day. Then she rang Nick.

'I've just been talking to my parents,' she said. 'I told them about you.'

'Wow. Does that mean I'm going to meet them?'

'No, but it does mean they know I want to spend most of Christmas with you. I did promise I'd go to church with them on Christmas day.'

'That's excellent. When are you coming over?'

'How about now?'

This Christmas, Deborah would fuck Nick Cane out of her system. While she enjoyed herself, should Deborah find out anything else about Andrew Saint, who they were seeing on New Year's Eve, it would be all to the good. Then, at New Year, she'd invent a crisis of conscience about the relationship: race, religion, whatever; dump Nick and return to Leicester, with kudos for getting a result at the last minute. She wasn't done yet.

Chantelle took to sex like a convert to a new religion. Twice, she made him late for work. She complained when he had to give an English lesson on his day off, but he placated her by agreeing to go shopping with her afterwards.

He met Jerry in the city library's café.

'You look tired,' she said, after they'd finished with the play.

'Not getting enough sleep,' he admitted.

'Is that because you're caning it or do you just have a great love life?

When he didn't answer, she said. 'Sorry, too personal.

Students are always going on about that stuff. They're worse than the girls in the hostel.'

'Are you seeing someone?'

She shook her head before replying, in a softer voice. 'I still feel like damaged goods. I don't trust anyone who tries to get too near.'

'You'll get over it,' Nick assured her. He hoped this was true. Jerry had only been in one relationship, and it had come to a violent, messy ending.

'I have nightmares about the police showing up in college, arresting me in front of the whole class.'

'It's not going to happen.'

'I have worse nightmares than that, too. You don't want to hear them.'

Nick hesitated. He had done more than enough for Jerry already, but they would always be connected, and it was hard to step back.

'You can tell me anything you want. There are things you can't tell anyone else. Or shouldn't, anyway.'

'You know, sometimes, you act like you're my dad.'

Nick shuddered, in what he hoped was a comic way. Jerry smiled.

'For now I want to work hard, get to uni. That's what a dad would want to hear, isn't it? Your girlfriend, is she a tall woman with an Afro?'

'Sounds like her.'

'She must be keen. She's followed you here.'

Nick turned to see Chantelle, beaming at him. 'I got off work early,' his lover told him. 'I'll just wait at another table until you're done.'

Nick introduced them.

'We're finished,' Jerry told them. 'But it was nice to meet you.'

Chantelle smiled graciously. Nick was annoyed she'd turned up. True, the lesson was over, but he liked his conversations with

Jerry. He wanted to know if she had plans for Christmas. There was nobody in her life. No adults, anyway, apart from him.

'I'll text you about a lesson in the new year,' Jerry said, and took her leave, dirty blonde hair obscuring her friendly grin. 'Have a good one.'

'You too.'

'Doesn't she pay you?' Chantelle asked when Jerry was gone.

Nick wasn't going to explain the relationship he had with Jerry, who was his landlady. A former lover had given her the flat, which she had no current use for.

'She pays at the start, not the end.'

Just like a pro, he could see Chantelle thinking. He put his arm around her and they left the library. It was a bitter afternoon. A freezing wind whistled up Waverley Street. Too cold to carry out a conversation. A familiar Merc was parked up the road, near the house. Its driver hid behind a newspaper.

Nick was turning the key in the front door when Andrew appeared.

'I've been sat in my car waiting for you to come home.'

'Sorry, had my mobile turned off.'

'I had to visit our friend at short notice.'

Chantelle gave Andrew a curious look. She didn't know about Terence, or that Andrew was shagging Nancy. Nick would rather she didn't find out.

'I was hoping we could go for a drink later,' Andrew added. 'I have to stay over.'

'Sorry, I'm on shift from seven.'

'You can take me for a drink if you like,' Chantelle told Andrew.

'Great!'

Nick wasn't sure how sincere this response was, but invited Andrew in.

'I need to freshen up,' Chantelle said, once they were in the flat, and left them alone.

'Sorry if I'm getting in the way of... whatever,' Andrew said. 'Here's the thing. I had to do some business with Terence so I went to see Nancy again. I tried to persuade her to sort herself out. I think I'm starting to get somewhere.'

'Yeah?' Nick was dubious about his friend's motives.

'Obviously, Terence won't be happy if she goes. Nancy's his best earner. When she leaves, that's *if* I persuade her to leave, I can't be connected to it.'

'You want me to collect her, take her to rehab in the country?'

'Not rehab. She won't go there. My place in London.'

Nick took in what this implied. 'Why not put her on a train?'

'Would you trust her to get that far without a pipe to smoke?'

'I don't know,' Nick admitted. 'What are you going to do with her in London? How will you look after her?'

'I'll get some professional help. I like her, Nick. She's a smart cookie. You wanted me to help her and I am. In my own way.'

'What will Gill Temperley say when she finds Nancy's living with you?'

'Gill never comes to the house. Will you help me?'

The Sunday before Christmas, when Nick was still sleeping off his Saturday night shift, Chantelle arrived just after noon and brought him tea in bed. By the time they got out of bed it was dark. Nick decided to cycle to the Vegetarian Pot and collect an early dinner. Then he saw that it had begun to rain, quite heavily.

'I can go for the food if you like,' Chantelle said. 'After my shower.'

'If I was on your insurance, I could drive.'

She thought for a moment. 'After Christmas, when I have to renew it.'

There was something slightly off about the way she said that. She'd have to declare Nick's conviction if she put him on the insurance. As a result, she might be turned down, or have her premium bumped up. Maybe that was all it was. Nick didn't mind.

Cycling kept him fit, although it could be a pain this time of year.

'I'll go. It's less than a mile. I don't mind getting a bit wet.'

Two streets away, on the cut-through to Forest Road, he glimpsed a guy who looked like Andrew. He was knocking at the front door of one of the big, terraced houses. Why was Andrew still in Nottingham? He'd said he was driving home after his drink with Chantelle.

'How was your drink with Andrew?' he asked her, half an hour later, over aubergine masala. He'd decided not to mention seeing Andrew earlier.

'All right. He doesn't open up a lot, though, does he? The thing he most liked to talk about was what you and him got up to in university days. I found it a bit creepy, if I'm honest.'

'We were kids then,' Nick said, then wished he'd not used that word, because Chantelle wasn't much older than he and Andrew were when they graduated. 'Did he talk about his girlfriend?'

'That Tory MP? No. I asked about her but, between the lines, I get the impression she's stringing him along. He pays her a fortune, you know?'

'He told you that? How much?' Nick was surprised at how good Chantelle was at digging for information.

'40K a year for doing fuck all. He likes boasting about money, your friend, but he doesn't like to talk about how he makes it.'

'He never brags about money when it's just me and him.'

'He didn't want to talk about why he was in Nottingham, either.'

'Ah.' Nick decided to tell the truth. Part of it at least. 'That's because he's trying to help Nancy.'

'You roped him into that?'

'He offered to pay for her rehab, remember. When I failed to persuade her, Andrew said he'd have a go. That's what he's here for.'

'Andrew doesn't strike me as a Good Samaritan.'

'Me neither,' Nick said. 'But people can surprise you.'

19

Sunday, when Sarah walked back to The Park after shopping in town, was the first time it felt like winter. Icy winds whipped round Nottingham Castle.

Sarah ought to walk more. She was putting on weight. Her days of belonging to a gym were a distant memory. Since she stopped being a minister, she had more time for exercise, but less inclination. Her life felt like it was on hold.

Walking helped her think. And remember: how, in Spain, Dad once hinted about a dark secret he'd like to share but didn't want to upset her with. Which was fine at the time, because Sarah had had enough of her father's misdemeanours. If he'd told her that he'd been a spy back in the 1960s, would she even have gone into politics? How electable was the daughter of a traitor, one who had been caught and kicked out of the country? Her majority was miniscule. If the story got out, she would never get back in. And what about the damage the revelation would do to her grandad, who was unable to defend himself. Dead men's reputations made easy targets.

Before she contacted the Public Records Office, Sarah needed to talk this over with someone. Technically, Pete Rugby, the East Midlands regional whip, should be her first port of call. That was if she were to go through official channels. But whips liked to boast that they knew where the bodies were buried. Tell Pete, and he would always have something to hold over her. Sarah didn't want that. She trusted her old boss, the Home Secretary. He had responsibility for the security services now, but no direct influence over the Public Records Office. There was another drawback: the Home Secretary already knew Sarah's biggest secret: that she'd had an affair with Paul Morris.

Morris's murder was unsolved, so the taint of a scandal already hung over her.

There was another senior politician she could turn to. They had once been lovers, and he would not turn her away. He might have the clout to stop the story. But Sarah was under no illusions. If she went to him and he was able to fix this, it wouldn't end there. No matter how civilised the transaction, he would own her, and Sarah did not like to be owned. She wanted to sit at the top table on her own terms, as an equal, or not at all.

The obvious person to call for advice was Steve Carter. The Junior Transport minister was her closest friend in politics, but so far this session Steve had only found time for a brief coffee with her.

There was only one person who had nothing to lose by helping her. But nothing to gain, either. Yes, she was a Tory. But this situation had nothing to do with party politics. Sarah had never seen Gill Temperley socially outside the Commons. She had, however, been given an invitation to her fiftieth birthday party. Gill's home phone number was on the invite. Sarah doubted that she still had it. The event clashed with a prior commitment. Also, if Sarah rang Gill at home, her husband might answer the phone, and he was a politician too, albeit a Euro MP. Gill joked that being a Euro MP was like being a neutered dog: you could run around all you liked and bark as loud as you wanted, but your fucking days were over. Even so, Sarah would rather he didn't know her business.

Tomorrow, Sarah would call Gill as soon as she got in: see if she had any advice on how to suppress a story from the Public Records Office.

'When are we going to meet her, this new girlfriend of yours?' Caroline asked, after Sunday dinner.

Caroline was looking good. She'd let her hair grow again. Eighteen months after Phoebe's birth, she had her figure back, too. Nick was reminded of how strongly he used to fancy her.

Still did, after a few drinks. His niece sat in a high chair to her left, wearing a purple bib.

'Chantelle's coming to the New Year's party. I think you'll like her.'

'It would be hard for me not to like her more than the last one.'

She meant Nancy. Nick didn't want to start that conversation, so he shared a confidence.

'Between you and me, I'm thinking of asking Chantelle to move in.'

'Really? How long have you been seeing each other? Seriously, I mean.'

That was a tricky one to answer. They'd spent a lot of time together since September, but, if, by *seeing each other*, she meant sex, well...

'Three months,' he said.

'That's kind of quick,' Caroline pointed out, in a friendly voice.

'I think she wants me to ask her.'

His sister-in-law turned away from spooning slop into her daughter's mouth and gave Nick a look that mixed her usual condescension with a rare burst of affection.

'Don't take this the wrong way, Nick, but you haven't got a great record of figuring out what women want. I'd leave it until after Christmas, if I were you. Spending the holidays together tells you a lot about a relationship. Maybe take her away on holiday. You'd give Nick some time off, wouldn't you, Joe?'

'You what?' Nick's younger brother had already finished his dinner and was absorbed in the Sports section of the Sunday Times. Caroline repeated the question and Joe answered without looking up.

'Just give me a week's notice. You can have one day's paid holiday for every month you work for me.'

'I should be able to manage a week off by Easter, then.'

Would he still be with Chantelle at Easter? Did they have

enough in common to sustain a relationship? Caroline was right about one thing: women were a mystery to him. His sister-in-law knew him better than any of his exes ever did, bar Sarah. He and Caroline had a thing years ago, before she married Joe. He'd been seriously into her. They were well suited: both teachers, her three years his junior. Then he found out that she was only sleeping with him as a way to stay close to her ex, his kid brother, the professional footballer. When Joe decided he wanted her back, Caroline kicked Nick into touch, but only after she'd made him promise never to tell Joe about the affair. Nick had felt constant, low-level Catholic guilt about this lie ever since, while – as far as he could tell – agnostic Caroline never gave it a second thought.

He trusted Caroline, and not just because of the secrets they shared. If Joe weren't sitting there, nursing his Sunday hangover, he'd have liked to take the conversation about him and women further. But Joe and women was an even more awkward subject, one that neither he nor Caroline would broach. Nick looked at his watch. He had a tutorial to give, the last of the year. The number of students he taught fluctuated between three and seven. Next year, he'd have to get that number up or find himself a better job. He wanted to be able to look after Chantelle in the style to which he'd like her to become accustomed. Take her on holiday, like Caroline suggested.

'Another glass of wine?' Joe offered.

'Gotta go, sorry.' He explained why. 'Thanks for lunch.'

'You're always welcome,' Caroline said. 'Next time she stays over, invite Chantelle to Sunday dinner. I'd like to meet her properly, not just at the party.'

Deborah's flat felt barren. She'd left most of her stuff at home, in Leicester – everything that she didn't need or couldn't bring: possessions that belonged to Deborah, but didn't fit Chantelle. Not that she'd ever invited anyone back to this flat. Unless you counted Saturday, when Andrew Saint insisted on giving her a lift home, then waited like a gentleman while she let herself inside.

The drink with Andrew had yielded less information than she'd hoped. Nothing in the conversation indicated that he was suspicious of her, but he wasn't going to tell her his business in Nottingham. When she pressed him, in a jokey way, he mumbled something about a friend with personal problems. What friends did Andrew have in Nottingham, other than Nick? He hadn't lived here in fifteen years. She hadn't pressed him on that, and Nick had revealed who he really meant: that tart, Nancy.

If Deborah was right about Andrew's real trade, he had to have a Nottingham number two. It wasn't Nick. Deborah had kept a close eye on him, checked his mobile messages, was able to account for what he did when he wasn't with her. Could it be someone connected to Nancy, was that why Andrew was taking such an interest in her? It was a possibility. Time to phone Mike. Make her last report. Her assignment was officially over, but she had been allowed to wind things down on her own terms.

'Back in Leicester yet?' was his first question.

'Not yet. Still tidying up loose ends. You ought to know that I had a drink with Andrew Saint the other night, just me and him.'

'We've been over this,' Mike said, his voice verging on irritation. 'Saint is not the focus of this operation. Still, what did he tell you?'

'He's back in Nottingham this week. You might put a tail on him.'

'I'd need more detail, and more evidence, before I could swing that.'

Deborah explained about Nancy, and the brothel. 'Nick tried to make it sound like Andrew was being a good Samaritan, but the way I see it: Andrew Saint, a brothel, there are bound to be drugs involved.'

Mike thought for a moment before replying. 'That sounds more promising. I'll request local plod on stand-by. Get back to me with more information as soon as you have it.'

'Will do.'

'Have you given in your notice?'

'I finish this week. I have to hand back the keys to the flat by the end of the first week of the new year.'

Deborah decided not to mention the party on New Year's Eve, the one that both Andrew Saint and the MP were expected to attend. She didn't want to push her luck. Why was the police investigation still so focussed on Nick Cane? Because the Chief Constable wanted him out of the way? Nick, as far as she could tell, was clean. More than once, he'd told her how tough he'd found his five years in prison. He'd learnt his lesson. Nevertheless, it was easy for ex-cons to fall foul of the law. It was bad enough that she had to dump him without a proper explanation. She didn't want his life ruined a second time.

20

The two women had agreed to meet in the members' room at the Royal Academy. Gill Temperley insisted on making a pot of tea. Sarah had no patience for this calming ritual. She got straight to the point.

'This is awkward. I need someone to confide in. An MP I trust.'

'Shall I be mother?' Gill poured Assam into bone china cups. 'Other people's secrets are a burden. You should only share yours if you have to.'

'I need advice,' Sarah said.

'Is it about a man? I can tell you this – without knowing anything about him – they never leave their wives, no matter what they say. Not for the mistress, anyway.'

'I wish it were that simple. But, yes, it is a man. My father.'

'I thought your father wasn't around.'

'He isn't. He left Mum nearly thirty years ago, died in 1985. It's what he did before that's coming back to haunt me, and I need to contain the damage.'

'Spill,' Gill said.

When Sarah was done, Gill thought for a while.

'Tons of public records are released at the end of every year,' she said. 'There's a choice about what morsels are fed to the press in advance, and certain things are always held back. Unless Labour has changed things, the decisions are made at various levels, so it may not be too late to stop this coming out. But you need to know the whole story before you can decide how to play it. Were your parents divorced?'

'They never actually got divorced, no.'

'So, as his widow, the public records people approached your mother first. But you're the relative most closely connected and they should have consulted you, too. Do you know the name of the person from the Public Records Office who spoke to your mother?'

'I'm afraid not. She's not been terribly alert these last few weeks.'

'I know somebody there who will talk to you. There are two ways of handling this. You either go through Number Ten, which, I suspect, means their press guy, Alastair Campbell.'

'I'd rather not be in his debt. I don't think this is on Number Ten's radar yet. They've got bigger fish to fry.'

'Or you can try to sort it out yourself, directly.'

'That's what I want to do.'

'How many people do you think knew about your father?'

'Beyond my mother and grandfather, I've no idea.'

'If it didn't ruin Hugh Bone's career, it shouldn't ruin yours.'

'It didn't ruin his career because it didn't come out. I'd like to make sure that it still doesn't come out. Or...'

'The news may hinder your making a speedy return to government.'

'I don't know about *speedy*, but eventually, yes, once my mum's fine.'

'You do realise it might be better to lance the boil? To get this in the public domain and out of the way so that it can't hurt you in the future.'

'I've considered that. But, first, I need to know how bad it is. I need to know what really happened.'

'You're right. Less than two weeks to new year. Your options are narrowing.'

They left together. On Piccadilly, Gill asked. 'Have you seen our mutual friend recently?'

'Andrew? No. But I'm having dinner with him on New Year's Eve.'

'Do give him my regards. Was he able to help you over that Spanish property business?'

'He took it in hand for me, yes.'

'He's such a helpful man.' She said this with a wry smile that Sarah couldn't read. Was it an *I know that you know that I'm screwing him* look? Or something more complicated?

Eve hadn't called for a few days. Nick rang and left a message to invite her and Geoff to the party on New Year's Eve. That made two of his exes on the guest list, Caroline might point out. Three, if he counted her. But so what? In his book, anyone who stuck by him after a five year stretch qualified as a friend for life. He had also invited Tony Bax, an old political ally, and, of course, Andrew.

What Nick still couldn't work out about Andrew was this: did he have a new number two in Nottingham? Was that who he was seeing when Nick thought he spotted him the other night? Nick wasn't in a position to ask. Andrew ought to have somebody in place by now. Why, otherwise, the repeated visits to Hyson Green? Andrew once told Nick that he hoped to be legit by the millennium. At the time, Nick believed him. Now he wasn't so sure.

The Andrew of today was not the Andy Nick first encountered half a lifetime ago. If they were to meet for the first time now, they wouldn't get on. They remained friends because they had always been friends. Yet the only areas they still had in common were the very ones Nick wanted to escape from.

Chantelle was coming round soon. She felt like the future. Despite this, he worried, from time to time, that she wasn't complicated enough for him, that he needed to be with someone who, like him, had been to university and had learnt to see the world in shades of grey. Someone like Sarah.

But that was the old Nick thinking. Chantelle's straightforwardness was what made them right together. She had principles and was still sorting out her take on life. They could be a good team. She would make him change, and he needed to change. Hell, if she wanted, Nick would even go to church with her.

Nick had stopped going to church when he was in the sixth form. Roman Catholicism was an all-or-nothing religion. He'd come down on the side of nothing. Still, if accepting God was the price Chantelle charged for becoming Nick's life partner, bearing his kids, perhaps it was a price worth paying. Most believers faked faith some of the time. He'd learnt that, not from church, but from reading Graham Greene. Only fools didn't doubt.

What kind of Christian would he be? Nick had never done stuff he considered truly bad, but bad things had happened around him. Sometimes he had not done enough to stop them. Sins of omission. These often related to Andrew. His best friend might expect to be the godfather of any child that Nick fathered. That would be a curse of biblical proportions. And Chantelle, he suspected, was the sort of Christian who believed in eternal damnation.

His girlfriend arrived, weary from work. Nick didn't have a shift tonight, but it had become their habit to go straight to bed, then share a shower, and that was what they did.

Later, when she was coming, riding him harder and harder, she used the words for the first time.

'I love *this*! God! I love *you*.'

'Oh yes,' Nick said in return. 'Yes!'

Nick knew better than to take words spoken in orgasm as a permanent truth. He was careful not to say them back. When he used those words, they would be loaded with meaning. They would be a precursor to his asking her to move in. When he was sure. Move in and more.

'It's great being like this,' she said, afterwards, opening a bottle of red. 'Couldn't you change your shifts so we can have more full evenings?'

'I'll ask, when someone leaves.'

He rolled a joint. She liked to smoke after sex.

'Is Andrew coming back this week?' she asked.

'He said he might, but he hasn't called and this is my only night off, so if he wants to go for a drink, he's screwed. Unless you want to go out with him again.'

Chantelle gave a wry look. 'Not so soon after last time. He can be hard work. I tried to make conversation, but he closes so many things down. For instance, have you got any idea what business he's doing in Nottingham?'

Nick shook his head. 'I learnt long ago not to ask direct questions about Andrew's business. If he's got something he wants to tell me, he'll tell me.'

'You don't think it's something, you know... dodgy?'

Chantelle was smart, all right. He couldn't lie to her.

'It wouldn't surprise me in the least. So let's not ask, eh?'

On cue, the phone rang. Andrew.

'I'm still working on trying to get Nancy into rehab. Willing to help?'

'Of course,' Nick said.

'I'm visiting there tomorrow. If she agrees, I want you to bring her to London on Thursday. I'll join you on Thursday night, in time for you to get the last train back. You'll only lose an evening. Can you manage that?'

'Sure. I'll switch a shift. If she agrees, that is.'

'I can be very persuasive.'

'I know you can. Will you come round here tomorrow?'

'When I'm done there. Fourish?'

They agreed the time and Nick hung up. Chantelle gave him a wry, quizzical look.

'What's going on?'

He told her.

Sir Giles was one of those civil service old boys who seemed to belong not just to an older generation, but to a different century. His thick eyebrow hairs were long, grey and proudly wild. He had once been very handsome and retained a distinguished, old school, masculine allure.

'You're a friend of Gill Temperley's. I remember Gill in her first parliament. My, she was a beauty. Still is, of course, and very, very bright.' He paused. 'She speaks highly of you. So, naturally, I'll do what I can to help.'

Sarah chose her words carefully. 'Have you had any instructions from... on high... as to how much information should be released?'

'Not as such. Which surprised me a little. But you are no longer a member of the government and the story is not about you. Were your grandfather still alive, he would, of course, have been consulted. As it is, your mother was the closest relative, so we alerted her in good time, should she wish to argue that any of the information be redacted.'

'By *redacted*, in this context, you mean...?'

'Withheld. There are certain guidelines that allow us to – I suppose the word the press would use is *censor* cabinet papers to remove information that remains sensitive.'

'This is certainly very sensitive for me,' Sarah said.

'I appreciate that the situation is embarrassing, but it is of historical interest. How much has your mother told you?'

Sarah summed up what she had been told. 'I don't understand, however, why, if Dad was exposed by '68, which is when Grandad left the State Security committee, he didn't leave the country until 1970.'

'Therein lies a tale,' Sir Giles said. 'And one that doesn't fully emerge until the cabinet papers for 1969 and 1970 are released.'

'You're telling me that I'm going to have to put up with more revelations next year and the year after as well!'

'I'm afraid so.'

21

1970

Hugh suggested that they meet at his club, The Acropolis. The PM agreed, saying he fancied a change of scene. However, his security detail advised against it, so they met on the third floor of Number Ten as usual. Hugh arrived by the garden entrance. The PM had already poured two large brandies. For ten minutes, they discussed that day's cabinet meeting. Then they moved on to the opinion polls. At last the percentages were beginning to move back in Labour's direction.

They were onto their second drink when Harold said, 'The Security Services. Have you gleaned anything, yet?'

'I had a word with some former colleagues. Of course you have opponents there, people who can't stand you. But nothing to worry about.'

Hugh got out a notepad on which he had already written a message. *You're probably being bugged. Suggest you need a breath of fresh air when I get up to go and I'll tell you more in the garden.*

Harold met his gaze for a moment, and nodded. Hugh began to talk about the opinion polls. 'There's still a big deficit to turn around but, you never know, anything's possible.'

Harold gave a loud yawn. 'Over a year before I need to call an election.'

'You're tired, Prime Minister. I'll see myself out.'

'No, no. I could do with a breath of fresh air. Let me walk down with you.'

Only when they were in the garden did they resume the conversation. Hugh told the PM what he had learned.

'There are plenty of old timers in MI5 who want you out, but at the moment they think you're going to lose the next election and are happy to bide their time. One chap I trust hinted to me – more than hinted – that Number Ten has been bugged since you got in. Five's justification being that there are plenty of reasons to think you're a Soviet plant.'

Harold guffawed. 'And they say I'm paranoid.'

'Indeed. They'd think the same of any successful Labour leader. The point is that they're bugging you so that they'll have something to use should they want to force you out.'

'There's nothing to find.'

'Isn't there?' Hugh gave him a look that said, *we're both men of the world* and Harold gave the smallest shake of the head. He didn't put it about. 'Just be careful. If they don't find sex, they'll come after your finances. Or party donors. Whatever it takes.'

Party donors would be the tricky one. Every party made promises to the people that funded them. Deniable promises that, nevertheless, had to be kept.

'You think I should have the place swept for bugs, get rid?'

'Then they'd know that you know.'

'Nonsense. A show of strength is how it could be portrayed.'

Nearby, an owl hooted. There was rain in the air.

'Too risky a gambit,' Hugh said. 'The people I'm talking to have no suspicion I'm talking to you. You could expose me and we wouldn't get any more intelligence from them.'

'I take your point.' Harold thought aloud. 'Ultimately, I'm in charge of MI5. They've all signed the Official Secrets Act. What's to stop me from letting them know that I know they're plotting? Threaten to put all those behind it in prison for the rest of their natural lives unless they desist and shut up?'

'You'd need proof. I don't have that. It would be easier if I had a formal role that would allow me to interrogate officers who I don't already know.'

'I'd prefer you to keep at it on the hush-hush. The fewer people are aware of these suspicions, the better.' Harold knew that Hugh retained the hope of becoming Home Secretary. As things stood, the incumbent Jim Callaghan had his feet firmly settled under the table. But Jim was a rival, who might one day challenge Harold for the top job. Hugh was a loyalist. And he had a secret weapon: his friendship with Peter Wright.

Harold went on. 'That said, many things may change after the next election. If we manage to win.'

The minute he got home, Hugh rang Peter and arranged to meet. He needed some new dirt that would cleave Harold closer to him. Peter liked to talk, but he remained in active service as MI5's Chief Scientific Officer. He had to be careful what he said. Luckily, Peter hated Harold so much that he was easy to goad into indiscretion. He still harboured suspicions that Harold was a spy.

Times were tough, but Hugh was rooting for Harold. The PM, a lame duck mere weeks ago, could yet hang onto power. None of his rivals, not even Jim, had dared raise their heads above the parapet. They might not like Harold, much, but they respected him. More than that, they feared him. In his current position, the PM could do more damage to them than they to him.

It was time to play the family card, he decided. Sarah and her mum should visit Number Ten while Hugh was a minister. Not Kevin. Now that homosexuality was legal and Kevin worked for Driberg, Hugh's hold on his son was gone. At least Kevin kept in touch with Sarah, visiting Chesterfield every few weeks. Good for the girl to have a young father. Not so good for Felicity, who couldn't stand the sight of her estranged husband.

Hugh rang Felicity, arranged for her to bring Sarah over at half term, then wrote a note to Harold, asking if they could 'pop in' to Number Ten. He knew that the PM would agree. Harold was sentimental about families and felt for abandoned wives. There had been a hint, just a hint, long before the split, that Harold was aware of the rumours about Kevin. The PM had his spies everywhere.

Hugh should know. He was one of them.

22

Peter Wright was waiting in the Cardogan club, nursing a G & T in which the ice had already melted. Hugh ordered him a refill, a double.

'How's the hometown?'

'Still there.' Wright, taller than Hugh, with intelligent, hangdog eyes, had been born in Chesterfield, where Hugh lived, and always affected an interest in the place. Hugh dug out a few snippets about local politics to satisfy him. Wright didn't have many friends in MI5. Bad at following orders, he was, nevertheless, too good an intelligence officer for them to let him go. At least that was how Peter saw it. MI5 tended to give him his head when he wanted to investigate someone.

Since Hugh left MI5, the two men had met for a drink once or twice a year. Their meetings had become more frequent since Hugh became Minister Without Portfolio. Peter and his wife had even been to stay in Chesterfield.

Hugh waited until the drinks had been served before he began the real conversation.

'There was something I needed to ask you, about our old friend.'

They could not be overheard, but Hugh still preferred circumspect language. Probing delicately, however, didn't work with Peter. Wright wagged his long chin with excitement.

'I told you I investigated you-know-who for murder?' he began.

Hugh remembered the tale. The sudden death of Wilson's predecessor as party leader, Hugh Gaitskell, still excited those who liked to think that the Russians were behind everything. The theory went that Wilson was indirectly responsible for the secret poisoning of the Labour leader. The KGB did it in order to install one of their own agents as the new Labour leader. Wilson.

In other words, the PM was a Russian spy. The only trouble with this theory being that it was, not to put too fine a point on it, bollocks. Hugh knew the Russians. They weren't capable of that kind of thinking, or behaviour. A Prime Ministerial plant was much more like the CIA, and they had no motive for backing Wilson. Rather the opposite as, in recent years, the PM had refused to let the UK be drawn into the American imbroglio in Vietnam.

Hugh let Peter ramble on about the Gaitskell conspiracy for a few minutes. It was a rare opportunity for the old boy to sound off with a friend who, like him, had signed the Official Secrets Act. Hugh, in contrast to Peter's colleagues, had no axe to grind. In the end, Peter had to admit that he'd found no evidence against the PM. Hugh ordered another round of drinks.

'What I'm looking for is something more recent,' he told Peter. 'Not a threat from Henry Worthington, but a threat *to* him. Doesn't have to have been a viable threat, but it has to sound like a credible one.'

Henry Worthington was the PM's codename at MI5. Wright had a mischievous smile that came out on rare occasions. He used it now, before his expression settled into frank suspicion.

'On whose behalf are you asking?'

'Who do you think? This can't backfire on you, Peter. I promise.'

Peter thought for a moment.

'There was that nonsense with Cecil King in '68. Nothing came of it, and Cecil lost his job not long afterwards. But they tried to bring Mountbatten in. They were serious, according to him.'

'Serious about what?'

'A coup, aimed against Wilson.'

'Tell me more.'

After their conversation, Hugh went for a short walk to think things through, make sure he'd got the story straight. The discussion, according to Wright, had taken place in early summer. He had not been entirely clear on everybody who was there: Cecil King, certainly. Ironic that the proprietor of the Mirror newspaper group, who you would expect to be friendly to Wilson, had instigated the whole thing. Solly Zuckerman, the government's chief scientific adviser, was present. So was Lord Mountbatten, war hero and mentor to the heir to the throne, the young Prince Charles. This was certain, for the meeting had taken place in Mountbatten's London flat.

According to Peter, Zuckerman stormed out as soon as King broached the coup idea, shouting that it was treason. Mountbatten heard the discussion out but did not commit to the plan. Nothing was finalised, but someone present must have had words elsewhere. For, a few days later, King was ousted as chair of the Mirror group. The ostensible reason was that his colleagues were tired of King's constant attacks on the Prime Minister, who the paper strongly supported. But the timing suggested knowledge of the putative coup.

It wasn't much of a conspiracy. What was this information worth, Hugh wondered. News of the coup conspiracy might fuel Harold's paranoia about the establishment, but it was not an imminent danger. Unless Labour were re-elected. Then these bitter men would become the people to watch.

'You're sure of all this?' he'd asked Peter.

'Of course I'm sure. If this were a communist country, everyone involved would have been lined up against a wall and shot. But Five and Six are soft as shit. Full of lefties who haven't got the conviction or the nerve to take on the right.'

Peter was a Tory through and through. It wouldn't surprise Hugh if he had been somehow involved in the plot, which was why he hadn't mentioned it before. He'd changed the topic, letting Peter revisit an old saw about how he had part of his pension stolen when he joined MI5. When the old spy paused for breath, Hugh had invented a meeting he had to get to. This allowed him to escape before he was too squiffy to forget any of the detail.

The lift in Mansion Gardens wasn't working. His flat was on the third floor. Never mind. A bit of exercise would do him good. He'd planned to sell this flat to raise some cash, but now that he was a minister, that had to wait. He was pleased to find that he was not out of breath when he reached his front door. His heart beat only a little more strongly. Not bad for a man past sixty.

Hugh put his key into the front door, only to find that it was unlocked. Nobody but the cleaner had a key, and she never came in the evenings. Hugh collected himself for a moment, then opened the door as quietly as he could. There was an umbrella stand to the right of the door. It held a stout stick that, in extremity, might make a good weapon for defence or attack. Hugh reached for it. Then the light came on in the hallway.

'Dad! Hell, you gave me a shock.'

Kevin Bone wore what looked like a woman's blouse, a frilly affair in blue cheesecloth. His curly hair was longer than Sarah's. Add to this his red, flared cotton jeans and he looked like a clown. A guilty clown. Hugh took a deep breath, collected himself, and took off his coat.

'How did you get in here?'

'I borrowed Felicity's key. She won't miss it. Who were you expecting?'

'I wasn't expecting anyone. What are you doing?'

Hugh strode past him into the study. His son did not reply, or try to stop him. Two drawers of the bureau were open, including the one that Hugh always kept locked.

'You found the key, then?'

Kevin nodded. 'I'm sorry. I needed money.'

This was a lie. The money was in the safe, and Kevin knew

that. He did not know the combination. Hugh glanced at the government papers on the desk. Some were marked *secret*, but there was nothing that would be of any interest to a hostile power or even a tabloid newspaper. If there had been, they, too, would have been in the safe. The only secrets in this flat were securely locked in Hugh's head. Kevin stroked his thick moustache.

'I suppose you want me to go. You've got that look on. Don't tell me, your mistress is about to arrive. I'll bet she's got a key.'

'I don't...'

'Or a call girl. I know what you're like. Highly sexed. I inherited it from you. Don't tell me you haven't got a woman here. Or women.'

'We're not all at it like dogs on heat,' Hugh said.

'No, you haven't suddenly been liberated, like my clan. I feel sorry for your generation, had to do most of your shagging just before the pill. Severely limited the outlets for your libido, I'm sure.'

Kevin was pushing something deeper into his trouser pocket. A camera, Hugh would bet. He wanted Hugh to get angry, so he would throw him out without further interrogation. But Hugh was good at keeping his temper.

'How's old Tom? Has he not got tired of you yet?'

'You don't understand anything, do you?' Kevin was loud and whiny, like the petulant teenager he had never grown out of being. 'People like me and Tom, we aren't interested in having each other. We go on the prowl together. We take boys back to his place. And I've had boys here, when you've been in Chesterfield. You had no idea, did you?'

There had been times when Hugh suspected.

'Give me the key,' he said. 'Give me Felicity's key.'

'It's not *her* key, you silly old bugger. I had it copied and returned the original.'

'Nevertheless, I want it.' Hugh knew his son's meanness. He would only have had one copy made. Reluctantly, the boy handed it over.

'I'm going to go now,' he said. 'I'll see you in Chesterfield at the weekend.'

'What do you want to go there for?'

'To see Sarah, of course. And don't come up with any threats, or I'll tell her, and your local party, that my dad is sleeping with my wife.'

23

1998

Sir Giles looked at his watch. The glance implied another appointment, or an early dinner date. Sarah needed to make her pitch quickly.

'When push comes to shove, my father was a very minor player, wasn't he? There were hundreds of spies in the 50s and 60s. So why pick on him?'

'There *were* plenty of others, but they weren't spying on the chairman of the State Security Select Committee.'

'When did my grandfather find out what my father was up to?'

'Not until 1969.'

Sarah tried to process the information. 'But Dad had been exposed before that, otherwise this wouldn't be in the '68 cabinet papers.'

'That's correct.'

'What am I missing here?'

'The newsworthy event took place in 1968. I'm not at liberty to say what further events might have taken place in subsequent years.'

Sarah tried to concentrate her mind. 'When did the... *newsworthy event* come to light?'

Sir Giles smiled. 'You're quite good at forensic questioning, Ms Bone. I wonder that you didn't become a barrister, or a police detective.'

'I used to be a police officer, as I expect Gill told you. Help me out here. Who found out that Dad was a spy in 1968? My grandad?'

'No.'

'But it was discussed in cabinet, or it wouldn't be in the papers.'

'Not in cabinet as such. There is a documented meeting between the Prime Minister and the Home Secretary when the Home Secretary brought the matter to the PM's attention.' Sir Giles looked at his watch again. 'I really have to...'

'Just one more thing. How was my father exposed?'

'That information is not contained in the 1968 papers.'

Sarah stood to take her leave. She didn't know if Sir Giles realised it but, for the first time, he had mentioned somebody she could talk to, somebody who was still alive.

'Thank you for your help,' she said.

'At your service.'

Outside the Kew offices, Sarah had to wait several minutes for a taxi. It gave her time to think. The man she wanted to see was in his eighties, so was unlikely to be in his office so late in the day, especially during the parliamentary recess. But if she went there now she would, at least, be able to leave the former home secretary a note, stating that she had urgent business with him. With luck, he would be there tomorrow. She got into a black cab.

'House of Lords,' she said.

Chantelle rolled out of bed on Wednesday morning.

'I'm tempted to call in sick. If it wasn't my last day, I would.'

'I didn't realise the surgery was closed tomorrow,' Nick said.

Chantelle hesitated. 'I've managed to fix it so that I'm off until new year.'

'Nice. Only thing is, I might have to go to London tomorrow.'

'Why?'

'Long story. I'll tell you tonight, if you're coming by.'

'When will you know?'

'This afternoon, when Andrew's been.'

'So it's the *rescue Nancy* thing.'

'Yeah.'

'You don't still have the hots for her, do you?'

'No. I only have the hots for you. I can't speak for Andrew.'

Chantelle stretched her legs out from the bed, and tugged on her woolly tights. 'You mean Andrew isn't acting entirely out of... what's the word? Altruism.'

'I don't think Andrew knows the meaning of the word *altruism*. But he's the best hope of getting her clean.'

'Have you told Eve?'

'Not yet. The news would make a nice Christmas present for her, if things work out.'

Again, a slightly shifty look. What wasn't she telling him?

'Am I missing something here?' he asked.

'I told Eve I wouldn't say. But I don't like having secrets from you.'

Nick had no idea what was coming. She changed the subject.

'Andrew wouldn't be sampling the goods, by any chance?'

Nick sighed. 'I wouldn't put it past him. You don't get to see Nancy in person unless you pay, and Andrew likes to get his money's worth.'

'So does Eve's husband.'

His eyes met hers. He hadn't misunderstood.

'Oh shit.'

'We saw him there. Eve already suspected. Have you heard from her since the afternoon the three of us went round?'

'I put a note in her Christmas card, saying I hoped to have news soon.'

'She'd still be glad if you got Nancy off the game, if only because it keeps her away from hubby. But nobody's motives in this are altruistic.'

'Yours are.'

Chantelle shook her head. 'I wanted to make sure that you weren't still interested in Eve or Nancy. You're involved because you're guilty about Nancy and you've still got a thing for Eve.

Oh, don't deny it. You've got this warm thing going on when you talk about her. And she still fancies the pants off you, that's obvious. I was protecting my territory. Eve saw that. She respected it.'

'As long as you know I'm faithful to you.'

'Men are only faithful when it's their best option,' Chantelle said. 'I intend to stay your best option. What time's Andrew coming over?'

'Around four, he said. He's going to the brothel to set things up.'

'I don't understand why he can't take her to London himself.'

'These are violent people Nancy works for. He doesn't want them to know it was him.'

'But it's alright if they work out it was you?'

'They won't, because nobody will see us leave town together, and she won't be living with me.'

'Even so, no point in taking unnecessary risks. If Nancy agrees to go, you should take her in my car.'

'You're the best,' Nick said. 'How can I thank you?'

'I can think of a very good way.'

24

Lord Callaghan was eighty-six. His tall frame had taken on a pronounced stoop.

'A pleasure to meet Hugh Bone's granddaughter.' The former Prime Minister waved Sarah to a seat in his spacious office. He offered her tea, which she refused. 'Your note said this had to do with cabinet papers.'

'Not the cabinet, as such, but a meeting that took place between you and the prime... Harold Wilson. The subject was my father, Kevin Bone.'

'Ah.' The former PM sat down opposite her. 'When was this?'

'1968.'

'Of course. The thirty year rule.' He gave a reassuring smile that suggested she had nothing to worry about. His lordship was good at reassurance. The papers had once christened him "Sunny Jim". 'But if the story of this meeting is about to come out, why are you here to ask me about it?'

'There are aspects that don't make sense to me. Also, I'm worried that there are further... events to be revealed, in 1969 and 1970. I don't want to whinge, but, if there are highly negative stories about my family in the papers every New Year for three years, it will affect my career.'

'Of course. You want to get back into government?'

'I might. And I've got one of the most marginal seats in the country.'

'Understood. What have they told you?'

'That my father was a spy. That he stole secrets from his own father for money. It's not entirely clear how he was exposed. And I don't know why he didn't leave the country for two years. I was hoping you could help me.'

Callaghan stood. He was the only man who had ever held all of the great offices of state: Chancellor, Foreign Secretary and Home Secretary, as well as Prime Minister. He had been a success in every job but the last, for which he had waited too long. The old man walked slowly to the narrow window and gazed at the gabled buildings of the parliamentary estate.

'It was a very long time ago,' he said. 'I would have to ask to see all of the papers, to be sure. I have access, of course. I used them for my autobiography. However, since time is of the essence, memory will have to suffice.'

Sarah waited while he stared out of the window. Callaghan nodded, to himself it seemed, then returned to his comfortable chair.

'The secret services were in a bad way in the 1960s. After Burgess, Philby and McLean, there was press speculation about a fourth man. Secretly, we already had the fourth man, Anthony Blunt. He was allowed to remain *in situ* because he provided useful intelligence when we were looking for other spies. There was paranoia about a spy somewhere at the very top – the fifth man, if you like – but the whole system was fatally compromised. We knew there were dozens of spies and we'd never expose them all, but we had to keep up appearances for the Americans. There were endless investigations, going round in circles. It's all been documented in lurid books.'

'None of them mention my father or grandfather, though.'

'My recollection is that your grandfather was investigated initially. Not because he was under suspicion. He had been given positions that required enormous trust precisely because of his reputation for integrity. He'd worked for the Security Services after the war, before he became an MP. That experience was why he was put on the National Security Committee, and subsequently became its chairman. In which role he was privy to regular briefings from my office and others, hence he underwent biannual security clearance checks. Hugh had access to all but the most sensitive papers.

'The first time he was vetted – although we didn't use that word then, we would have called it "screened" – he came through clean, but the second time, in 1968, certain leaks were suspected and we were much more thorough. Hugh was given a document containing information about the Polaris missile that the Russians would have been very interested in. We were clandestinely monitoring their communications. Within a month, it was clear that the Russians had the faked briefing. So Hugh was put under close surveillance. And it emerged that the person selling the secrets wasn't him, but his research assistant. Your father. Which left me with something of a dilemma.'

'How did you resolve it?'

'It was Harold's idea. First, we fed Hugh more fake information. Never to the committee itself, but in the background briefings that Hugh received. But disinformation has its limits, and its risks, because you have to mix it with real secrets in order to make it convincing. After a few months, Harold promoted Hugh to the government. The job he was given was a nebulous one, with far fewer secrets. Hugh was given his own staff, so had no need for a research assistant. Your father could have walked away at that point. He'd served both sides and was of little further use to either of them. We weren't interested. There were spies everywhere in those days, hard as it may be to believe now. Prosecuting him would have served no purpose. It was your father who blew the whistle. He caught Kevin photographing secret documents that he kept at home and told the PM. After that, it was only a matter of time before we prosecuted your father, but, as I recall, the matter kept being put off. Then we lost the election and your father... what happened to him?'

'He fled the country. Never left Spain after 1970.'

'That would explain why the matter didn't cross my desk again.'

Sarah left a silence for him to fill, but Callaghan had told her as much as he was going to. She thanked him warmly. 'You've explained a lot. Can I ask your advice?' she added. 'How should I proceed?'

'You're right to want the story killed off. It will keep coming back to hurt you. I'm surprised that it's been sanctioned for release. Which team are you on: Brown or Blair?'

Sarah had never heard this rift put so bluntly by someone so senior.

'Neither. I get on with both men but I'm not in the pocket of either.'

'That explains it. You've no protector. Well, I might be able to help you out this time. Leave it with me and I'll see what I can do. After all, the story ended on my watch.'

'How do you mean?'

That familiar, comforting smile. Then the punch in the mouth. 'I sacked Hugh when I took over as PM. Told him it was time to make way for a younger man. I owed him nothing and I had a few debts to pay. But I felt bad about doing it. He was a very able man, and a loyal one. He sacrificed his own son, after all.'

Nick spotted the Audi 80 on his way back from giving an English lesson. The daughter of a newsagent on the Alfreton Road got out of Games on Wednesday afternoons in order to spend two hours with Nick. Forty notes for half-writing her assignment on *Of Mice and Men*. Nick's route home took him along Radford Boulevard, past Radford Road, where he planned to pick up a couple of things at ASDA. He couldn't resist a glimpse down the dead end street where Andrew was seeing Nancy.

Andrew's Merc wasn't there. He would have left it in the ASDA car park. But Shaved Head's Audi was parked at the end of the street, with its owner at the wheel. The guy had to be following Andrew. Why? Andrew wasn't making a delivery today. He never did stuff like that in person, never did anything he could be arrested for. Nick crossed the road and turned into ASDA. He got his phone out. Best to warn Andrew that he was under surveillance. There was no doubt this time. Andrew would take it seriously, act accordingly. He hoped that the brothel had a back exit. Nick didn't want Shaved Head shadowing Andrew to his flat. Again.

Before he could tap in the number, Nick saw the police cars. Two Ford Focuses turned onto the narrow road and blocked it off. Six officers – four men, two women – charged out of the cars, toward the brothel. The lead officer knocked once and shouted a warning. He waited two seconds, then nodded to the ones with the battering ram, who broke down the door.

Radford Road was a busy thoroughfare so, despite the December chill, it didn't take long for a crowd to gather. Easy for Nick to slip in among them. One of the first people dragged out was Terence. The pimp stared straight ahead, murderously angry. Then came the punters. Two middle-aged men followed by a third, who pulled a coat over his head to avoid being recognised. Next, and last, Andrew.

Andrew allowed himself to be ushered into the police car. When both cars had left the street, Shaved Head drove off, too. The crowd dispersed, unaware, perhaps, what kind of house it was. Not knowing, therefore, that the main attractions were still inside, Nick decided to go and look for Nancy.

Three days into recess, the parliamentary estate was quiet. Sarah looked for Gill to thank her for helping with the Public Records Office. She wouldn't tell her about Jim Callaghan. That was between the two of them. Sarah had done as much as she could, short of grovelling to Tony or Gordon, and she wasn't sure how effective that would be. She needed to keep her head down and her nose clean. The former PM was probably right. Her embarrassment hadn't figured into calculations about whether to release the story. She was irrelevant.

'How did it go at the Public Records Office?' Gill asked, when Sarah found the Tory, who was alone in her office.

'Not as well as I hoped, but I got a clearer picture of what's going on.'

'If there's anything else I...' Gill's mobile began to ring, so she didn't finish the sentence. Her ringtone was, if Sarah's scant knowledge of opera sufficed, something from *Madame Butterfly*. Gill listened. A frown began to cross her face, then decided to stay there.

'I see. Thanks for letting me know.'

'Bad news?' Sarah asked.

'Yes, a mutual friend of ours is in a little trouble.'

Sarah lowered her voice. 'Andrew Saint?'

'The police just raided a brothel in a part of Nottingham called... Hyson Green, would that be right?'

'Yes.'

'They're planning to name and shame the punters caught in flagrante.'

Sarah recalled being briefed on this *publicise the punters* press initiative, but she thought it only applied to kerb crawlers, who were a public nuisance.

'Can they do that?'

'So it would seem. Your old friend was one of five men arrested.'

Sarah swore. 'Is there anything we can do?'

'Not unless you want to draw more bad publicity on yourself. Did you know that he was in the habit of—?'

'—No, of course not.'

'Most men have the sense to choose somewhere more classy, places that have an arrangement with the police. Maybe he's got a thing for rough trade.' Gill sighed. 'Men and their sexual predilections never cease to surprise me.'

'You and he never...?'

'Good God, no.'

Sarah didn't conceal her surprise. 'I'm sorry, you gave the impression.'

'That was what he wanted, and I played along. But tubby bearded men aren't my cup of tea at all. Which isn't to say that he didn't try, in a roundabout way, or that I didn't let him think that, in the fullness of time, when I knew him better... Do you think I ought to stop working for him? It's all rather seedy. Though, to be honest, I suspected something worse.'

'How do you mean?' Sarah asked.

'When I took the job, John wasn't keen. He looked into the company's finances and they were... less than transparent. To be on the safe side, I hired an investigator to check up on Andrew. That's who just phoned.'

Sarah's mobile rang. She looked at the caller ID. Andrew. She showed Gill.

'Don't answer. He'll be after you to talk to your Chief Constable friend, see if his name can be kept out of it.'

Sarah hesitated. Gill snatched the phone from her, pushed it into her bag. 'Let it ring out. If you reject the call, he'll know, but you mustn't answer. Unless, that is, you want to save him.'

Sarah thought about calling Eric. But, no. She was still pissed off with the Chief Constable for setting Nick up with Chantelle, or whatever her real name was. She wasn't going to owe him one in order to save Andrew from embarrassment.

'Andrew might just have a good excuse,' Sarah said, as the phone stopped ringing, 'though I can't think what it would be'.

'Check your messages in a minute. See how good his explanation is.'

25

There were five women. The youngest, still wearing a see-through pink negligee, looked about fourteen. The oldest must be at least fifty. Nick would have taken Nancy for his own age, had he not known that she was seven years younger. She sat opposite him, next to a woman of similar vintage and look: hollow-eyed, heavily made-up. Nancy wore a grey, vintage overcoat with, he suspected, nothing underneath.

'Can we talk?' he said.

She shrugged. 'Nothing better to do.'

'Let's get out of here.'

'I'll get dressed,' she told him, and left the room.

The other women eyed him with something approaching interest. The girl in the negligee pulled it tighter over her buds of breasts, wanting him to take a good look.

'How old are you?' he asked.

'Sixteen, innit?'

'Do you live here?'

'Nah, a hostel. What are you, a social worker or summut?'

At least she didn't take him for a punter. She would live in the kind of hostel that Jerry lived in when Nick first met her. The city's official statistics said that more than half the girls in care ended up selling their bodies. Which meant, in practice, the vast majority of them. There seemed to be nothing that anybody could – or would – do about that situation. One of the other women, a blonde of nineteen or so, spoke.

'You're a dealer, aren'tcha? Saw you with Terence before. Got something to take the edge off? It's been a rough afternoon.'

'Is that what the police raid was about? Were they looking for drugs?'

The fiftyish woman, who was black, and fleshier than the others, maybe not an addict, answered for all of them. 'Terence won't allow any drugs on the premises, mister. And you don't mess with Terence.' She pulled down her blouse to reveal a three-inch long scar on the side of her left breast. 'I came to a private arrangement with a client once. But only once. You a friend of his? Are you going to look after us, or just Nance?'

'I don't work for Terence, I'm afraid. If he doesn't allow drugs here, what did they arrest him for?'

The woman Nancy's age had a supermodel body, but sunken eyes. Her smile revealed two gold-capped teeth. 'He's been running a house of ill repute, duck.'

That would be it. Selling your body in a private house wasn't a crime, but it was against the law to live off the proceeds of immoral earnings. Terence had been arrested for being a pimp.

'What about the punters, what did they arrest them for?'

'Said they were going to take their pictures for the Evening Post,' the teenager said. 'Good thing you didn't come round any earlier, or you'd be in there too.'

Nick looked at his watch.

'Nancy's cleared off,' said the black woman. 'Think she was going to go somewhere with you, Mister? You got another think coming.'

Before Nick could decide whether she was telling the truth, the teenager got up and began to rub herself against him. The other white girl, not much older, joined her and did the same.

'Two for the price of one?' the younger said, in a thick Nottingham accent. 'We can put on a show for you, if you like. I'll bet you like to watch.'

When Nick shook himself loose, all four women began to laugh. Their bitter, mocking cascade drove him out of the house, onto the empty street. There was no sign of Nancy. Nick walked rapidly back to the ASDA car park, where he collected his bicycle and cycled home. Only when he got in did he realise that he'd forgotten to shop. He had nothing in for dinner.

26

Opinion at the cabinet table was divided. Many thought that a June General Election was too risky. Labour was still behind in the polls, and the economy was likely to have improved by October, the other possible date. There was also the matter of the World Cup in June. England had won the football trophy four years ago, when they were the home side. A good performance in Brazil would boost the party in power. A bad one would have the opposite effect.

Half the cabinet were inclined to wait until October, but the mood seemed to be shifting towards June. Dick Crossman had changed his mind to favour the earlier date. Hugh, who hated to get things wrong, had yet to come down one way or the other. He argued that Harold should wait for the local election results before deciding. That poll was only a week away.

'Opinion polls are all very well,' he argued, 'but we need to see how people vote in real elections.'

Nobody disagreed with him.

Afterwards, he asked to have a private word with Harold. He wanted to prepare the ground for his coup revelation. *Coup* was too strong a word. The danger was not imminent, though the plot was bound to be revisited should Labour be re-elected. Trouble was, Kevin's treachery interfered with Hugh's timing. Were he to give Harold a few juicy details today, at the same time as he told him about Kevin, the intelligence might mitigate the embarrassment of Hugh's own son being a traitor, but that was all. He wanted more.

Harold, as it turned out, was not keen to talk to him.

'I'm sorry to press you, Prime Minister, but it is a very

sensitive and urgent matter.'

'Very well.' The PM explained that he had to take a conference call with LBJ, the US president, but agreed to see Hugh that evening.

When Hugh returned, after dinner, Harold took him into the garden, which meant that he still took Hugh's bugging intelligence seriously, but hadn't had the bugs removed.

'You said this was urgent.'

'It is. You'll want to pass it down to MI5, but you had to hear it from me, first. It's about my son, Kevin.'

The PM frowned and lit a small cigar. The night was mild but overcast. The flame from Harold's lighter cast eerie shadows across his face.

'I'm listening.'

'I got back from a meeting with one of my contacts last night.' Hugh mustn't say anything that might identify Peter. 'I found Kevin going through the papers on my desk. I think he had a camera.'

'You *think?*'

'I saw him putting something away. He made a very serious threat that caught me off balance, so I let him go. Last night, there was no high grade intelligence in my desk, but there is from time to time and it was clear that he's been at it for a while. He'd had a key cut.'

Hugh paused to take in the PM's reaction. Harold blew smoke into the night air.

'I wondered how long it would take for you to find out.'

'You knew?'

'MI5 have been looking into him since before he started working for Tom Driberg last year. Tom's not been above suspicion himself.'

'I know Tom's queer but… a spy?' Hugh calculated quickly. 'Is he being blackmailed by the Russians?'

Harold gave an expansive shrug. 'What Tom gets up to is an open secret. More likely he needed money. Your son likes boys too, doesn't he?'

'I'm afraid so. I thought that was why Driberg hired him.'

'No. He hired him because he was your son, and you're in the cabinet, with what most people assume is an intelligence role.'

'I see.'

Harold put his left arm round Hugh's shoulder. 'Don't look so crestfallen, man. Once we knew the lad was spying on you, we made sure that you didn't have any access to papers we didn't want the Russians to see. We did feed you one or two things that we wanted them to take seriously.'

Hugh shook off the PM's arm, humiliated. 'Why didn't you tell me? I'd have done whatever you asked.'

An apologetic smile. 'People get sentimental where family's involved.'

Hugh played for time. 'There must be more to it than that.'

'We had to be sure that you weren't involved. You used to be in Five, at a time when traitors abounded. Nothing to worry about: you were cleared. As far as your son goes, if he knows that we know, we'd better pick him up. I'll get Jim to talk to Five. You'll need to be debriefed. OK?'

'OK,' Hugh said. 'Only...'

'You want to avoid a scandal. Kevin's got something on you?'

'I'm afraid so. It's... personal, not political or financial.'

'He knows that you're having an affair with his wife.'

How the hell did Harold know that? A lucky guess? No point in asking.

'I'm afraid so. The other night, he threatened to tell my granddaughter.'

'Lovely little Sarah. She's too young to take that kind of thing in, isn't she? We'll try and get rid quietly.' The PM took one last suck on his cigar then dropped it onto the path, where he stubbed it out with his shoe. Sparks flew. 'You do realise that all of this will come out one day?' he added.

'Yes, but, please God, not until we're both of us long in our graves.'

27

'Has Kevin been in touch?' Hugh asked Felicity.

It was nearly midday. He had been at Five until the early hours. The spooks knew everything, including that he had been talking to Peter. Just old friends, sharing a few bevvies, Hugh had told them. They seemed to buy that.

'Not a dicky bird,' Flic told him. 'Why, have you seen him?'

'Yes. Two nights ago.' How much to tell her? 'I want you and Sarah to spend the weekend with me. Pick her up from school and bring her over.'

'You want me to close the office early?'

'Whenever you like. Go home and pack what you both need.'

'What's going on?'

'Probably nothing. I'll be home by the time you get there.'

From St Pancras to Chesterfield, he slept, only waking after the train left Derby. The flat, dull Midlands landscape trundled by. He accepted a cup of tea from the First Class steward. Anxieties smoothed by sleep, his mind began to work again. Over the years, Hugh had learned to value those times in the day when his brain was sharp and all of the cogs turned as they should. Now he found that he could see the situation clearly. Kevin would be arrested sooner or later, so would have to leave the country. His son would not rush to tell Sarah the filthy truth, as he had threatened, but might one day be tempted to sell the story to a newspaper. Hugh would have to make sure that Kevin didn't run out of money, for the threat would not diminish over the years.

Hugh had some savings, and a pension pot. But he also had fourteen years left on a big mortgage. He had been thinking of calling it a day at the next election: sell Bone Mansion, put Edith into a home, whisk Sarah and Felicity away to somewhere far distant, start all over again. But he'd left it too late. He'd need to keep working until the next election now, maybe the one after. The house was expensive to run. An invalid wife was costly enough without the added burden of his son's family to assist.

There were worse things in life than being the MP for Chesterfield. Politics was full of middle-aged men who'd kill to secure a safe Labour seat. Moreover, Flic's job would remain safe for as long as he held onto his.

At Chesterfield station, he looked for a taxi and was surprised to find his daughter-in-law waiting in her blue Cortina. Flic smiled anxiously.

'I thought we could pick up Sarah from school together, go straight to the house.'

'Good idea.'

As a couple, they were always awkward in public. Passers-by knew who Hugh was. It would not do for him to be seen kissing his secretary, even though she was family. She had been secretary first. He hadn't fancied her when he appointed her. She was so young then, younger than his only son. Why would such thoughts cross his mind? But after Edith's stroke...

Once they were in traffic, Hugh risked squeezing her thigh. It amazed him sometimes, that this woman, barely thirty, was his lover. Famous artists and the like might get away with muses half their age, but Hugh wasn't Picasso. He was an ageing politico with a beer gut and a wheelchair ridden, barely cognisant wife.

While they waited outside Sarah's school he told her what he had caught Kevin doing. He held back nothing, not even the MI5-backed plot to unseat Wilson.

'But you didn't tell the Prime Minister about it?'

'No. I'm saving that story up. I can claim to have found it out during the campaign and ask for an urgent meeting on security matters before he gets round to the cabinet reshuffle. By then, Kevin's betrayal will be old news.'

'If this was Russia,' Flic said, 'they'd have executed him by now.'

She said this as though it were what she wanted to happen. Then Sarah charged out of the school gates and jumped into the back seat of the car.

'Are we going to Grandad's?' she asked.

'Yes, we are,' Felicity said.

'I wrote a story today,' Sarah said.

'What was it about?' Hugh asked her. 'Perhaps you can tell it to grandma.'

'A prince who kidnapped a princess from the neighbouring kingdom because she wouldn't marry him.'

'That sounds a bit naughty,' Hugh said. 'Did the princess marry the prince in the end?'

'No. She escaped and told the prince's father, the king, what he had done, and the king was very angry, so he chopped the prince's head off.'

'Isn't that rather... *extreme*?' Flic asked her daughter.

'No, because the King falls in love with the princess and marries her and they have more children together and everyone lives happily ever after.'

'I see,' Flic said. She gave Hugh an amused glance. He decided not to ask Sarah what had become of the king's first wife.

Hugh relieved the nurse and took Sarah to see her grandma Edith, who was propped up in bed, staring at children's TV. Hard to tell if she took anything in. Her lips drooped. Her eyes were dead. Some days, the home help found it impossible to persuade Edith to get up.

Sarah was happy to join Grandma on the bed. When Bill and Ben had been and gone, she would tell Edith her story and Edith would fail to understand, but Sarah wouldn't mind. She accepted that Nana Bone didn't know who she was and never showed affection for her. But one day she would begin to mind. She would resent the time she spent in this over-heated room with its underlying smell of pee. One day, Hugh might feel driven to take one of the fat pillows that propped Edith up and use it to smother her sad, insensible face. She had been like this for thirteen years. The doctors said she might last another thirteen.

The phone rang. Flic answered it. At first, she didn't call him. Then she bellowed his name. This was a big house, but Hugh refused to have bells. You needed to shout.

'It's Kevin.'

Hugh took the call upstairs, with Flic listening in on the other line. His son was terse and to the point. 'They told me to leave the country. Before the election's called. A new government might not look so kindly on me.'

'They're being very kind. Where will you go?' Hugh asked his son.

'Spain. Majorca, maybe. Buy me a house and I'll agree to be at fault in the divorce.'

Hugh's son thought that he was a good negotiator, but he had nothing on Hugh. 'The most I can spare is seven thousand. That should buy you somewhere more than decent in a cheap country.'

'I need ten.'

'Seven and a half is the most I can do. But it'll be a lifetime tenancy, held in trust for Sarah.'

'You really don't want me to come back, do you?'

'I'll make you an allowance while I'm still in parliament, so you should be good for another four or five years. By then, I'll expect you to find a job.'

'I can teach languages. That's not an issue. But if you want Sarah to inherit, we'd better make sure she gets somewhere nice. Ten thousand.'

'I can just about manage eight. Spain's dirt cheap. Choose the right area and you'll be able to afford to put in a swimming pool.'

'Yes, Sarah would like that.' They haggled over the allowance. There was no need to discuss why Kevin was choosing Spain. It did not have an extradition treaty with the UK. General Franco wasn't friendly to homosexuals, but that was a surmountable problem. Kevin had always been discreet.

'I'll come over this weekend to say goodbye and collect some cash.'

'I'll talk to my bankers tomorrow.'

When he went back to the bedroom, children's TV was over and Sarah was telling Edith her story.

'He's a bad prince', the King said. 'His mother always said he'd come to no good. I'm going to have his head chopped off.'

'But he's your only child,' the princess said. 'I don't want to marry him, but you don't have to execute him.'

'Oh, but I do,' the King told her. 'You see, my wife the queen died in childbirth and I have been sad for a long, long time. Now I have seen how brave and beautiful you are, you have put new life into me. I want you to become my wife. We can have more children but their elder brother would always be their enemy, so he must die. Will you be my queen?'

The princess thought about it. The King was quite old and she wasn't ready to have children, but he was a nice man, she did want to be queen and didn't care about the Prince one way or the other.

'Yes,' she said. 'I will.'

After they married she had lots of children. When her father died they joined the two kingdoms together. Then, when the king died she married her favourite groom and they rode horses together and were happy for the rest of their days.

'Bravo!' Hugh said, and clapped his hands. 'A very satisfying ending.'

Edith continued to stare at the TV, even though Sarah had turned it off. Sarah got off the bed and gave her old grandad a cuddle.

'When I'm older,' she said, 'can I have a horse? There's room for one in the field at the back.'

'We'll see,' Hugh said, wondering how many horses a house in Spain with a swimming pool would pay for.

The local election results were good. The Tories lost 327 seats while Labour gained 443. You couldn't ask for a better omen for a General Election. But the big news of the day was that Will Owen had been acquitted of treason. Peter reckoned the Labour MP was guilty as hell. Owen didn't deny talking to or taking money from the Czechs but claimed he was taking them for a ride. Ten days of court time were used to show that he had passed them nothing confidential. Of course the jury believed him. He was a member of parliament. Owen, however, wouldn't be standing for re-election. You didn't come back from a trial like that.

How would Kevin cope, Hugh wondered, if they were to put him on trial? His son was more like him than not. How would Hugh handle the humiliation of a court appearance, the exposure of family secrets? Defiantly. And Kevin would probably do the same.

But it needn't come to that.

Kevin rang to tell him when he was coming to say goodbye to Sarah.

'Have you booked your flight?' Hugh asked.

'The election's not been announced yet.'

'It will be, this week. Latest opinion polls show Labour pulling ahead. It's too good a chance to resist. Third Thursday in June, I reckon. You need to be gone as soon as possible. I can't risk the story coming out during the campaign.'

'I'll miss the World Cup,' Kevin whinged.

'I believe they have televisions in Spain.'

The election was called for the date that Hugh had predicted.

Then, just before the football tournament began, the England captain, Bobby Moore, was arrested, accused of stealing jewellery from a shop. Mad. An incident so mad that he might just have done it. No, it was a set-up, Hugh was sure. Sport was even more open to corruption than politics. Someone wanted to nobble the current champions. England were already without their regular goalkeeper, another world cup winner, Gordon Banks. Food poisoning. A single ball had yet to be kicked, but the team's chances were fading. Luckily, Labour's were still on the rise.

Hugh had another drink with Peter before returning to his constituency for the duration. The old boy got grumpier and grumpier.

'Why didn't you tell me about Kevin?' he asked his old friend.

'Who?' Peter had no idea about Kevin's betrayal or any of the other areas that Hugh wanted to cover. A wasted visit. But the old spymaster had an urgent question of his own.

'Did you tell Wilson?'

'About the coup plot? I thought I'd leave it until after the election.'

'Then, if he wins, you'll line them up against a wall and offer to shoot them for him?'

'Something like that.'

'Bear in mind that the wily old sod probably knows already.'

Of course he does, Hugh thought. He already knew about Kevin, and Flic. I'm not cut out for all these secrets any more. It's a young man's game. The more secrets you hang onto – your own and other people's – the more of a burden they become. Much easier when you're younger and sharp enough to remember exactly what lies you told, and who you told them to.

'Retirement gets more and more appealing,' Peter said. 'Will you be doing another stint?'

'Need the money, old chap.'

'Can't be much fun, opposition. I'd've thought you could earn more on the outside than on a backbencher's salary.'

Hugh was counting on a cabinet minister's wage, not the meagre backbench stipend that he'd be on if the Tories got in.

'You don't think Labour's going to win?'

'Don't know, don't care. I plan to retire to Tasmania sometime in the next five years. I hope you'll come and visit us.'

'What on earth will you do in Tasmania?'

'Start a farm. Maybe write my memoirs.'

'Now there's a book that nobody would ever be allowed to read.'

28

Andrew showed up at Nick's flat just after six. He'd brought a bottle of Highland Park.

'It'll be in the fucking paper tomorrow,' Andrew complained, while Nick found suitable glasses. 'And TV news tonight. Gill might even hear about it.'

Nick poured them each a generous measure of malt. 'It'll only be on local news, so I doubt that. The Evening Post doesn't even have a website.'

'Chantelle is bound to find out,' Andrew said.

'She'll understand. She knows why you were there.'

Andrew gave him a sharp look. 'Does she?'

'She was in the car with Eve when I visited Nancy.' Nick explained why that was. 'Let's hear the worst. Did they catch you with your pants down?'

Andrew didn't make eye contact. 'Near enough.'

'Had you got to the point where you told Nancy that I was meant to take her to London tomorrow, so you could put her into Christmas rehab?'

'I mentioned it, yes. She didn't say *no*.'

'Is rehab how you explained it, or did you offer to be her sugar daddy? *Come live with me in my big house in Notting Hill.*'

'And what would be so wrong with that?' Andrew growled.

Nick wasn't used to Andrew taking his anger out on him. Maybe this was the wrong time to challenge him. Andrew collected himself.

'If I get her off the game, and she cuts out the crack, we could be good together.'

'Really?'

'Don't get high and mighty with me, Nick. Nancy has her problems but she's still got plenty about her. Not all of us can pull women like Chantelle. Where is she, anyway?'

'We don't live together.'

'You said she was coming round after work, going to lend you her car to drive Nancy to London tomorrow.'

'Seeing as how Nancy walked, I can't see us needing the car.'

'Nancy didn't know you were in on the plan. It's still on, far as I'm concerned. I'll call her mobile, sort things out. She might have an idea where Terence is, too. He's going to be mighty pissed off, but we still have business.'

'Why are you dealing directly with people like Terence? I thought you had a number two who did this kind of thing?'

Andrew grimaced, then shook his head. 'That's not how I work any more.'

'What about all that guff you gave me when you tried to persuade me to take on the job? A tight cell structure, everybody on a need to know basis...'

'I still pay for deliveries. Never have contact with the goods. But money, that's a different matter. This is still a cash business. Only way you can be sure the deal can't be traced. It's lucky no money changed hands today.'

'Meaning it was meant to?'

'The police got there before the money man did.'

'One time you told me that you might be legit by the end of next year.'

Andrew gave a wry smile. 'The legit business is still losing money.'

'Probably because you're paying Gill Temperley forty grand a year to sleep with you.'

Andrew frowned. 'Where did you get that figure? Ah, my drink with Chantelle. She's good at asking questions, that one. Does she knows I'm here this afternoon?'

'Of course. Because of the Nancy thing.'

Andrew frowned, like something new was bothering him. Nick read his mind. 'It wasn't her who grassed you up, if that's what you were thinking. You've got a shadow.'

He told Andrew about the bald guy in the Audi.

'Why the fuck didn't you mention that before?'

'Once could have been coincidence. This was twice.'

'I'm going to phone Nancy now. Mind if I go in the other room?'

Andrew wanted privacy while he talked to Nancy. Nick didn't feel any envy. He'd never been in love with Nancy. He could see how she and Andrew might be right for each other. Even so, after Nancy's disappearing act this afternoon, Nick doubted that their relationship was any more solid than Andrew's thing with Gill Temperley.

Andrew returned to the room with a smile on his face.

'The bust convinced her. She wants to come to London with me. Terence is still inside. There's never been a better time for her to leave. We're going tonight. I'll drive her myself.'

Brian Hicks from the Evening Post called Sarah for a comment on the Hyson Green brothel bust. She referred him to the constituency MP.

'Already spoken to him. He's all for legalising brothels in controlled zones to keep the girls safer. I'm after an alternative view from someone not associated with the issue.'

'Men who use prostitutes are exploiting them, is my view,' Sarah said.

'But it's the world's oldest profession. Isn't it unfair to humiliate these men, some of whom have wives and families? One of the punters they picked up today is a well-known businessman. You were at university with him.'

'I'm not going to comment on individuals, Brian.'

'... Andrew Saint. Do you know him, by any chance?'

'I was at university with a lot of people. Brian, my mum needs help. I've got to go. Off the record, the whole business of legalising prostitution isn't something I want to be associated with, on either side. If you want a quote, what I find worrying is that the number of men who use prostitutes seems to be going up. One in twenty admitted to it ten years ago. The latest research suggests that it's more like one in twelve.'

'Maybe that's because there's less stigma attached so the men surveyed feel more free to say what they really do.'

'Either way, I find it worrying. There are women being trafficked to Nottingham to work as prostitutes. It's not Julia Roberts in *Pretty Woman*. It's violent, organised crime.'

'Good line. I'll use that. Do you think it applies to the brothel in Hyson Green?'

'I've said enough. I've got to go.'

She hung up.

'Using me as an excuse to get out of difficult conversations?' Mum asked. She put dinner on the table, lamb chops with carrots, peas and mashed potatoes. Sarah sat down. She'd had a big lunch earlier, shouldn't tuck into a second full meal, but it would be rude not to.

'There's a bottle of red if you want a glass,' Mum said.

'Better not.' If they opened a bottle, Sarah was liable to finish it. Mum could stick to one or two glasses. Sarah couldn't. She helped herself to a generous serving from the gravy boat, then told a white lie.

'I met somebody who asked to be remembered to you yesterday.'

'Who was that?'

'Jim Callaghan.'

'I only met him the once, I think. He sacked your grandfather.'

'I know. He was quite apologetic about that.'

'And where did you bump into him?'

'In his office. I was asking for his help with the cabinet

papers thing.'

Mum looked up from her chop. 'You haven't let go of that.'

'The press are going to report that my father was a traitor.'

'He was. You're going to have to get past it. The story will be a nine-day wonder. Forgotten by the time you're up for election again.'

'Except the guy in the public records office said that there were connected developments in 1969 and 1970.'

'Did he?' Mum didn't seem too surprised by this news.

'He wasn't allowed to tell me what they were. Perhaps you can.'

'I have no idea what he was talking about.'

Sarah wished she'd found a way to get more information out of Jim Callaghan the day before. A handwritten note from the former Prime Minister had been waiting for Sarah at Norman Shaw house this morning.

I've done what I can. Fingers crossed.

'That's it, then. Andrew's taken Nancy to London?'

'It's what he said he was going to do.'

'I've got you to myself for Christmas.'

'All yours.' Nick told Chantelle.

'What are we eating tonight?' she asked.

'Sorry, I forgot to get anything in.' He didn't explain why.

'Chippy?'

'Fine by me.'

'I'll get them,' she offered.

'I'll come with you.' Nick got his wallet.

'Which one shall we go to, Alfreton Road or Ilkeston Road?'

'If we're going by car, might as well make it Ilkeston Road.'

Outside, a 4x4 with shaded windows swerved across Mount Hooton Road and parked in front of her Cortina.

'This doesn't look good,' Nick told Chantelle. 'Go back inside the house.'

'No. I'm not leaving you.'

Terence got out of the front passenger seat, wearing a black donkey jacket that made him look bulkier than usual. He was followed by another heavy from the back seat. Nick stood upright. He didn't want to have this conversation in front of Chantelle.

'Can I help you?' he asked Terence.

'Where's Nancy?'

'I don't know.'

'You were looking for her earlier. She didn't come back. Which means you found her.'

'No, I didn't.'

Terence beckoned the driver, who came and stood directly behind Terence. Nick expected one of the heavies to intervene, to rough him up. He weighed up the odds. Three of them. This wasn't prison, where you had to fight back or be deemed a pussy for the rest of your stretch. Even so, Nick didn't want to look weak in front of Chantelle.

Terence remained calm. He turned to his henchmen.

'Take the girl, put her in the back.'

'No!' The two men moved smoothly around Nick, ignoring his protest, and grabbed Chantelle before he could do anything about it. She resisted, to no effect. One pinned her hands behind her back, while the other dragged her to the car. When Nick went to intervene, Terence stepped between him and them. He grabbed Nick's arm with a tight, painful grip.

'Don't even think about it.'

Chantelle began to yell. Odd that she only did this now, when she was halfway into the car. Shock, Nick supposed. Terence ignored her screams.

'You used to be with Nancy, the girls told me. You wanted to help her. I understand that. And, I don't want to mess up my relationship with our mutual friend. So, OK, this new woman is black. White is more expensive, but I prefer black meat myself. She's younger than Nancy and she's fresh, not got that druggy look. So I can make good money off her. You want to make it an exchange, we'll call it quits.'

'That isn't funny, Terence.'

The pimp kept a straight face. His voice remained business-like. 'She might take a little breaking in. Me and my boys will do that tonight. Then I'll pump her so full of smack, she'll do whatever I tell her to. Your call.'

Terence's face was stern, angry. Nick could only stop this by giving up Andrew. Surely Terence wouldn't dare mess with Andrew, his supplier. Therefore, Nick had no choice but to betray him.

'This is what I know. Nancy's on her way to London, to our mutual friend's place. He took a fancy to her. I had nothing to do with it.'

Terence considered this. 'Let's say I believe you. You know his address?'

'I can give you Andrew's mobile number if you don't have it.'

'I have it. You keep the address, I keep the girl.'

'Let Chantelle back into the house, then I'll tell you.'

Terence waved to his henchmen. One opened the rear passenger side window. 'Let her go.'

Chantelle ran past Nick, into the house. Nick told Terence the address. 'They only left an hour ago. He won't be there yet.'

Terence got in the car and the four men drove off. Nick wanted to rush to Chantelle, but had to take a few breaths, calm himself down first. Now he knew what betrayal felt like.

29

Deborah sat on the stairs in the hall, shivering. *I ought to be better than this. I'm trained not to let stuff like this upset me.* But when the guys in the back seat were molesting her, she wasn't allowed to be Deborah. She had to be naive Chantelle, freaked out by the rough hands squeezing her breasts while another pair forced her legs apart. This situation didn't come up in training. A tongue in her ear and bad breath telling her what orifices they're going to explore. *Right Here. Right Now.* Hand on skin. Scratching. A snapped bra strap. *Why can't Nick protect me?*

Acting was hard. So tempting to say *you are molesting a police officer,* which might have given them second thoughts, but would have blown the whole operation – what little of it there was left. Maybe this was the sign, the confirmation that the whole undercover op had been one big mistake.

Where was Nick? She ought to get out of the house. But she couldn't, not until the men were gone, not until she'd changed her wet knickers.

Then he was there. She looked at Nick through blurry eyes. He squeezed her tight.

'It's alright, honey. They've gone now. It's all right.'

'I was so scared.'

'I'm sorry, so sorry. No need to worry. I told him what he wanted. He won't bother us again. It's all right. I love you. I'm going to look after you.'

'I love you, too,' she told him, and he held her until she stopped shaking, then took her upstairs and helped her into the shower.

Afterwards, she put on clean clothes and said she needed to go home, to her parents.

'It's the only place I feel safe right now.'

'I'll drive you.'

'No. It's OK. I'll call you. But I've got to go now.'

'I understand,' Nick said.

Afterwards, she remembered nothing about the drive home, just getting there. On Englefield Road, in Leicester, Mum and Dad could see that something was wrong but knew better than to ask what it was.

'You still going to be away for Christmas itself?' Dad asked. 'Is it work, that's keeping you in Nottum, or a fella?'

'I don't know,' Deborah told him. 'I don't know what I'm doing.'

At least Nick managed to get to Andrew before Terence did. On Nick's second attempt, he answered his mobile. There was traffic noise in the background while Nick explained what he had done and why. His voice became higher with every word, like that of a whining schoolboy.

'His two goons had Chantelle in the car! They ripped her clothes, bruised her. God knows what they threatened to do. She wouldn't talk about it, just had a shower and went home to her parents. I had no choice, Andy.'

'You gave that fucker my address.'

'Terence is your business partner. You're not that hard to track down, even without my help. And you'll come to an accommodation with him. Call him first, make it look like a misunderstanding. Which, in a sense, it is.'

'I'm going to pull into the services. I'll call you back in five.'

When the phone rang, Andrew appeared to have calmed down.

'Tell Chantelle I'm sorry about what happened. I'll deal with the fall-out from Terence. The point is, I got Nancy away. He's pissed off because he's in this country illegally and now he's on the police's radar, which means he's at risk of deportation. But that raid's hurt me too. My name will be in the papers.'

'Only in Nottingham.'

'Nottingham's not far from London. I'm supposed to be having dinner with Sarah on New Year's Eve. Guess what? She cancelled. I just got her text.'

'I'll explain when I see her,' Nick said. 'It was bad luck, that's all.'

'You make your own luck. I haven't had any today. I'll find out why.'

'Worked out who sent the guy following you?'

'No, but I will.' Andrew became plaintive. 'Tell me what to do with Nancy. We're not there and she's already strung out, desperate for the pipe.'

'Can't you take her to that rehab place you told me about?'

'She won't go. I'm thinking of helping her score, just to keep her quiet. It's best to cut down slowly, isn't it? Cold turkey's only for masochists.'

'You're asking the wrong guy, Andrew. I've never had a problem.'

'But you used to be a drugs counsellor.'

'You want the official advice? Persuade her to go to rehab. If she could cut down through free will, she already would have done. Nancy's an addict. She needs professional help. Anything less, you're just enabling her habit.'

'What about if I give her a drink, will that calm her down?'

'A little, maybe. But it might intensify the cravings.'

'Then I'll stop off at Ladbroke Grove, find a place to score. Better call Terence before he calls me. Maybe he'll have worked out who shopped us.'

Nick turned on the evening news. The local bulletin mentioned the raid on the brothel. It said that four men had been arrested. Which was odd, because Nick had seen five taken away. Had Andrew found a way to bribe himself out of the bad publicity? That wouldn't surprise Nick in the least.

30

On Christmas Eve, Sarah joined her team for lunch at Hart's, in The Park, where she'd had her first date with Eric. She'd meant to go back sooner, but never got round to it. Her taste for fine dining had taken a bit of a knock in the last few months. A year ago, this place would have seemed too plush, too upmarket for the office team. These days, everyone was feeling that bit better off, comrades included.

The mood was upbeat. The whole table had enjoyed the recent downfall of Trade and Industry minister Peter Mandelson, and his millionaire chum, the Paymaster General. Geoffrey Robinson had secretly lent Mandelson money to fund an expensive house. Both had been forced to resign.

'It's a very New Labour sin, isn't it?' Winston argued. 'Getting sacked because you secretly borrowed money in order to look rich.'

'It's the latter half of the equation that got him into trouble,' Sarah argued. 'If he'd borrowed it to pay off debts or...'

'Pay for private education!' Jolene interjected.

'Or even a private operation that the NHS wouldn't fund.' Sarah said.

'Like a heart transplant!' Jolene added.

'I almost feel sorry for the guy,' Winston said. 'It was no big sin.'

'He'll be back,' Sarah told him. 'Just wait and see.'

'And what about you?' Carl wanted to know. 'Will you be back?'

'That, I don't know.'

'Are you in Tony's good books?'

'I think so.'

'Is there a way of getting the message through: *my mum's OK now, please have me back in government, preferably in the cabinet?'*

'I won't get into the cabinet. I might have to re-enter at a lower level than before, a PPS maybe, in order to get back on the greasy pole. Sometimes I'm not sure if it's worth it. Maybe I should concentrate on being a good constituency MP, giving myself half a chance of being re-elected.'

'That won't be down to you,' Winston said. 'National trends.'

'My personal vote was two percent higher than the national swing last time,' Sarah reminded him. 'Otherwise the seat would have been too close to call. In a normal year, Nottingham West should be a safe Tory seat.'

'Nobody would think worse of you if you were to go elsewhere,' Jolene said. 'They say Tony Benn's going to stand down before the next election.'

'And you are a Chesterfield girl,' Carl pointed out.

'I am,' Sarah said. She was fed up of being told about this opportunity. 'And we're not quitters.'

That put a lid on that. They talked about Pinochet, Christmas TV, the local football teams. At the end, when the bill was due, Sarah popped to the loo, then circled the room and stopped at reception, where she settled up.

'Sarah! What brings you here?'

Eric. She hadn't heard from him for a while. He sounded well-oiled.

'Work's lunch. Left it a bit late but we managed to snag a table. I'm sorry I haven't called. I've been meaning to...'

'No, no. Busy life. I understand. Have you got a moment, though? There was something I wanted to tell you in private.'

'Of course.' Sarah signed the credit card slip, approving the 12.5% service charge, and joined Eric by the empty bar.

'That little falling out we had,' Eric said. 'You were right. I did have... let's call them mixed motives when I approved the Drugs Squad placing that young woman in that situation. I wanted you, strictly between the two of us, to know that it's over.

She was instructed to ease herself out by Christmas.'

'Thanks for telling me', Sarah said. 'I hope Nick isn't too heartbroken'

'Can I introduce you to someone?'

'Sure, but I'll have to make it brief.'

Eric walked her to his table, at the other side of the room from her party, where a fortyish woman wore a silk blouse that was slightly too low-cut for her tailored, tweed suit.

'I'd like you to meet Mary Harris,' Eric said. 'Of Harris and Butler. Mary, this is—'

'Of course I know who you are,' Mary interrupted, and stood to shake Sarah's hand, a little too firmly. The solicitor had an expensively cut bob and was slimmer than Sarah. 'Great to meet you. I admire all you've done to...'

She was struggling for words, so Sarah helped her out.

'How nice to meet you. I'm sorry I can't stay to chat but the people at my table all want to leave and they won't dare until I give them the nod.'

'I told you she can be a dragon when she chooses,' Eric said.

'I'm not sure how to take that,' Sarah said. 'Merry Christmas.'

Eric looked like he was going to kiss her cheek but Sarah didn't give him the chance. So that ship had sailed. Probably a good thing. And Nick, whether he knew it or not, was about to become single again. Useful to know, if dangerous to act on. She returned to her table.

'We know where you've been,' Jolene teased.

'I'm sorry?'

'We just tried to pay and they told us it was already settled,' Winston said. 'What do we owe you?'

'Nothing. And no complaints. I know how much you guys have carried me for the last three months and I appreciate it enormously. This is the very least I can do. Thank you, thank you, thank you.'

They gave her a little round of applause. She exited the room rapidly, without looking back at the man who might have been, and walked into town. She had to get a Christmas present for Mum. It didn't take her long to pick out a cashmere sweater in Monsoon. Wine at lunchtime made shopping more fun. At Weaver's on Castle Gate she got a good bottle of Bordeaux to go with Christmas dinner, and a decent Sauvignon Blanc, to drink tonight. On her way back to the flat, she picked up a copy of the *Evening Post.*

The story about the brothel bust was on page three. Any other day, it would have been front page, but they had gone with a soppy Christmas story instead. There was Andrew's name. He was listed as one of the punters arrested and later released without charge. The implication was that he had been caught in the act, but the paper was careful not to say this. Kerb crawling was an offence. Soliciting was an offence. Living off immoral earnings was an offence: a man called Terence Tailor had been arrested and bailed for this. Buying and selling sex remained legal. It was what it was: a sordid, commonplace transaction.

She had a doze, then got the bottle of white out of the fridge, poured herself a glass. The plan was to drive over to Mum's in the morning, when the motorway was quiet. Sarah could use some company tonight, but the only really close friend she had in Nottingham was Nick. Come to think of it, if Chantelle had dumped Nick, he'd probably be as lonely as she was this evening. A second large glass of wine and she thought *fuck it.* She got out her mobile and called him.

'Nick's phone.'

'Oh. Hello. It's Sarah Bone here. Is Nick not around?'

'He's in the shower. Want me to get him to call you back?'

'No, no. Just wish him a merry Christmas for me and tell him I'm looking forward to the party. I'll see you there, yes?'

'I wouldn't miss it for anything. I look forward to meeting you properly. Nick's told me so much about you.'

Sarah poured another glass and turned on the TV, kept

changing channels until she settled into a Ruth Rendell mystery. At the second ad break she emptied the bottle. An hour later, when her landline rang during the late news, she hoped that it would be Nick, calling her back, even though she'd said for him not to. But it wasn't Nick. It was Andrew.

'I got your text yesterday. I hope you don't mind me calling.'

'Not at all,' Sarah lied. At least she was too drunk to be embarrassed that they were having this conversation.

'Nick said he'd tell you what really happened. Has he had a chance yet?'

'No.'

'Thing is, it wasn't what it looked like. I was there to do a favour for Nick. Did you know an old girlfriend of his called Nancy?'

Sarah had heard of her. The story that unfolded was salacious, but not incredible. It reinforced her view that Nick was one of the good guys. He had persuaded Andrew to help get his ex-girlfriend out of prostitution. He couldn't do the deed himself because his probation conditions meant that he could be thrown back into prison at the smallest excuse. Unfortunately, however, Andrew's visit coincided with a police raid that led to his being named and shamed in the local paper.

'I would have had to cancel coming to Nottingham on New Year's Eve anyway, because, unless I can persuade Nancy to check into rehab, I'm still going to be looking after her. But I didn't want you to think badly of me.'

'I don't,' Sarah said. 'I didn't even think particularly badly of you when I thought you'd done what they said you did. I know what men are like when it comes to sex. Even so, it's best I'm not seen with you in Nottingham for a while. Somebody might make a news story out of it.'

'Understood. As long as we're still friends.'

'Old and valued friends,' Sarah said, taking another slug of Sauvignon Blanc. 'And trusted. Between us, I'm worried about

Nick. It's not something I can raise with him directly. Do you know if he's still into anything dodgy?'

'How do you mean?'

'The kind of dodgy he was into before. Drug dealing of some kind.'

'Not that I'm aware of. Why do you ask?'

'Because... I don't know. I thought he was in the clear but then, when I rang him up tonight, she answered the phone. I'm worried about him, is all. Are you sure that he's not dealing again? If he isn't doing anything illegal, he can't get into trouble, can he?'

On TV, a Celine Dion concert began. Sarah couldn't find the remote, so stumbled over to the TV and pressed the 'off' switch. It was good to talk to somebody else who had Nick's best interests at heart. Andrew's voice was warm, reassuring.

'By *she*, you mean Chantelle, right? I don't think he's in trouble, but why don't you slow down, tell me what it is that's bothering you?'

31

1970

'I'm being buggered in Belper,' George Brown said.

Labour's deputy leader was popular with the faithful, and had guaranteed a good house at the community centre earlier. In the pub afterwards, all he wanted to talk about was the Boundary Commission. It had proposed changes to the shape of his constituency, but they'd been delayed. There were thousands of new Tory home-owners in Belper. He might lose.

Of course, George blamed Harold for the delay.

'The Tory bastard Stewart-Smith has had four years to work the constituency, while I've been busy in government. Do you know how many speeches I'm down to give during this campaign? Nearly a hundred. While I should be back home, nursing my vote.'

'It was very good of you to come to Chesterfield, George,' Hugh said.

'At least you're close enough for me to get home and sleep in my own bed. Derbyshire MPs have to stick together. As do old working class socialists.'

Hugh listened to the pudgy owl begin a rant about Anthony Wedgwood-Benn, the most upper class of the new breed of Labour men. Benn had renounced a peerage and the first half of his double-barrelled name to remain an MP. Hugh didn't have a problem with Benn. Drink could turn George into a bore. Hugh tried to bring him back to earth.

'What will you do if you lose?'

'Win the seat back after the boundary changes.'

'It might be five years.'

George shrugged, as though time was immaterial to him. The landlord called last orders and the deputy leader demanded another round.

'Not for me,' Hugh said. 'I have to drive my own car home.'

'I'm sure there isn't one policeman round here who'd arrest you.'

'Maybe so, but nor is there a policeman who can stop me scraping the Jag against the gates when I turn into the drive because I've had one too many. What can I get you?'

George accepted a quick short. Hugh turned the conversation back to the campaign. 'You've been all over the country, so you must have a feel for the situation. The poll figures are good, but how do you think it's going?'

'Another small majority would be my best guess. Fifteen, twenty seats. Belper could be crucial.'

Back to himself again. Then came the rant about how, if Labour had devalued when George wanted, when he was chancellor, we wouldn't have got into this economic mess and should be looking at a sweeping majority.

George's driver came into the bar, and tapped his watch. George went for a pee. Hugh took the opportunity to call Flic from the payphone in the hall.

'Is everything clear?'

'Clear. She's flat out.'

Once, Sarah had caught Hugh visiting late at night. They'd had to make up a story. She had seemed to accept that Grandad was half undressed because he'd got wine on his shirt and Mummy was cleaning it for him. But she was a very bright girl and would one day work out why Grandad made late night visits only when Granny was away in respite care.

Hugh saw George to his car, congratulated him again on his speech, then drove to Chatsworth Road. He wished that he had George's skills as an orator. It would stand him in better stead for promotion – or, if the worst came to the worst and Labour should lose the election – give him a better chance of being elected to the shadow cabinet in October. Hugh was articulate and presentable, yet he somehow lacked the common touch.

Hugh parked up on a side road and made sure there was nobody about before he entered the ginnel that led to the alley behind the small gardens of the terraced houses. Flic's garden gate wasn't locked, and she had left the back door on the latch. He let himself in and locked the door, then took off his shoes before he ascended the stairs. Flic was waiting in bed.

'How was George?' she asked.

'Tired and emotional.'

She laughed. Lately, *Private Eye* kept using that phrase, which George's agent had used to explain one of his wilder outbursts.

'And how are you?'

'What's the word for it these days? *Horny.*'

'Better show me your horn, then.'

Felicity was the best thing in Hugh's life. She made him feel like a teenager. Sex with Flic was even more exciting than those early days with Edith, who had been as inexperienced as him. She was still the only other woman he'd ever been with. Hugh couldn't believe his luck. Flic could pick and choose if she wanted, yet she chose to be his mistress. In return, Hugh did his best to be a good lover. He read the latest books. He knew about the G spot. He always took his time. Sometimes, he definitely gave her an orgasm. Other times, like tonight, when it had been so long since they had last done the deed, he found he couldn't hold back. He couldn't...

The flash of a camera. A silhouette in the door.

'Oh, what a pretty picture you two make,' said a mocking voice. 'Let's have one more for the papers.'

A second flash, Hugh looking at the photographer this time. His own son, taking a full frontal photograph of his bare breasted wife, in flagrante delicto with her father-in-law. Kevin put the camera down.

'See you at home, Dad. Tell Sarah I'll be round in the morning, Fliss.'

32

A week to go. The morning papers had Labour leading by up to twelve points. Kevin was still in bed. Hugh thought about raiding his room, finding the fucking camera. What was Kevin's game? He must want money. Or to be allowed to stay in the country. He had created a counter to bargain with.

Harold was under the impression that Kevin had already left the UK. He had advised Hugh that, while MI5 were happy to let things slide under the current government, the situation might not be the same if the Tories got in. It was one thing for them to let an aristo like Blunt linger unexposed, but this homo was merely the son of a northern Labour MP. A new Tory government might decide that the publicity would make a useful smokescreen the next time they dropped a clanger on the economy. There were no guarantees.

His son came downstairs at five to eleven.

'Mum been taken to Scarborough again?'

'That's right. When are you off to Spain?'

'When you write me a big enough cheque and give me your car keys.'

Hugh rolled his eyes. 'You want the car as well now, do you? What's wrong with yours?'

'The mini's not big enough to take all my stuff. There's a ferry you can get, to Santander. From there you can take another ferry, to Majorca. I've heard that there are less fascists on the Iberian islands.'

'Plenty of very cheap property to be had, anyway.'

Kevin sneered. 'What Fliss still sees in you I don't know. You'll be drawing your pension soon.'

'I've got a good few years in me yet.'

'Not if I give the photo I took last night to the *News of the World*. The good voters of Chesterfield would put you out on your ear, wouldn't they?'

'Only if the paper publishes them. I have a lot of influence.'

'Fine. Take that risk.'

Hugh didn't like having his bluff called. They made the inevitable compromise. He signed the car over to Kevin, and took his son's mini, which was enough to be going on with. Hugh never drove in London.

'That'll be enough for the deposit,' Hugh said, when he wrote the cheque. 'Once you've found a place, have the Spanish lawyer contact me and I'll pay the rest provided you make Sarah's inheritance secure. Understood?'

'Understood.' Kevin all but snatched the cheque.

'Now give me the bloody film.'

'Can't. Already sent it off to be developed.'

'You did what? You've only just got out of bed!'

'Don't worry. Very discreet place. They never look at the pictures. I'll let you have it when you come to visit me in Spain. Bring Sarah, won't you? I'll get over there now, actually. Say goodbye to Sarah for me.'

Hugh had a sudden attack of heartburn, which silenced him. Kevin didn't notice. He took the keys to the Jag and was out of the door before Hugh could find the energy to argue.

33

'What happened to your Jag?' A reporter from the *Gazette* asked.

'Do you know the price of petrol?' It was the fifth time Hugh had made the joke that day. Flic drove him from polling station to polling station. She'd offered to use her car but he insisted on sticking to the Mini. He'd bought the car for Edith, new, in '59, and passed it on to Kevin after her stroke. At least it was British, unlike Flic's oddly shaped Peugeot. Trouble was, the hours they'd spent in it were taking their toll. His spine felt stiff and his lower back ached like buggery. At each station he made sure that he had a good walk around to stretch his legs.

It was a glorious June day. Good weather always benefitted Labour at the polls. Their voters were more fickle, less political. And they owned fewer cars. The party organised lifts to the polling stations, but most voters were too proud to use them. Today, despite the weather, the polling clerks all agreed that voting was down. By evening, they said, things were bound to improve. Wives waited for husbands to return from work. Then loyal couples would come out for a warm stroll before supper.

By 6.30pm, Hugh was sure that it was going badly. The campaign reminded him of '64, when everything started so well, but enthusiasm lagged during the final week. Then there were some truly dreadful trade figures, which made the Tory government's tale of economic recovery far less convincing. This time, England had been knocked out of the World Cup by the West Germans after extra time in the quarter finals. That hadn't helped Labour. Still, in '64, Labour had scraped into government, and got a full majority two years later. They might do the same again.

Flic insisted on cooking Hugh a late dinner before he went to the count. Sarah returned from the neighbour who had been looking after her. This was the first election that she was old enough to understand, and the eight year old was full of questions.

'What will happen if you lose, Grandad?'

'I'm not going to lose. My party might lose, and that will mean that we go into what is called Opposition. We fight the government in Parliament and try to stop them doing silly things, but we have very little power.'

'Then why would you stay?'

'I can still help Chesterfield people with their problems. The main thing is to make a fuss if the government do bad things and make sure that everybody knows, so that they don't get elected again.'

'I hope the Labour Party wins.'

'So do I. Have you heard from your father?'

She shook her head. 'He said he'd send me a postcard when he gets to Spain, but he's been gone a week.'

'I think he's on one of their islands, Sugar Plum. The post can be very slow from places like that. I'm sure you'll get a postcard from him soon.'

Flic persuaded Sarah to go to bed.

'I wish I could come with you,' she said. 'I should have arranged for Sarah to stay the night.'

'Then I'd have felt bad about going back to Edith, leaving you alone.'

'Do you know for sure that Kevin's in Spain?'

Hugh shook his head. 'He could have a nasty surprise if he isn't.'

'How do you mean? Is it to do with that photograph?'

'Don't remind me about that.' Hugh hadn't seen his son since the morning after George Brown's visit. He'd led Flic to believe that he'd destroyed the film. 'Thing is, if the Tories get in, my ability to protect him ceases. He could still get done. So he'd better have left the country.'

As soon as the count began it became clear that turn-out was down. Jeremy, Hugh's agent, had brought in a little transistor radio, even though, technically, this was against the rules. Guildford was the first result in. A swing to the Tories of just over five percent. In Birmingham, Enoch Powell increased his majority despite – or perhaps because of – his speech about rivers flowing with blood when more commonwealth immigrants were allowed into the country.

By the time Hugh got his result – majority down two thousand, not bad, considering – it was clear that Labour had lost. Soon the BBC were talking about the Tories having a majority of a hundred. When Hugh got up in the morning, however, it was down to less than forty. A hundred or forty, it made no odds: Labour were out.

George lost his seat. When Hugh rang to commiserate, the deputy leader was sanguine, said he might go the Lords rather than hang around, hoping to come back. Four or five years of opposition stretched ahead of them. Hugh empathised with him. He had no appetite for opposition, not again. He should have retired. If it weren't for Kevin, he might have done.

34

The big car was outside the house when Mum drove Sarah home from school. At first, she thought it was Grandad. Then she remembered, Grandad no longer had that car. He drove an old, grey Mini. The big car looked like Grandad's old one, though, except it was very dirty. Up close, she could see its inside was piled high with cardboard boxes and plastic bags.

Daddy was in the kitchen, waiting for her. He wore the striped, pale blue cheesecloth shirt she loved, and tight, purple trousers with enormous flares. His moustache had become very thick. Sarah jumped onto his lap.

'Daddy, daddy! You've come back from Spain.'

'Not quite, my sweetheart. I haven't gone yet. Do you think I would go without saying a proper goodbye?'

'Don't go, then. Stay!'

He hugged her. Daddy wore stronger perfume than Mum did but that was OK; Sarah liked patchouli.

'I did try to stay, believe me. But I have to go today – tonight, in fact.'

She clung to him tighter. 'Take me with you!'

'I can't do that. You have school.'

'Term finishes soon. I could go on holiday. Take-me-with-you!'

'I wish I could, sweetie.'

Sarah was not one of those girls who burst into tears whenever she didn't get her own way. So she was surprised to find herself crying. Daddy held her tight. He stroked her hair.

'I'm so sorry, sweetheart, but you still have Mummy, and Grandad. When you're older, you can come and visit me.'

'Want to visit you now!'

'I need to find somewhere to live first. And you're too young to travel home on your own. Don't worry, everything here will be just fine. Grandad will look after mummy. Why don't I take you upstairs and read you a story?'

Sarah was too old to be read to but she didn't tell Daddy this. She loved the smell of him, the drawl of his voice that used to be Derbyshire but now sounded like somebody in a film, almost American. She liked it when he called her "his only girl" and she didn't mind that she didn't have any brothers or sisters because then she'd have to share him.

Daddy read *The Weird Stone of Brisingamen* to her for nearly half an hour. Then it was time for him to go.

'I have an early morning ferry to catch, sweetheart. I just need a few minutes with your mummy, then I'll come and say goodbye properly.'

Although she'd promised not to, Sarah followed Daddy downstairs and listened. She wanted to suck up every last bit of him.

Daddy's voice kept getting louder.

'I know I promised to go then, but not all promises have to be kept, do they? Have a divorce if you want. I won't stop you, but the scandal will do for the old fool, you do realise that? Well, that's his look out. Oh, he told you about that, did he? Well, I'll tell you something about your precious...'

Sarah must have started crying again, for, at that point, the door opened, and Mum saw her.

'I told you she'd come down. See, you've upset her. Now, now, Sarah, you know how your dad and I argue sometimes. It doesn't mean anything.'

But Sarah could tell that it meant a lot. They had used the 'divorce' word and Daddy was never coming back and she was too young to go and see him in Spain.

More than ten years would pass before she saw him again.

35

1998

New year's eve

Nick had the party tapes sorted. Most people wouldn't dance until gone midnight, but a few were bound to get their groove on early. He'd sequenced plenty of crowd-pleasers onto the first C90. The second cassette was hidden behind a speaker so that nobody could dick around with the music. The midnight tape began with Prince's *1999*, the full length version, and stuck to the tried and tested for the next 90 minutes.

The third and final tape was more idiosyncratic, with some of his particular favourites. *There, There My Dear* by Dexy's Midnight Runners. Junior Murvin's original version of *Police and Thieves* segued into The Clash's *London Calling*, followed by The Jam's *A Town Called Malice*. By 3AM, when this tape ran out, Nick doubted that there'd be many people dancing. Or, if there were, they would either have taken control of the music or be happy with a repeated tape from earlier.

The party officially kicked off in five minutes, at nine. Nick got out the background cassette, a mix of jazz, hip-hop, reggae and pop. It began with Madonna and *Cherish*. Back in the day, Nick remembered dancing to this song with Sarah. He wondered who she'd bring tonight. Originally, she was meant to come with Andrew, but he'd had to pull out because of Nancy.

Nick felt bad that he hadn't spoken to his oldest friend over Christmas. He wanted to know how Andrew and Nancy were getting on. Several times, he had thought about phoning them. But Andrew was probably still pissed off with him for giving Terence his home address. If Nick called and they argued, it'd start the night on a sour note that he'd find hard to shake off.

Nick couldn't wait to see Chantelle. She'd come over to spend the morning with him on Christmas Day, then returned to her parents and not been back since. The goons who'd manhandled her outside his flat had shaken her more than she had first let on. If only she hadn't been there when they came. At least, since Christmas, she'd rung him every day. Until today.

'It's not that I don't love you, baby, you know I do. It's just I got freaked out, and things have been going a bit fast between us. Sometimes I feel like I like you too much.'

By which – he suspected – she meant that, as a good Christian girl, she felt guilty about how many orgasms she was having.

'I don't think you have to worry about Terence,' he'd told her. 'Andrew sorted things with him. Say you'll stay at mine for the New Year weekend.'

'Course I will.'

It was decided, then. Tonight he would invite her to move in.

The doorbell rang. Caroline was still upstairs, while Joe was at the next-door-neighbour's, tucking up Phoebe for the night. Chantelle had promised to arrive early. Nick pressed 'play' on the warm-up tape, then went to the door. It wasn't Chantelle, but an ex-County player, with his busty, over made-up wife.

'Can't stay long so thought we'd get here early. We're not the first, are we?'

'You are. Come in, come in!'

'Mike, Janey, fantastic to see you.' Caroline made her entrance down the stairs, in a black cocktail dress with a single string of pearls. She looked stunning. The doorbell rang again.

'Am I first?' Tony Bax. An old comrade of Nick's from his Labour Party days. Knocking on sixty now, Tony was Sarah's predecessor as Labour candidate in Nottingham West. He lost badly in '92. While Nick was inside, breast cancer had taken Tony's wife. The two men went for a drink every few weeks.

'Not at all,' Nick said. 'It's great to see you. Come and have a drink.'

Joe returned with four people he'd found waiting at the doorstep. The house filled up. Most guests were friends of Joe and Caroline's, but Nick knew a few, either from the football field or the cab company.

Jack Drew, who Nick used to teach with, turned up with his boyfriend, Simon. Nick had bumped into them at the PJ Harvey gig a couple of weeks before, invited them to the party, but now found he had little in common with either. They got the dancing going, though, and Nick was distracted by the arrival of Eve. The deputy head scrubbed up well, in a sheer, blue dress that was almost as revealing as Caroline's. She dragged him onto the dining room dance floor, where they had a slow one to the Commodores.

'This is meant to be background music,' he said.

'Works fine for me. Where's Chantelle?'

'She'll be along later,' Nick said. 'Where's Geoff?'

'I kicked him out.'

'Ah. I could do with a smoke. Want to pop outside, tell me about it?'

Three ex-footballers were in the garden, but kept their distance from Nick and Eve. He lit a spliff while Eve gave him a rundown on how Geoff took his marching orders – badly, of course. To Nick's surprise, when he offered her the spliff, Eve took a couple of pulls.

'I haven't touched this since the 70s,' Eve said. 'Ooh, it's got stronger.'

'I'd never have thought of offering you a smoke when we were...'

'*Lovers*. You can say it. We had a good time, didn't we? And I ended it because I'd met Geoff and I thought he was a safer choice, even though you were so much more exciting.' She took another deep pull on the joint. 'I don't know which is worse, cheating, or using prostitutes – exploiting women that way. Worst of all, going to Nancy, despite knowing all her problems.'

'I know what you mean,' Nick said. 'Another friend of mine…' He stopped himself. No need for Eve to be told the full story of Andrew and Nancy. 'What I meant to say is, I know someone else who paid to have sex with her, who thought that there was nothing wrong with doing that. Can you stay friends with someone who thinks that way? I don't know.'

'Me neither.' She handed back the spliff. 'Maybe I'm too uptight. I know what men are like. I already divorced one for being unfaithful. Geoff can't understand why I kicked him out, says it doesn't count.'

'I don't know about that,' Nick said.

'No need to worry, by the way, I didn't mention that I found out about it thanks to you. I let him think it was a female friend he didn't know.'

'Would it have been so bad if it had been someone other than Nancy?' Nick asked.

'Bad enough. Some would say he only needed to go elsewhere because things were bad at home. Which they were.'

'You're well rid, then.'

'Except I don't like living alone. I need to find someone better while I've still got my looks.'

'Plenty of time yet,' Nick said.

'The clock is ticking. I'm fifty-one. My kids are at university and I don't want to be a head teacher. The only career move I have left is retirement.'

If he was single, this was the point where Nick would have told Eve how fantastic she looked, and suggested that he took her upstairs, showed her what he meant. Instead, he squeezed her arm and puffed on the joint.

Eve shivered. 'Getting cold. I'm going back inside. There's

nobody here my age. Who's that guy standing by the door? He looks familiar.'

'Tony Bax. He's on the city council. I didn't think he'd come. Not sure he knows anyone. We had a talk about the new tram system earlier. He's a good bloke, actually. Do you want me to introduce you?'

'I can do that myself. Go look for your girlfriend.'

Nick stubbed out the joint and followed her inside.

'I think I voted for you once,' he heard Eve telling Tony as he checked his watch. Half ten. Time for the first dance tape proper. He reached the dining room just as the auto reverse turned the background tape over. He caught it before the music started again and put the new cassette on. Curtis Mayfield, *Moving On Up*. Where the hell was Chantelle?

36

Tonight was it. Their last night.

Deborah sat in the back of her Cane Cars taxi, trying to work out how to drop Nick gently, as she had been instructed. The obvious way – the route that Mike advised – was not to show up at the party. All she need do was leave a phone message or send a text, saying she'd had a change of heart. If she spoke to Nick, she could explain that she'd told her parents about him over Christmas, and they didn't like the idea of her dating an atheist, especially a white ex-con who was so much older than her. She'd decided to move on.

Actually, her parents hadn't asked her anything about Nick's religion, or his ethnicity. They knew that she was undercover, and forbidden to discuss her work. They didn't know that she was only thirty miles away, in Nottingham. All they cared about was that she was safe. Her father approved of her exercising hard every day, staying fit. She couldn't explain why she had redoubled her efforts. If any of Terence's men came near her again, she meant to be in the best possible shape to defend herself.

Tonight, Deborah wanted to spend one last, delicious night with Nick. In her head, a hundred times, she had written the loving note that she would leave in the morning, while he still slept, saying how much he meant to her, but it wasn't to be, and that he must not try to track her down.

This New Year's resolution would be hard to keep. But what was the alternative? She could only continue to see him by explaining the sustained deception. How would Nick react? Hard to tell. At heart, he was an old fashioned romantic who liked to smoke a bit of dope. The stats said that five million people in the UK did the same. If Deborah fessed up about the undercover, and Nick accepted it, she could go on seeing him. As long as she kept it quiet in Leicester. As long as she kept her distance from Andrew Saint and Nick didn't tell his best buddy about the secret surveillance.

Bullshit.

She had developed an immature crush on Nick. It was an inevitable effect of such a long pretence. She had hoped to exorcise it by going to bed with him, but sex had only made her feelings stronger. They would vanish when the operation was over. Once she was back in uniform, seeing Nick would threaten her career. It would also get in the way of her meeting the right guy, who had to be out there somewhere.

'Over here, please.'

The taxi pulled up at Nick's brother's house, on the edge of the Sherwood estate. Deborah had been ducking invites for Sunday lunch from the wife, Caroline. Nick seemed fond of Caroline, unaware that he made her sound like a right dragon. No way to avoid her tonight. That was OK. Deborah was curious to complete an imaginary picture, the one where Nick invited her to move in with him and they played happy families with Joe and Caroline, Chantelle becoming an auntie to his niece.

She gave the driver a fiver and told him to keep the change, then got out of the car.

'Chantelle!'

Time to get into character. Deborah turned to flash a smile at whoever it was. And froze. There was no reason for him to be here, with one hand behind his back. Unless...

The cab had left. Nobody else on the street. In Joe and Caroline's house, somebody turned up the music. Madonna had made it through the wilderness. The surrounding homes were quiet, unlit. He took a step towards her.

'I've been waiting for you.'

She saw the baseball bat coming, but didn't have time to get out of the way. The blow struck her on the left side of her face. It was a mercy when he hit her again, and she stopped feeling anything at all.

37

Sarah got to Sherwood at ten to eleven. The party was heaving. She didn't recognise anyone. Was that Joe Cane, over there in the bell-bottomed jeans? She hadn't seen him since he was an arrogant teenager. A statuesque woman with long, wavy hair came over. She wore a low cut black dress that was either *Dolce Gabbana* or a very good knock off.

'Sarah, hi! I'm glad you could make it. I'm Caroline, Joe's wife. Let me get you a drink.'

'I thought I was going to be early. Most of the New Year's Eve parties I've been to didn't get going until after eleven.'

'Half of our friends have small kids. They'll be wilting by midnight.'

Sarah glanced at the dining room to her right. A dozen people danced to a loud hip-hop song. She hardly ever danced these days, though she used to love to, when she was with Nick. That was the last time that she really felt in touch with music, went to lots of gigs with him at Rock City: Elvis Costello, R.E.M., Kid Creole and the Coconuts...

'Red or white?'

'White,' Sarah said. She preferred good reds, but you rarely got good reds at a party, and white gave her less of a hangover. Caroline handed her a glass of something cold and drinkable. Pinot Grigio, possibly.

'I'm not sure where Nick is,' Caroline said. 'Do you know anyone?'

Sarah could see Tony Bax in the corner of the kitchen. He was always good company. Certainly the blonde woman in the blue dress seemed to think so. Sarah wasn't going to interrupt that tête-à-tête.

'I'll be fine,' she said, sensing the slight panic in Caroline's expression. She was happy to have a local MP at the party but didn't know what to say to her and wasn't sure which of her drunken friends to introduce her to.

'Here's Nick,' Caroline sounded relieved. 'Did you find her?'

'No. I tried her mobile, but it's turned off.'

'Sarah's here.'

'You made it. That's great.'

He planted a beery kiss on her lips.

'Something wrong?' she asked.

'Chantelle's not shown up. She said she'd be here early.'

'Ah.' Sarah didn't know what to say, so said nothing.

'But it's great to see you.'

'It's great to be here. I hope there's going to be lots of dancing.'

'Lots and lots. Some people are at it already. Not sure who you'll know. Tony Bax is here.'

'Seen him already. Who's that he's with?'

'Eve Shipton. Deputy Head at the school where I used to teach.'

'So the whole staff didn't turn against you when you were sent down?'

'Not quite all. They tell me I was a hero to some of the students.'

'I'll bet. Hey, I recognise this song. Why don't we have a dance?'

'I'd like that. Let me fill up your drink first.'

She'd downed a whole glass of white in less than five minutes, but – on top of the two glasses she'd drunk with her lonely dinner – it seemed to have had the desired effect. In the dining room, Sarah found that she still knew all the words to *Annie, I'm Not Your Daddy.*

If I was in your blood, August Darnell told Annie, *you wouldn't be so ugly.* Sarah tried not to worry about how the world would find out that her dad was a spy. She was not her father. By the time of the next general election, the story would be old news. Unless there were further revelations from 1969, and 1970... in London, the papers would be out. She could phone somebody there, ask them to buy an early edition.

She only knew one person in the capital who was likely to be home tonight: Andrew. They'd had a good, long, drunken conversation, one she could barely remember, on Christmas Eve. But if the story wasn't to be in the papers, Sarah didn't want Andrew to know about it.

Common People came on. A guy at the edge of the low-lit room nudged his boyfriend. *There's the local MP, singing along with Pulp and making shapes.* Sarah didn't care. *Yeah,* she wanted to say, *I know what it's like to have people look down on you because, compared to them and half the people I work with, I'm common. I didn't go to a public school or Oxbridge, I'm a Northerner, thank you very much and fuck off.*

The room filled up with dancers. Nick excused himself.

'Got to help with the fizzy wine for midnight,' he explained.

And he probably had to try and ring his girlfriend, find out where she was. But the phone number he had would never be answered again. Sarah hoped that Nick had had fun with Chantelle. She couldn't imagine that he'd have fallen very hard. They were so different from each other. Chantelle – or whatever her real name was – might be sexy and bright, but her culture was very different from Nick's. And she was a secret police woman.

It was the last part that offended Sarah most about the whole situation. If Nick knew what Chantelle really was, he would never have gone out with her, under any circumstances. It was Sarah's joining the police force that had split them up. And, in a sense, Nick had been right to finish it, for Sarah had made the wrong choice. She only lasted a couple of years in the job. But she would never have taken on the role that Chantelle had. The amount of deception involved in undercover work required a mind-set that Sarah couldn't imagine. Very few male officers did it. For a woman to go undercover, as someone's girlfriend...

Sarah knew Nick. He wouldn't be with someone for all these months if she wasn't sleeping with him. So what did that make Chantelle? Not Police, but another word beginning with a 'P'. And why? Because Eric was jealous and wanted Nick out of the way.

The operation was over. Chantelle was gone for good, back to another city, another life. Nick deserved to know the truth. Joe came in and turned down the music. A TV was turned on, displaying Big Ben. There was Nick, holding a tray full of champagne flutes, and his sister-in-law alongside him, doing the same. They made a handsome couple. The ex-footballer began the countdown, and the whole room joined in.

10-9-8-7-6-5-4-3-2-1

38

Not long after midnight, Nick found Sarah in the upstairs snug, listening to the news on Radio Four.

'What are you doing?' he asked.

She shushed him. 'Something I had to check.'

'You always were obsessed with work,' he muttered, and sat down next to her on the old sofa. A new story began.

'Cabinet papers released today detail government secrets that can now be revealed under the thirty year rule. The biggest revelation is that, thirty years ago, the government nearly returned the Falkland Islands to Argentina.'

The newsreader explained that the 1968 government eventually opted to delay returning the islands until the older generation of islanders died off. Other stories followed. The government had considered prosecuting Enoch Powell for a racist speech, but decided against giving him his day in court.

'Finally, the security services had to warn the Prime Minister that there was a chance he would be spied on... by his television. Bizarre as it may seem, Harold Wilson was not allowed to install one of the new colour televisions at 10 Downing Street, because the size and complexity of the sets meant that it would have been easy for foreign powers to install a bug inside one.'

Sarah turned off the radio. She was crying, Nick saw.

'Hey, what was all that about?' He handed her a tissue.

'Nothing.' She wiped her eyes and sat down again. 'Hold me.'

She felt good in his arms. After a while, she gave him a brave smile.

'How about a New Year's kiss, for old time's sake?'

They had a long, affectionate kiss. Odd to find that you could enjoy a wet kiss without wanting it to lead further. Sarah brightened.

'You're worried about Chantelle, aren't you?'

'I am. I think she must have dumped me, but I don't know why.'

He could hardly tell her about Nancy, and Andrew taking her, and Terence nearly taking it out on Chantelle.

'I do,' Sarah said.

'What?' He wasn't sure that he'd heard her correctly.

'She's not all she seems. I'm not meant to tell you this, but you're one of my oldest friends. I don't like having secrets from you. I complained, as soon as I found out that you were going out with her.'

'Complained about what?' Nick watched Sarah decide how much to tell him. She was drunk, and they had just kissed, and there was something else going on with the news bulletin that he didn't yet understand. Hence her hesitation. 'What is it that's so secret?'

Sarah made up her mind. 'Chantelle's an undercover cop. She was going out with you because the police believed that you might be heavily involved with drug dealing.'

Nick laughed. 'She's...? Oh, that's priceless. Chantelle, a cop? I smoked dope with her. We were sleeping together. She couldn't be...'

Sarah was not joking. 'I complained. But I was in a difficult position. I knew about her because I was on the board of the Power Project, and she was brought in from an outside force to go undercover there, because there were fears that it would be used as a front for drug dealing. As far as I was aware, her job ended when the project closed down. So you can imagine my surprise when I saw you with her, in town, holding hands.'

'Wait a minute,' Nick said. 'The guy you were with that day, was he in the police?'

'He's the Chief Constable.'

'I thought there was a weird dynamic between him and Chantelle, but then she made a joke and…' He put his head in his hands. 'Shit, shit, shit.'

'I'm sorry,' Sarah said. She tried to hold him, but he shook her off.

'You knew all this time!'

'I was in an impossible position. I'd thought about confronting her tonight, asking what she was playing at. But then Eric told me…'

'This guy, the Chief Constable, were you going out with him?'

'We had a few dates but he was too old for me, too straight. I know what you're thinking, but he didn't have any operational responsibility.'

'What am I thinking?'

'Did Eric have mixed motives in setting Chantelle onto you, because he knew that I still had feelings for you and saw you as a rival?'

Nick hadn't got that far. 'He knew that I used to go out with you?'

'It came up, yes.'

'Jesus Christ.'

'I'm sorry, Nick. I'm sorry. It's a complete mess.'

'Yes. It is. I need another drink.'

Nick charged out of the room, giving Sarah no time to get herself together and follow. Downstairs, he found Eve and Tony at the front door.

'Nick, it's been lovely. Thanks so much for inviting me. Tell Chantelle I'm sorry I missed her.'

Tony shook his hand. 'Eve and I are sharing a cab. I've had a great time. Pint in a week or two, yes?'

The dining room was heaving. Caroline waved, and urged Nick

to join her in a dance to ABC's *Poison Arrow*. Nick ignored her. He'd secreted two bottles of Czech Budwar at the back of the fridge. He opened one and glugged straight from the bottle. He needed to smoke a joint. Chill out. Get his head round Chantelle being a... what? She knew that Nick wasn't a dealer. He had held nothing back from her, except for Andrew's real profession... Shit, were the police on to Andrew? Of course! Chantelle had been keen to visit the Notting Hill house. She had even been out for a drink with him on her own, which Nick had thought odd at the time. Sarah didn't know the whole story. It wasn't Nick that the police were after. It was Andrew.

39

Gone one, and the numbers were thinning. This wasn't like the New Year's Eve parties of Nick's younger days, when people would still be arriving at this hour. Nick no longer felt like dancing. Neither, it seemed, did Sarah. She joined him in the kitchen, where he was smoking a cigarette at the open door. It had become too cold to stand outside.

'I think it's time for me to make a move,' Sarah said. 'Could you...?'

'One advantage of going to my family's parties, you can always get a cab quickly.' Nick used the wall phone to dial the private number for Cane Cars. 'On its way,' he told Sarah.

'You're still mad at me for not telling you, aren't you?'

'You did what you had to do. There are things I haven't told you, too.' Long-kept secrets flashed across his mind. All to do with women: he ought to see a pattern forming here.

'I wish we were close again,' Sarah said. 'I miss being able to talk to you.'

'Me too.' She was drunk, but not very drunk. The last hour had sobered them up. In other circumstances, he would have kissed her, taken his chance. 'I haven't asked how your mum is.'

'She's fine. Are you staying here tonight, or do you want a lift home?'

'I can't leave. I'm one of the hosts.'

'I think I'm the last of your guests.'

He'd only invited half a dozen friends, people he'd looked forward to showing off Chantelle to. He remembered something, and lowered his voice.

'Why were you crying when I found you watching TV earlier?'

'Long story. Maybe we can have a proper talk one of these days.'

'I'd like that.'

'What I told you earlier, about Chantelle, you can't let on to anyone that you know.'

'I understand,' Nick said, without making any promises. A horn sounded. 'I'll see you to the door.'

In the porch, with nobody watching, Sarah kissed him. Not a goodnight peck. She left her mouth a little open. Nick felt a tentative sweep of the tongue. He pulled away.

'You can come with me if you want,' Sarah said.

'You'd regret it in the morning.' The words slipped out. He should have said, 'I'll get my coat', like in that sketch show. Yet, if things were ever to start up with him and Sarah again, it mustn't be like this. Right now, he wasn't even sure if he wanted to be with her again. He hadn't let on to Sarah how much Chantelle had meant to him. He wanted her back. No, that wasn't it any more. He wanted the fictional Chantelle that he had fallen for. He couldn't bear the thought of never seeing her again. At the very least, he wanted to have it out with her, to tell her how much she had hurt him.

The taxi door slammed. While he was staring into space, Sarah had left. Nick returned to the party. There was only one thing to do in a situation like this. Get totally bladdered.

40

Sarah woke at half seven and took two Solpadeine capsules to clear her head. Her first fully formed thought was *did I really make a pass at Nick last night?* And, if so, why? Guilt about Chantelle? Sarah didn't do guilt. But she had felt elated when the spy story wasn't on the news. The other possibility was *in vino veritas*: she really wanted to be with him, despite having decided countless times that she couldn't. Not while she was still an MP.

Her next thought was, where can I get a paper? That the spy story wasn't on the radio news did not mean it hadn't been released. She had *The Independent* delivered when she was in Nottingham, but, on a Saturday, it didn't arrive until nine. If Sarah had the internet she could do a search on herself and her father, check the daily papers' websites to see if the story was out. However her six year old computer didn't have a modem.

Sarah got dressed and walked to town. At the newsagents underneath the Friar Lane roundabout she bought the *Times*, *Telegraph* and *Daily Mail*. Might as well get the bad news from the enemy papers, who would have the sourest take on it. She couldn't wait to get home to read them, so followed the tunnel to the Wimpy on the corner of Friar Lane and Maid Marion Way. An elderly man sipped tea next to the window. Otherwise, the place was deserted. She ordered a large coffee and spread the papers out on a Formica table top.

The 1968 revelations were deep in the inside pages: the same stories that were on the news last night, plus minor ones about House of Lords reform and the reasons for Ray Gunter's resignation. Nothing about spies. If Sarah had Jim Callaghan's home phone number, she would call him now, offer eternal obeisance. She left her coffee unfinished. The girl at the till called her back.

'You've forgotten your papers!'

'I thought another customer might like them.'

'They can buy their own. Take your mess with you.'

Sarah picked up the papers and was back home by half past eight, with nothing to do for the rest of the day. She went back to bed.

Nick needed to see Chantelle. He couldn't leave it the way it was, with his knowing but not being meant to know. How would he act if he didn't know? Worried.

He'd left two messages last night, asking where she was. Today, he'd rung her mobile twice. Both times it went straight to voicemail. What was he supposed to do in this situation? Assume he'd been dumped, or call the police? The former, probably. He'd feel used, insulted, crapped on. The easy reaction would be to do nothing. Take it on the chin and learn to forget her.

But what if something bad *had* happened to her? They'd been all lovey-dovey on the phone until two days ago. He found it hard to believe she'd exit without a faked farewell. Also, whatever the situation, the police were bound to be keeping an eye on him. He had to act like he didn't know what she was.

Which meant he had to go and see her. Definitely. Only he'd never had Chantelle's home address. She'd told him that she lived with her parents and didn't want him to meet them. That was probably nonsense, but he ought to act as though he believed it. He could try to get the address from the dentist's where she worked. At least he knew where that was. But it would be closed until Tuesday. Then he remembered that he knew somebody who had given her a lift home.

Eve took a while to answer the phone.

'It's nice to hear from you,' she said. 'Thanks for a lovely party. I met some interesting people.'

'You and Tony seemed to get on well.'

'He's a very smart guy. He thinks highly of you.'

'I'm glad somebody does. I think that Chantelle's dumped me.'

'Oh.' Short pause. 'I did wonder why she wasn't there.'

'Remember that night we tried to help Nancy, you gave her a lift home?'

'Yes.'

'Can you tell me where you took her?'

'It was a back street in Arnold. Don't you have her address?'

'No, she never took me there. She's not answering her phone and I want to go round and see her.'

'I didn't notice the name of the street, I'm sorry.'

'But would you remember where it was?'

'I expect so, though I'm not sure I can describe it. You're really desperate to see her, aren't you?'

'Yes.' Although he wasn't expecting to still find her there.

'Give me half an hour. I'll pick you up, see if I can remember the way.'

Nick shaved and dressed. He took with him the one photo that he had of Chantelle. Andrew had taken it despite Chantelle's complaint that she was camera-shy and truly, truly hated being photographed. Now Nick knew why. In the photo, he was grinning. Chantelle's head rested on his shoulders so that her smiling face was partially covered by his. Clever girl.

Eve was as good as her word. She arrived just after two, and they set off at once.

'I like Chantelle,' Eve said. 'She's feisty and smart, a lot better for you than Nancy was, even without her... proclivities. There's probably a straight forward explanation for her no-show, like she's been throwing up all night.'

'She'd have called or texted.'

Eve turned left. 'I think it was one of these. Of course, it was dark...'

They were off the High Street, in a maze of old semis and terraces.

'I dropped her at the end of the street, but I waited until she went in. So, yes. I'm sure it was this one.' They turned onto Gilbey Road. 'I remember her walking past that post box.'

She pointed at two modern semi-detached houses in the centre of the street. There was a metre gap either side of them, just big enough to wheel a bin down. Nick got out of the car and tried the first one. No reply. He tried to look through the net curtains. This was the sort of house he could imagine Chantelle's parents living in, just big enough for three of them. Would Chantelle go undercover in her own city, when she could be spotted by someone she knew? Unlikely, but not impossible.

He knocked on the door of the other half of the building. This side was in need of paint. The alleyway held a flight of metal steps. The man who answered the door was in his seventies, at least.

'Sorry to disturb you. I'm looking for this woman, a friend of mine, and I wanted to check if she lives next door.' He held out the photo.

'Aye, I know her. I don't know her name, but she's not next door.'

'How do you know her, then?'

'She lives in the flat upstairs.'

Result. 'Is the entrance up those stairs?'

'It is. You won't find her in.'

'Why not?'

'She went out last night, just after ten. Taxi picked her up. She hasn't come home yet. I'd of heard her come in.'

'Is that unusual?' Nick asked.

'No. She's often away. Specially recently.'

'Did you see what kind of taxi it was?'

'A saloon, not one of the big black cabs.'

'Happen to notice the firm?'

He hadn't. Nick went up and tried the door anyway. No reply. At least, now, he knew where it was. She did not live with her parents, but maybe she had returned to her family for the holidays. He would come back tomorrow.

Sarah spent New Year's Day in a pair of flannelette, stripey pyjamas that she had stolen from Nick some fifteen years earlier. Not that he ever wore them. They used to belong to his dad, who had died young, and whom she'd never met. She knew Nick's mum, a Sheffield woman who worked in a cutlery factory before having her sons and returned to it as soon as Joe started school. She was long dead, too, though Sarah didn't know when or what from. She and Nick had lost touch by then.

Liz Cane approved of Sarah as a girlfriend for Nick, let them share a bed in her council house home whenever they visited, which was more than Sarah's mum did. But then, Sarah's mum had two spare bedrooms and the use of Grandad's place as well. Nick's home on Rock Street, Pitsmore, had just three bedrooms and his schoolboy kid brother occupied one of those.

Sarah was tempted to ring Nick. They needed to have a sober conversation. She was worried about him tracking down Chantelle, then giving away what Sarah had told him. Why did she tell Nick? To comfort him about her disappearance? Or to clear the decks for them to resume their relationship?

Madness, to start things back up with Nick. She wouldn't be giving him a second thought if it weren't the parliamentary recess, which gave her time to think, nor if she'd had sex in recent memory. The phone rang and she found herself wanting it to be him. But it was Mum, wishing her a happy new year.

'No story in the papers.'

'No,' Sarah allowed a hint of triumph into her voice.

'Clever girl. Come for your dinner tomorrow lunchtime, and we can finish talking about all this business.'

41

The next time Nick rang Chantelle, he left a message.

'Where are you? If this is your way of dumping me, at least have the good grace to text. I'm worried.'

He decided to cycle to hers before Sunday dinner at Joe and Caroline's. If that failed, he'd try the dentist's when it reopened. After what Sarah told him, he didn't expect Chantelle to be there, not now the case was over. But phoning her at work was what a jilted boyfriend would do. If he wanted to see her again, he had to act like he didn't know she was a police spy.

The more he thought about it, the less Nick understood the undercover operation. There would have been some logic to Chantelle seducing him while he was in charge of The Power Project – if the police thought the place was a front for drug dealing. But they only started seeing each other after he'd left. If it *was* Andrew the police were after, why go to the trouble of setting Nick up?

But Chantelle *had* suggested visiting Andy in London and Sarah *did* know the Chief Constable. Then there were all those months when Chantelle held him off in the bedroom department, citing the religious stuff. Also, Nick had spotted a guy spying on Andrew, which suggested that the Saint was under investigation.

Maybe I should turn back, he thought, as he cycled through persistent drizzle. *All I'm asking for is trouble.* Except he wanted to see her, to confront her. He wanted her to lie to his face one last time.

There was a light on in her flat that hadn't been on the day before. Nick locked his bike to the metal staircase and reminded himself that his lover would be surprised to see him. She didn't know that he knew where she lived. He rehearsed what he was about to say, then climbed the metal stairs. What would he do if she didn't let him in? No idea. He rang the doorbell anyway.

'How did you keep the story out of the paper?' Mum wanted to know. She had *The Guardian* spread out over the dining room table.

'It wasn't me. Somebody did us a favour.'

'Somebody who owed you?'

'No. He did it out of the goodness of his heart, I think.'

'Politicians never act out of the goodness of their hearts. They always have a motive.'

'This was a retired one.'

'So that's why you saw Jim Callaghan. Politicians never completely retire. They have scores to settle and reputations to protect. Your grandfather always kept his guard up, even at the very end.'

'Hardly surprising, when he knew that his only child was a spy.'

'I don't think that bothered him much. You don't know what it was like. There were spies everywhere in the post war years. The sides had been confused, you see. Lots of left wing people loved the Russians. Then they became the enemy.'

'Dad had no great affection for communist Russia.'

'But he liked to live well, and he liked to get one over on your grandad, to make him look bad.'

'Is that why he did it – for a lark, and the money?'

'I never had the chance to ask him.'

Sarah got out the scrapbooks that she had looked at while Mum was in hospital. 'You know, I did a lot of thinking about you and Dad while you were sick. I tried to understand what made your marriage tick. I can't really remember what you were like together. I tried, and I looked at the photos in here, but they didn't help. Dad's hardly in them, for a start.'

'We soon realised the marriage was a mistake. If we hadn't had you, we wouldn't have stayed together long.'

'I don't understand what possessed you to get together in the first place. Dad must have had a fair idea that he was gay, or, at least, bisexual. All right, in those days, lots of gay men married to convince themselves and the world that they were normal. Dad wanted to be independent, yet he married his father's secretary. That tied him closer to his parents, helped keep him in Chesterfield. And the two of you had so little in common. I can't understand what you saw in him.'

'I can't speak for your father's motives, but he was a very good looking man, and I was young and naive. Looking back, I suppose I hero-worshipped your grandfather. I wanted to marry into the family.'

'By marrying my dad, you were also marrying Grandad.'

'That's one way of putting it.'

It was time for Sarah to confront a suspicion that had been growing since she looked at the scrapbooks. 'After Dad left and Grandma died, did you and Grandad... were you and he... involved?'

'Of course we were.'

Mum held up the scrapbook so that Sarah couldn't see the look on her face. Sarah's mouth hung open. She had a dozen questions and didn't know where to start. She meant to hide her distaste, but it was her grandad they were talking about.

'Grandad was thirty years older than you.'

Mum put down the scrapbook. Her expression was that of a sulky teenager. Do people ever grow up, Sarah wondered, or do they just get better at putting on an act?

'Age isn't very important', Mum said.

'He was your husband's father!'

'Not much of a husband. Hugh was more of a father to you than Kevin was.'

'No, he was a proper grandad. And you...' Sarah remembered

once how Nick, after visiting Chesterfield, asked if there was anything going on between her mum and her grandad. She had closed the conversation down with such determination that Nick had never brought the subject up again.

'When did it start?'

'I'm not sure you really want to know,' Mum said.

'No, I...' Sarah knew what Mum was like. She had to get the story out of her today, because Mum would never discuss it with her again. Mum had a hundred ways of avoiding difficult or dangerous subjects.

'Was it going on while I was still living at home?'

'Yes, it was.'

'And it kept going on until he died?'

'He was the only one, yes. Hugh was the love of my life.'

Sarah was still formulating her next question when the phone rang. Mum answered it.

'For you. That Chief Constable.'

Sarah took the phone. 'Eric, what can I do for you?'

'Do you remember the last conversation we had?'

'About Chantelle Brown, yes.'

'Did you share the information I gave you then?'

'Of course not,' Sarah lied. 'Why?'

'Because she's disappeared.'

'How do you mean, *disappeared*?'

'She told her parents that she would be returning for good yesterday. She was due back in uniform tomorrow. She spent most of Christmas at home, so her parents knew exactly how things stood. When she wasn't back by midnight, they called her handler. He was the only way for them to get in touch when she was undercover. He couldn't raise her either, so we went to her flat today. She hasn't been seen since just after ten on New Year's Eve.'

'Are you sure she isn't with Nick?' Sarah asked.

'We're sure. But that doesn't mean he hasn't done something

to her – especially if he worked out she was a plant. We'll be questioning him today.'

'As it happens, I was at a party with Nick and some old friends on New Year's Eve. He was quite upset when Chantelle didn't show up. I don't think he has any idea about what she was up to.'

'OK, I'm sorry to have disturbed you, Sarah, but, obviously, we're worried when we lose one of ours, and I was stupidly indiscreet with you.'

'No, you were thoughtful to tell me. And I hope you locate her soon.'

'What did your boyfriend want?' Mum asked.

'Nothing important. And he's not my boyfriend. In fact, he's seeing someone else, a solicitor.'

'Another one you let get away.'

'I suppose,' Sarah said, 'but he was never going to be the love of my life. And I'm too young to settle for less, aren't I? You said that Grandad was the love of your life. When did you...?'

'I've said all I've got to say about that.'

42

The front door had a central panel of plastic, imitation smoked glass, through which Nick could only make out shape and colour. But the form behind the glass wasn't Chantelle. It was a white man in a brown mac. The door opened.

'Yes?'

'I'm looking for Chantelle.'

'And you are?' he asked, in a Nottingham accent.

'My name's Nick Cane.'

'Ah. Would you mind waiting there for a minute?'

Nick stepped into a small, empty vestibule. No coat on the hook, no notes on the small cork board to his right. There was a telephone table. Beneath the landline was a small pile of takeaway menus.

The man who greeted him next was older than the first. He had a more cultured voice, suggesting seniority.

'Mr Cane, we were going to come and see you. Thanks for saving us the trouble. You'd better come in.'

The living room was not quite empty. There was a TV and a mini CD system, with a few discs. No pictures on the walls. Some books along the window ledge. Self Help guides and, the dead giveaway, a *Jane's Police Review* crammer for sergeants and inspectors' part 1 exams. The officer saw Nick looking at them, said nothing.

'When did you last see Chantelle Brown, Mr Cane?'

'Christmas Day.'

'And when did you last speak to her?'

'New Year's Eve. No, the day before. She was meant to come to a party at my brother's on New Year's Eve but didn't show up and she hasn't been answering her mobile. Do you know what's happened to her?'

'No, we don't. Her parents called us and that's why we're here.'

'They don't live round here, then?'

'Ms Brown seems to have disappeared. You don't have any idea why that might be?'

'I don't. We were very close. It isn't like her.'

The senior guy nodded. 'It's cold in here. She'd turned the heating off. Perhaps you wouldn't mind coming to Oxclose Lane station with me, answering a few questions that might help us to find Chantelle.'

'Of course,' Nick said, then thought aloud. 'If she'd turned the heating off, she can't have been intending to come back here on New Year's Eve.'

'No.'

It was comforting to know that Chantelle meant to spend the night with him, even if it would have been the last night they ever spent together. She didn't dump me, Nick told himself. Someone got to her before she could pull out. Which meant she was in great danger. Or worse.

What day was it? Deborah had lost track of time. She might have been in this room for 24 hours or three days. He had raped her three times. She was sore and soiled, inside and out. The exercise she'd done over Christmas, the self-defence classes she'd taken, counted for nothing when you were knocked out and tied up.

He had told her, again and again, that he was going to kill her. After he'd had his fun.

Not much noise. The distant rumble of traffic and the dripping of a tap, which had her constantly wanting to pee. He hadn't told her where she was. The only clue was a church bell, faint but familiar, like one she could hear when she stayed overnight at Nick's flat.

He had given her water, and offered her a cold burger, which she'd refused. Now she was hungry. And cold. Her prison felt like it was a cellar. No windows. The only ventilation came from the gaps around the frame of the locked door. He only removed the gag on the few occasions when he allowed her to drink. If she tried to scream, he told her, nobody would hear, and he would hit her. The bruises from Friday night were only just starting to heal. She didn't want more.

With her hands tied behind her back, Deborah had enough flexibility to pull down her knickers when she needed to use the bucket to piss and shit in. He took the bucket out to empty just before he raped her. Once, he arrived to find that she had accidentally knocked the bucket over. He hit her for that.

Deborah tried to work out what he wanted, long term. Would he really kill her once he got tired of raping her? At Hendon police training college, she'd been to an under-attended lecture that dealt with the psychology of women as victims. She'd had to overcome an inbuilt, irrational contempt for women who let themselves be used and abused by men, who felt in some fucked-up way that they deserved whatever they got. Now she needed to empathise with the victims. Hard to fake such a pathetic role. But it was her only chance. She'd managed to fool Nick. This guy wasn't as clever as Nick, but he probably knew more about women, and how their minds worked.

He terrified her.

43

Nick wanted to cycle to Oxclose Lane police station but the police insisted they take him in their Ford Focus. A uniform asked for the key to his bike lock.

'We'll have a van collect the bike for you, have it waiting at the station before we're finished.'

The guy talking, DI Rawlins, came over as suave, verging on smarmy. Nick knew better than to allow himself to relax, for even a moment.

'Can you account for your movements on New Year's Eve?'

Nick had been in company the entire evening. He told the officers this, without mentioning Sarah. He still hadn't got to the bottom of why he'd found her watching TV, or why the news had had such an effect on her.

While answering the police's questions, he thought about the answers that he needed. Did Chantelle's disappearance have something to do with Andrew's taking Nancy? Were the police looking for Terence?

He finished his account. 'I got a cab home at about half three. There'll be a record of it.'

Rawlins wrote something down then looked Nick in the eye.

'You said you spoke to Miss Brown every day except for New Year's Eve. Did you try to get in touch with her on New Year's Eve?'

'Yes. I phoned her two or three times when she didn't show. She wasn't picking up.'

'Did you leave a voicemail?'

'Once. After that, there was no point. She knew that I was expecting her. So I assumed that she was sending me a message.'

'And what message would that be?'

'That she'd changed her mind... about me, the party, whatever.'

'Were there tensions between you?'

'I didn't think so.'

'But now you seem to think she finished the relationship.'

'Only because of what's happened since. We're from different cultures and I'm quite a bit older than her. She'd just spent a few days at home with her parents and I suppose that might have given her second thoughts.'

These were all the things that had been running through Nick's mind before Sarah told him the real reason for his girlfriend's non-appearance.

'You didn't try to contact her at her parents'?'

'No. She didn't want them to meet me. She never gave me their address, so I had no way of contacting them.'

He didn't mention that she had misled him about living with them. Never give the police any information that they haven't directly asked for.

'I'd like a list of all the people who can vouch for your movements on New Year's Eve.'

Nick gave as many names as he could remember, including Eve and Sarah. Chantelle's disappearance must have something to do with Andrew and Nancy, though he couldn't satisfactorily state why, and the police hadn't mentioned them yet. Perhaps this was all a set-up. Soon the police would spring a surprise witness on him: Ms Undercover, a.k.a. Chantelle Brown, and ask the killer question: what jobs did you do for Andrew Saint? To which the answer was: nothing that could land me back inside.

All right, there might be something illegal about the messages he had passed on Andrew's behalf. Conspiracy, perhaps. But any half decent lawyer would be able to demonstrate that Nick had acted in ignorance.

He finished his list. 'There were more ex-footballers there, with their wives or girlfriends. I don't know their names, but my brother would.'

'And you didn't leave the house once?'

'Only to go into the back garden for a cigarette, and, even then, there was always somebody about.'

'Who?'

Once more, Nick tried to remember who was where, when, without revealing that he had been sharing a spliff rather than smoking a cigarette.

'Now I'd like you to go over the whole day's events again.'

This was how they got you. They found small inconsistencies in your story, then hammered a chisel into the gap until it was a gaping hole. Nick began at the beginning.

'I caught a bus to Sherwood just after four in the afternoon...'

Sarah rang Nick before she drove to Nottingham, but his phone went straight to voicemail and this wasn't the sort of thing you left a message about. She tried again once she was back in her flat. Again, voicemail. She needed to see him before going to London tomorrow. She considered delaying her return. Recess wasn't over, but she'd arranged dinner with Andrew Saint. Andrew had completed arrangements for local builders to fix up the villa in Majorca. Regardless of his recent bad publicity, she couldn't cancel on him a second time. Also, she was curious about Andy's reinvention of himself as a Good Samaritan. Andrew being Andrew, she expected he had a self-interested angle. The girl was bound to be good looking, for a start.

It was infuriating that Eric had called when he did. She knew her mum, and she knew that she would never open up again the way she had started to before the call. Sarah's feelings about the relationship fluctuated. Grandad had been dead nearly fifteen years. It was hard to hold grudges on Dad's behalf. Kevin Bone had been gone almost as long, victim of a disease that didn't have a name while Grandad was alive. Grandma Edith had lingered for thirteen years after her stroke. Sarah had only known her as a brain-damaged invalid. Did Gran know about Mum's affair with Grandad?

No, she couldn't have. Nevertheless, a large part of Sarah's childhood had been turned on its head. For a second time. At what point had she realised that her father preferred to sleep with men? It began to dawn on her when she was sixteen, in a vague way. Everyone knew about homosexuality in the 70s, but there were no 'out' gay men in Chesterfield. Only a handful at Nottingham University in the early 80s. None of her friends understood how you could have a gay dad. Except Nick. He didn't judge Kevin Bone until he met him.

Interview over, Nick looked for his bicycle. No sign. The police offered him a lift home, but Nick wouldn't be seen in a police car. He called Cane Cars.

In Sherwood, Nick was in time for roast duck. While Caroline was serving, he turned his mobile on. Three missed calls. One was from an unknown number, two were from Sarah. He called her back.

'I need to talk to you,' she said. 'Can you come round later?'

He said he would. She offered to cook.

'No need,' he replied. Sarah wasn't much of a cook. 'I'm about to eat.'

'I'll make us something light.'

Nick refused wine with his Sunday lunch, wanting to keep a straight head. Caroline, he noticed, didn't drink either. Which made the announcement after dessert less of a surprise.

'We've got something to tell you,' Joe said.

'When's it due?'

'Middle of June,' Caroline said. 'Everybody reckons that a two year gap between siblings is ideal.'

'Not that we planned it or anything,' Joe said.

'You're a lucky guy,' Nick told his brother.

'I know. This'll happen to you, one day.'

'Do you reckon?' Joe knew that Nick would like to be a dad. 'Funny thing is, I'd started to wonder what Chantelle and my kids would look like.'

'Ah. That reminds me. The police asked me to check whether Chantelle phoned for a cab, so I went through the records. She did. Quarter past ten. And the car brought her here.'

'That's strange,' Nick said. 'More than strange.'

She did come to the party at the time she said she'd arrive. Nick found that oddly comforting. Only why had she not come in?

'Who was on the switch New Year's Eve?'

'Tess and Bill. Beardy Bob did the pick-up.'

'Is he on tonight?'

Joe made a call and found out. He was.

'Get him to collect me from here at twenty past eight, would you?'

44

Sarah washed her hair then put on black Levis. She found a clean, black Wonderbra and selected a Nicole Farhi sweater that wasn't too opaque: a dusky pink cashmere with a scooped neck. Five minutes before Nick was due to arrive, she heard a car pull up outside. She looked through the living room window. A taxi. It was a cold night, but Nick must be flush, if he was coming by taxi rather than walking over or cycling. The car didn't leave straight away. It was a couple of minutes before the doorbell rang. Nick wore a leather bomber jacket that had seen better days, supplemented by a thick, woollen scarf. His smile radiated affection.

'Have you been sat outside, waiting for it to be half past?' Sarah teased.

'Outside, yes. Waiting, no. I was quizzing Bob, the driver who picked up Chantelle on Friday night.'

'And?'

'He dropped her at the party. But she didn't come in.'

'Do the police think someone kidnapped her?'

'I don't know what they think. They questioned me for the best part of two hours, but they didn't let on that she was an undercover cop.'

Sarah considered this for a moment. 'She must have found out something that upset somebody.'

'She did meet Terence, the pimp who ran the brothel where Andrew was picked up,' Nick said. 'He threatened her, but only to get at Andrew.'

'Did you tell the police about him threatening her?'

'I couldn't tell them without bringing Andrew into it, which I didn't want to do. Anyway, Chantelle's one of theirs. They'll already know about Terence.'

'But they couldn't tell you without letting on how they knew. Do you know who Terence works for?'

'I don't. It could be that he just works for Andrew, but both he and Andrew keep the structural stuff pretty vague.'

They chewed it over a little longer, but got no further.

'Was this what you asked me over to talk about?' Nick asked. 'On the phone, I got the sense that there was something else going on with you.'

'There is,' Sarah said. 'But you'll have to promise it'll go no further.'

She opened a bottle of Chianti. Then she told him everything. It was a relief to get it out. Her mother apart, Nick was the only person who had met everybody concerned. He listened carefully, prompting her with the occasional comment.

'Blimey,' he said when she was done, 'I do remember picking up a weird dynamic between your mum and your grandad that time we stayed with him in '82. But when I broached it with you, you freaked out.'

'Of course I did. It's like…. reverse incest.'

'Then, when we met your dad, he was always hinting that he had big secrets to tell, if only we'd ask him.'

'He was showing off.'

'Maybe, or maybe he wanted to spill but knew you weren't ready. The thing was, that week in Majorca, he irritated me so much, I wanted to irritate him back by not asking. Him in his little corner of paradise. The last night we were there he got me so stoned I virtually blacked out.'

'Seems I own that villa now.'

'You what?'

Sarah told him about her inheritance. 'Dad's boyfriend Sergio had the place after Dad died. He passed away nearly a year ago, after a long illness, but I only just found out. Under the terms of Dad's will, it comes to me. So I need to go over there once it's been fixed up, check the repairs, then put it on the market.'

'You don't want a holiday home?'

'I already own two flats. And I never take holidays.'

'Maybe you ought to.'

'When the place has been renovated, maybe we could go there together,' she heard herself ask, 'to look it over? Just as mates, obviously.'

Or not so obviously.

'That'd be good. I haven't had a holiday since I got out.'

She poured him another glass. They resumed talking about Chantelle. Sarah couldn't get her head around why the police had let the girl go undercover for so long. Unless they had something on Nick.

'There was no flirtation while we were both working at the Power Project,' Nick said. 'The opposite, if anything. One night she gave me a lift home from a club and I came onto her. Took a while to persuade her to go for a drink. Then she offered to help me move flat. Looking back, we took it very slowly. We'd been seeing each other for five months before we, you know...'

'Maybe she stayed on the case because she got to like you,' Sarah suggested. 'You became her boyfriend, rather than her target.'

'Or maybe the police were using me to get to somebody else.'

'Who?' Sarah asked, not sure she wanted to know the answer.

'There's only one person it can be.'

When he didn't fill in the name, she said it for him. 'Andrew.'

'You knew?'

'I don't know anything,' Sarah said. 'I'm not sure I want to know.'

'I don't blame you.'

Their eyes met. She couldn't avoid this.

'Drugs?' Sarah asked.

'On a huge scale. Paul Morris used to run his Nottingham

operation. When Paul moved to London, there was a vacuum. Andrew tried to persuade me to be his new number two. I turned him down. Andrew took on some of the work himself. Not sure how much of that Chantelle worked out. Nothing from me, but she's smart. And she had the run of Andrew's place in London.'

Sarah had worked out that Paul Morris was killed because of his involvement in the drug trade. The police despaired of finding his killer. And she knew that Andrew dealt when they were students, not that anybody called it dealing then. It was helping out friends. Nick did the same, to some extent. Fair enough, people thought, if your friend made enough profit to pay for his own supply. Though, knowing Andrew, he did rather better than that.

'Do you think Andrew had anything to do with Paul's murder?'

'I'm certain that he didn't.'

'Are you equally sure he doesn't have anything to do with Chantelle's disappearance?'

Nick didn't answer. Sarah sighed. 'Do you know how long the police have been investigating him?'

'It's not the first time they've come after him. He was in some kind of trouble in '92 and had to get out of the country. But he doesn't have a record. I had my suspicions that he was being investigated. Lately he's been followed by a guy I spotted twice, shaved head, baseball cap. He didn't look like police. I figured he could be working for a rival gang.'

Or, for Gill Temperley, Sarah thought, recalling a conversation they'd had. But she'd keep quiet about this until she'd found out what Gill knew. There was something else she had to confide.

'I spoke to Andrew,' she said, 'just before Christmas, to apologise for cancelling dinner. I'd had a lot to drink and I don't remember that much about the conversation. I agreed to have dinner with him in London on Tuesday. And I think... no, I'm sure, that I talked about Chantelle. I wanted advice. I didn't have an inkling that he was still in the drugs business. He always gave the impression that he'd left all that behind at university. He talked about you like you were the reprobate kid brother who'd never grown up.'

'Did you tell him what Chantelle was?'

'I must have done. I think I remember him telling me not to tell you. He said it was kinder that way. I knew she was under instructions to finish with you at Christmas.'

Nick thought for a minute, head in hands, like he always used to when deep in concentration.

'At least, if the investigation was over, and Andrew knew that, he had no reason to hurt Chantelle.'

'You thought he might be behind her disappearance?' Sarah asked.

'Couldn't rule it out.'

'He's your oldest friend.'

'And he knew my girlfriend was a spy, but didn't tell me. It's still possible he knows what happened to her.'

'In that case,' Sarah said, 'one of us has to confront him.'

45

The walk home from Sarah's took fifteen minutes, the night chill eliminating the effects of the half bottle of wine he'd drunk. The way Sarah looked at him when he'd kissed her cheek goodnight, she might have let him stay the night. Nick had to be at work from midnight, but that wasn't why he'd left early. He couldn't use her that way, not while Chantelle was the one thing on his mind.

He'd been ready to settle down with Chantelle. For a while there, he'd thought he was in love. How had he let her take him in so completely? It couldn't all be lies. Was she a good enough actor to fake the way her body shuddered while she shouted words of love? Friday nights, wrapped in each other's arms like an old married couple, laughing at *Friends* and *Frasier*, were they a lie, too? The times she woke up smiling after he was relieved early from a night on the switch? She deserved an Oscar for those.

Nick's flat was nearly the way he wanted it. Decent art on the walls: a big Magritte poster and a psychedelic Rick Griffin screen print that covered the damp patches. He had two second-hand leather armchairs, a decent enough Persian rug in front of the gas fire. Yet, after an evening at Sarah's, his home felt like a shabby rental. Nick needed some framed black and white photographs to add personality, he decided – be-bop musicians might do it – and a more stylish sofa. Maybe one of those new widescreen TVs like Sarah had. Before that, however, he needed better paid, legitimate work to enable him to afford such things.

He poured himself a glass of water from the tap, then phoned Andrew. His end of the conversation was carefully planned.

'Happy new year.'

'Same to you. How was the party?'

'Good, thanks. Except that Chantelle didn't show up. She's

not answering her phone. I think she's dumped me.'

'I'm sorry to hear that. You two are good together.'

'You haven't heard anything, have you?' Nick asked, carefully.

'Why would I have?'

'You tell me. How's it going with Nancy?'

'Hard. She won't go into rehab and she keeps offering me all sorts of... treats if I'll go out and get her a little taste. I try to explain that I can't have it in the house. But, that first night, I got her a little to ease her through Christmas, so she knows it isn't a cast-iron rule.'

'Are you with her all the time?'

'When she's awake. She sleeps a lot. We have a drink together in the evenings. I haven't taken her out of the house.'

'You didn't take her to meet your folks over Christmas?'

Andrew had family in Leeds, but they weren't close. His parents were getting on a bit and his kid sister, last Nick heard, was an estate agent.

'I didn't take her anywhere. We watch a lot of films on DVD. Nancy can make some clever comments, when she's not nodding off.'

'She was always very sharp, before the crack took hold. Look, if you want help, I've got a couple of days off work this week. I could babysit Nancy while you get on with your business.'

'You'd do that for us?'

'I got you into this. I feel responsible. And I care about Nancy.'

'As long as you don't care too much,' Andrew said, in a wistful tone. He really was smitten.

'It would do me good to get away from the situation here.'

'Maybe Chantelle will phone, tell you she's had a fever.' Something slightly off in Andrew's tone when he said this. It took Nick a moment to recognise what this unexpected quality was intended to be: kindness.

'If she does, I'll get the first train back.'

'Do you know anyone who's got a grudge against her?'

Nick found himself caught in a morass of double-think. What could he tell Andrew without revealing that he knew Chantelle was a spy?

'There's one guy. He was going to Nancy and his wife found out, dumped him. Hang on though. He might have seen Chantelle behind the wheel of a car, but he wouldn't have known who she was.'

'What's his name?'

'Doesn't matter. He wouldn't know how to find her.'

'Like I say, there'll probably be a simple explanation.'

'Hope you're right. I'll come on Tuesday.'

When they were through, he rang Sarah.

'It's done. I'm on.'

'How did he sound?'

'Normal. I can't believe he has anything to do with this.'

Sarah went back to London on Monday. She found her secretary in the office, sorting the day's mail. They spent half an hour dealing with chronic cases, most of which she referred back to the office in Nottingham. Sarah made a couple of phone calls about urgent immigration matters. There tended to be more deportations at this time of year, when the Immigration Service knew that bleeding heart MPs were liable to have their eyes off the ball.

The phone rang. Gill Temperley.

'Time for a coffee?'

They met in the plush Pugin Rooms, which they had to themselves. Sarah wasn't sure that it was good for her to be seen so publicly cosying up to a senior Tory, but out of session they would only be noticed by parliamentary estate staff, who were much more discreet than the members.

'I'm having dinner with Andrew Saint tomorrow,' Sarah said.

'Is that wise, after what happened?'

'Andrew rang when I cancelled our dinner on New Year's Eve. He explained what he was doing in the brothel. He was rescuing a woman who'd fallen into drug addiction and prostitution.'

'If you believe that,' Gill said, with a sad smile, 'you'll believe...'

'... anything, I know. You're right to be suspicious. Only, another old friend confirmed the story. Andrew has the woman staying with him at the moment, I hear. She refuses to go into rehab, so Andrew is helping her through cold turkey himself.'

'A saint indeed.'

'I don't know about that, but I wouldn't judge him too harshly. Unless, that is, you know something I don't. Didn't you tell me you had him followed?'

'Until the arrest at the brothel, yes. Doing my due diligence. You have to be careful who you take money from.'

'You've not had him watched since?'

'The man I employed couldn't come up with anything definite against Andrew.' Gill paused. 'It was what he didn't find that worried me. I had Andrew looked into in both London and Nottingham. In London, there was little sign of him having anything to do with the property business that he's supposed to be running. In Nottingham, most of the people and places he visited were of a... shall we say, dubious nature. He saw a lot of one guy who'd served five years in prison for growing vast amounts of cannabis.'

'I know about him,' Sarah said. 'They're old university friends. Was there anything else?'

'I've put some extra doubt in your mind, haven't I? I'm sorry. I know that you and Andrew go back a long way, but you do have a career to protect. Would you like to borrow the report?'

'Please. If there's anything I can't explain, I might be able to bring it up with him tomorrow. Without letting on where I got it, of course.'

'It hardly matters,' Gill said. 'I've severed my connection with Saint Holdings. He'll get a registered letter. In our job, you can't be too careful.'

'She's asleep,' Andrew told Nick, when he got to Notting Hill.

The two men shook hands with the same tight squeeze they always used.

'Did you know someone's watching your house?' Nick asked. He had spotted a Merc with darkened windows on his way in, guy behind the wheel.

'Same guy as before?'

'Couldn't tell. Different car.'

'Not police?'

'I don't think so. Too expensive a car.'

'I'll look into it.' Andrew dismissed the subject. Nick remembered how annoyed Andrew had been when he gave Terence the address of this house. He wondered whether this had anything to do with the car outside. Best not to remind Andrew about all that. Instead, he held up his black Adidas carry-all.

'Which room am I in? I could do with a wash and change.'

'The one you and Chantelle were in. I'll put the kettle on.'

Nick had a quick shower in the *en-suite*, then put on a fresh shirt and underwear. On the landing, he ran into Nancy. She wore only a Sex Pistols T-shirt and black knickers. Her hair was matted, her eyes only half open.

'Andy, what time is it?'

'It's not Andrew, it's Nick.' When she didn't react to this, he added, 'Why don't you have a shower? There's lots of hot water.'

'Can't be bothered,' Nancy said, not evincing any surprise that Nick was here. 'I'll come downstairs with you.'

She seemed unsteady on her feet, but when Nick offered her his arm, she shook him off. He followed her down.

'Look who I met on the landing,' Nick said to Andrew.

He watched his oldest friend give his ex-girlfriend a cuddle. Andrew spooned sugar into a large mug of tea for her, then made a fresh one for Nick.

'Nick's visiting. He's going to look after you while I go out and do some business,' Andrew told her. 'How are you feeling?'

'Like tiny creatures have been crawling over me all night. Where are my cigs?'

'I'm not sure.'

'Let me roll you one,' Nick offered, getting out his tobacco.

'Why don't I run you a bath?' Andrew suggested, when she was lit up.

She didn't say "yes", but didn't say "no" either. Andrew went upstairs, leaving the two of them alone. Between sips of tea, Nancy shivered.

'Can I get you a dressing gown, or a blanket or something?' Nick offered.

Nancy bristled. 'I'm not a fucking invalid. If I want something, I'll get it myself.'

'Sorry.'

'If Andy had to get me a minder, he could have gone for someone younger and better looking.'

Nick gave her an amused smile. It was good to see her combative side. She sucked on the roll-up and her wide eyes became alert. She glared at Nick.

'All of this was your idea, wasn't it?'

'Andrew offered to get you into rehab. I didn't imagine he'd...'

'Fall for me?' she filled in. 'Does he often go for your cast-offs?'

'Never happened before. Anyway, it was you who finished with me. You went back to Carl, remember?'

'Carl liked smoking with me. You didn't.'

'I know.'

'How come you came looking for me?' Nancy asked.

'Eve asked me to.'

'Oh, right. Eve.' A shadow crossed her face. He wondered whether she was remembering that Eve's husband had been one of her clients. How often had Nancy serviced Geoff? Nick had never met the guy, but he and Geoff had been with two of the same women, which created an odd, unsettling kinship.

Andrew returned. 'I've put some of that bubble bath in. The herbal essence you like.'

Nancy didn't react. Andrew began to ask Nick about his journey, the party he'd missed, his brother and sister-in-law. Nancy didn't join in. Andrew went back out to turn the water off. He yelled down that the bath was ready. Nancy left, like an obedient child. Alone, Nick topped up his tea from the pot and looked for Andrew's mobile. No sign. He rolled himself a cigarette. Five minutes later, Andrew returned.

'I told her I was going to pop out soon. She seemed to take it in. I really appreciate this. Especially when you must be deep down in the dumps, with Chantelle going off like that. Did you try and call her at work yesterday?'

'She never told me which dentist's she worked at,' Nick said. 'I looked up dentists in Arnold. There are five of them. I could ring round, try to track her down, but it seems pointless. The police will have been onto them.'

'I suppose,' Andrew said. 'What do the police reckon?'

'If they reckon anything, they've not told me. Have you had any medical help...? I mean, with Nancy?'

'I talked to professionals. They say, watch her all the time but in the long run, if it doesn't come from her, it's hopeless. I'm thinking of taking her on holiday somewhere warm, somewhere she'll find it very hard to score.'

He looked at his watch. 'I've set up a meeting in half an hour. I'd better get changed. I'm seeing Sarah for dinner this evening so I'll go straight there from my meeting. If that's OK with you?'

'It's why I'm here.'

46

Andrew's house had a dozen high ceilinged rooms. Nick searched them methodically, careful not to make much noise. He didn't want Nancy to hear and put two and two together.

At first, he couldn't help but feel ashamed of what he was doing. After a while, though, he began to feel oddly detached. What was his relationship with Andrew these days? Why were they still friends? *Precious villain*, Othello called Iago after discovering his betrayal. Jerry once asked Nick to explain Othello's use of 'precious'. He'd struggled to explain to a sixth former how one could value an old friendship even when the friend was irredeemably corrupt.

Nothing of interest downstairs, but it took twenty-five minutes to be sure. There was no cellar and no easy access to the attic. Nick moved on to the master bedroom, two doors down from the bathroom. It had pink walls. There was a fug of body odour and stale smoke. He looked out of the window. The Merc was gone. Had it followed Andrew? Old newspapers and magazines were scattered across the green carpet. The duvet cover had an elaborate oriental pattern while the sheet covering the mattress was jet black silk. Nick started with the obvious places: under the mattress, at the back of drawers. He went through the pockets of each jacket in Andrew's wardrobe. There was some porn stuffed beneath the pyjamas at the bottom of it. Big tits and spread legs, not hardcore or particularly kinky. There were condoms and lube in the bedside cabinet. No sex toys or stimulants. No letters or notebooks.

In the spare bedroom beyond the bathroom was a computer, with a modem, and a printer. There was also a red box file with the word, 'accounts' written on it: probably not worth looking into if it was out in the open. Nick checked anyway. Andrew had a conventional savings account, about fifty grand in total, and had paid income tax on a declared salary of thirty thousand a year from Saint Holdings for the previous year. There were no books referencing the company itself. Those accounts were probably on the computer.

Andrew's PC was password protected. What word might he use? In the movies, the hero always made a clever guess on the second attempt. Nick thought hard, but came up with no ideas. He went back onto the landing and tapped lightly on the bathroom door.

'Nancy, you awake?'

'Worried about me drowning in the bath?'

'Can I ask you something?'

'Come in. It's not locked. Nothing you haven't seen before.'

He did as she asked, though he wasn't sure that Andrew would be happy about it. Nancy sank beneath the water, half concealing her plump breasts.

'Sorry, I was a bit of a bitch earlier. It was a surprise to see you here.'

'It's a rough time. How are you doing?'

'My head feels empty, and raw, like I'm a building where all the walls have been stripped. There are big gaps in the floorboards and half the windows are cracked, so the wind gets in. A hot bath helps. I have two most days. Drinking doesn't help much. Have you brought any spliff with you?'

'Sorry, no.' He'd figured that, if Nancy was allowed dope, Andrew would have some in.

'Pity. What was it you wanted?'

'The password to Andrew's computer. There's something I need to look up.'

'Which computer? He's got a laptop downstairs, but he lets me use the PC in the spare room. The password's *Jethro*, after my ancestor, the guy who invented the seed drill.' Nancy's surname was Tull. 'Before you get sucked into the internet,' she went on, 'bring me another mug of tea, would you? Just one level spoonful of sugar. Andy always puts too much in.'

'I remember how you like it.'

While the kettle was on, Nick double-checked the kitchen cupboards. There was one drawer, beneath the cooker. It held a pile of brown envelopes and printed papers. Utility bills mostly. He checked the phone ones. Andrew's calls weren't itemised. Next, he located the chunky black laptop, which was on the sofa in the living room. He moved it onto the coffee table and put a bunch of newspapers and magazines over it, the sort of thing – he hoped – that Andrew would think Nancy would have done. He took two mugs of tea upstairs, knocked, then placed one of them on the edge of the bath without once glancing at the body he used to lust after. Only then did he sign in to Andrew's PC.

'Heard from Nick recently?' Andrew asked Sarah when they were settled at their table in *Quo Vadis*.

'Not since the New Year's party. You?'

'He's at my house now, looking after Nancy. Think I can trust him?'

'He seems pretty hung up on his new girlfriend,' Sarah said. 'He tried not to show it, but he was very upset when she didn't show up at the party.'

'But you knew why that was,' Andrew said.

'What do you mean?'

'You told me, remember? You weren't that drunk.'

Her betrayal confirmed, Sarah felt herself flush. She didn't try to hide her embarrassment. Andrew gave her one of those aren't-we-clever, complicit grins that some vain men were prone to.

'I shouldn't have mentioned it,' Sarah said, after sipping some over-priced Pinot Gris. 'You didn't tell him that I told you, did you?'

'God, no, but it was tempting. He's cut up about her vanishing like that.'

'Here's the problem,' Sarah said, prepared to spin the lie she'd rehearsed. 'Chantelle, or whatever her name really is, was meant to return to uniform yesterday. But she didn't show up. The police went to her house. She hadn't been home since New Year's Eve.'

Andrew sipped his wine, then looked her straight in the eye. 'And you want to know if I had anything to do with it?'

'Pardon?' Andrew had jumped ahead too quickly for her.

Andrew took a deep draught of wine. 'It's a fair question. The only people you told were me and Nick. You have told Nick by now, haven't you? That why he's at my house today, going through my stuff. He's trying to find out what happened to Chantelle. Waste of time. All he had to do was ask.'

Sarah took a deep glug of wine. Andrew did the same.

'I'll ask, then. Do you know what happened to Chantelle?'

The waitress approached. For the second time, Andrew told her that they weren't ready to order.

'I'm afraid we can only let you have this table for ninety minutes, sir.'

'Fuck off.'

She hurried away. It was the first time since they were students that Sarah had seen Andrew lose his cool.

'I don't know for sure,' he told Sarah. 'But I expect I can find out. If we're going to level with each other, I suggest we go back to my place, where we won't be overheard, and Nick can join the conversation.'

He filled up his wine glass and drank it in one long gulp, then left a twenty on the table to cover the cost of the bottle. Sarah followed him out of the restaurant.

47

On Dean Street, Andrew looked for a taxi to flag down. Sarah really shouldn't be seen with him. Gill's surveillance had finished, but the police might well be observing him. A cab pulled up. She took the jump seat opposite Andrew, rather than sit next to him, then leant forward.

'Are you sure your house isn't being watched?'

'I'm not sure about anything any more,' Andrew muttered.

This is a mistake, Sarah told herself. I'm going to the home of a man who is known as a drugs distributor. Why didn't Eric warn me against Andrew, rather than Nick? He can't know that we're connected. She got out her phone.

'Texting Nick to tell him we're on the way?'

That had crossed her mind. 'Just checking my messages.'

'Don't mind me. Text him if you want.'

She put the phone away.

The Notting Hill house was shabby on the outside, and soullessly functional inside, like one of those shared, barely occupied houses rented by provincial MPs for the Westminster week. Andrew didn't announce their return.

'Drink?' he asked Sarah in the vast kitchen. When she hesitated, he added, 'if we're going to talk frankly, you can't let me drink alone.'

He opened a bottle of something expensive and white. Nick hurried into the room, a guilty expression on his face. They had interrupted his search.

'Andrew? You're back early.' He noticed her. 'Sarah?'

'Found what you were looking for?' Andrew asked. 'I got you a glass.'

'I'm all right,' Nick said.

'No, you're not,' Andrew talked while he poured the entire bottle into three glasses. 'I'll bet you couldn't believe your luck when you pulled Chantelle. She's the kind of woman you always fancy, but who's never interested in you – built like an Amazon, high minded. After years of settling for bronze, you thought you'd won gold.'

'What does that make me?' Sarah asked, trying to take the sting out of Andrew's attack. 'Base metal? Or am I one of the bronze also-rans?'

'You're better than gold. Platinum. Better for Nick, too, than any of the women he's had since you. Especially the latest, way things turned out.'

Andrew got up, opened a drawer and pulled out an oblong, sealed wooden box, together with a small plastic device, whose function she could not at first work out.

'We're talking openly now. It's better that way. We're Nick's closest friends. He must have told you how I make my money.'

Andrew tore the seal from the box and opened it: five, long, fat cigars.

'He did,' Sarah said. 'I can't say I was too surprised.'

'I'm glad you're not shocked. Legalisation of cannabis was on your election manifesto when you stood for student union president. Remember?'

'I still support lowering cannabis from class B to C as a controlled drug. But it's not just dope you handle, is it? It's coke, ecstasy, God knows what else.'

Andrew pulled open the plastic device to reveal two metal blades, resembling a guillotine, with a half-moon hole in the centre of each.

'If I don't do it, somebody else will, Sarah. Simple as that. Any government that pretends otherwise is guilty of gross hypocrisy.'

'Politicians specialise in hypocrisy. It's the only way to get elected. Nick and I aren't here to debate drug policy. This is about Chantelle. Do you know what happened to her?'

Andrew put the tip of the cigar into the guillotine and snapped it shut, neatly cutting off the sealed tip of the cigar, which he put in his mouth.

'No.' He pushed the cigar box towards Nick, who shook his head.

'But you must have some idea,' Nick said.

Andrew lit the cigar with a long match. He took his time, waited until the fat end glowed red. 'Some idea, yes.'

'Do you know how we can find her?' Nick pressed.

'If I'm right about who's got her, Terence's boss is sending a message.'

'Who to?' Sarah asked.

'The police, of course. And, by extension, your lot.'

'The government? What message would that be?'

'*Fuck off and leave us alone.*' He blew smoke at her.

'Wouldn't that be your message too?' Sarah asked.

Andrew flared with anger. 'If I were behind this and wanted to make an impression, I'd dump her dead, naked body on the steps of County Hall and make sure that the press had photos before the police got there.'

Nick knocked over his glass of wine. Before Sarah could stop him, he took a swing at Andrew. The smaller man tried to duck, but wasn't quick enough. Nick caught him on the side of the face. Andrew fell off his chair, landing hard on the wooden floor.

'What the fuck is going on in here?'

The new arrival was a slender, busty woman with long dark hair, wearing only tights, knickers and a see-through bra.

'Sarah,' Andrew said, reaching for the edge of the kitchen table in order to haul himself up, 'I'd like you to meet my girlfriend, Nancy.'

48

1976

He'd heard it said, if you really want to punish a man, give him the thing he most wants. Hugh was back in the cabinet, doing a proper job. Defence. Which meant minister for cutting the army. Until now, he had not known what it was like to be loathed. These were like the last days of the '66 – '70 Labour government, only worse. The party had fought two elections in '74, winning a slender overall majority in the second. Two years on, the economy was back in the khazi. Inflation was 26%. The Chancellor was threatening to impose maximum wage increases of 10%. Bernard Donaghue was working on a voluntary flat rate increase of £6 a week. Harold liked the idea of a voluntary flat rate because it sounded socialist, but the Treasury wanted legislation.

If things were bad for Hugh, they were worse for the PM. The press had it in for Harold, always had done. The smears got worse and worse. During the four-year Heath government, there had been stories about Harold and the Soviets, most of them planted by MI5. *Private Eye* magazine had taken an almost pathological dislike to Wilson, and were happy to publish any lie the spooks fed them. Not Hugh's problem. These days, Ted Short, the Paymaster General, was the PM's conduit for dealing with the security services.

Hugh was surprised to get a summons to Number Ten. At short notice, too. During the years of opposition, his tenuous friendship with the PM had fallen into abeyance. He was still on the Christmas card list, and Harold had sent a sincere note of condolence when Edith died, succumbing to a second stroke sixteen years after the first. Hugh had been expected to retire, but couldn't afford to. Not after paying off Kevin. Not unless he sold the house. He'd only been an MP for seventeen years. He needed to build up a bigger pension.

Tonight, Harold looked plumper than usual, more tired. He offered Hugh a cigar, but did not smoke one himself.

'How's Defence?' the PM asked.

'I've had worse jobs,' Hugh replied, and took the cigar cutter.

'This was the best I could give you. It had to be somebody utterly reliable, you understand that.'

'I do, and I was flattered to be offered it. Pity the role can't be expanded to include security liaison, though.'

'Exactly what I wanted to talk to you about. Not a cabinet reshuffle. That won't be until the spring, but I need your security expertise now.'

'Always at your service, Harold.' Hugh thought that this was going to be about one of Wilson's former protégés. Recently, John Stonehouse, who used to borrow the Wilsons' cottage in the Scilly Isles – a favour that had never been offered to Hugh – had faked his own death, then done a runner to the other side of the world. Rumour had it that Stonehouse was a double agent who had taken money from the Russians. The Australians had deported him back to the UK, where he was now awaiting trial for fraud.

'That story you told me. I didn't believe you at first.'

'The coup plot? I hardly dared believe it myself.' Hugh had saved his intelligence about the Mountbatten coup attempt until Harold had his overall majority, eighteen months ago. He'd timed the revelation well, so that Harold felt in his debt, and offered him a cabinet job. Not the one Hugh wanted. Jim Callaghan had that. Harold went on.

'I kept it to myself, saving it up, if you like, in case I needed a weapon.'

'And did you?' Hugh still didn't know what was coming. Why would Harold need a weapon against Five, or Six? Peter had retired earlier this year. Gone to farm in Tasmania. Hugh no longer had a decent source in either security agency, a situation that left him feeling vulnerable, exposed. The PM changed his mind about the cigar. He chose one from the wooden box and trimmed it. Only when the Corona was fully lit did he speak again.

'Let's go for a walk in the garden.'

So he was still worried about being bugged. They went outside and took a turn around the trees.

'Yesterday, I decided it was time. I called in Hanley.' Sir Michael Hanley was the head of MI5. 'I put your conspiracy theories to him.'

'You did, did you? Good man.'

Harold nodded, as though he appreciated Hugh's approval.

'He told me, in essence, that everything you suggested was true. That there had been a motley group behaving oddly, or out of turn. Not the majority, but a significant number. He also said that the threat was long gone. Most of them had retired now, or were on their way to retirement. Does that ring true to your experience?'

'More or less, yes.' Hanley was probably including Peter in that group, which was fair enough. Peter had always loathed Wilson. Never found any evidence against him, though. 'What are you going to do about it?'

'Haven't decided yet. Why waste energy on a threat that has passed? Hanley told me something else, which is why I called you in. Something so flabbergasting that it put the other thing out of my mind. He said there was an allegation that one of the former heads of MI5 was a Soviet mole.'

'Christ! What did you say?'

'Now I have heard everything.'

'He didn't come up with any evidence, I take it?'

'The investigation was inconclusive, but MI5 was badly undermined by the whole affair; so they won't be any threat to me for a while.' Harold paused, allowing Hugh room for a question that he did not formulate. Hugh knew who had been under investigation: Peter's old boss, Roger Hollis. According to Peter, he had accused Hollis to his face of being a spy. The spymaster didn't deny it: he merely refused to reply.

Hollis had been dead three years. There was no proof of his betrayal. There would never be any proof. Harold became impatient.

'Well? Anything you feel the need to tell me?'

How much did Harold know? Hugh found it very hard to tell.

'I'd heard rumours, but you know what Five is like: paranoia upon paranoia. It's a disease. I have no idea whether it's true or not.'

Harold blew smoke at him. 'Truth'll come out after we're all dead.'

'It's not the truth you get when all the witnesses are dead. It's history.'

The two men walked and smoked in companionable silence until they were back at the door to number ten.

'How's that boy of yours?' Harold asked. 'Still lapping up the sun?'

'Last I heard, yes.'

'And your beautiful daughter, Sarah. She must be at secondary school now.'

'Granddaughter, you mean. Yes, Sarah's thriving. She'll be starting her GCE's in the autumn.'

'Any idea what she wants to do with her life?'

'Last time we discussed it, she wanted to be an astronaut.'

'First woman in space, eh? There's bound to be one. Why shouldn't it be her, eh? Shall we go back inside?'

Hugh followed the Prime Minister into the old building, with its ghosts and its listening devices. Harold stopped on the threshold.

'There are going to be big changes in a week or two. Nothing will stay the same. Be prepared.'

'Thanks for the tip, Harold.'

The PM gave him an ambivalent smile, then saw him to the door. They shook hands like old friends. Hugh wasn't sure if he had just been promised a promotion. He wasn't sure about a lot of things, any more.

49

'I seem to have knocked Andrew over,' Nick said. Wine was splashed all over the table and floor, but Andrew's glass, miraculously, hadn't broken. Nick went to the sink and got a cloth to mop up. Sarah stared at the three of them, agog. She'd already had a bit to drink, Nick could tell. He and Nancy were the only sober people in the room. And Nick wasn't thinking straight. He couldn't be, for he'd just hit his oldest friend. Precious villain. Nancy found some Nivea cream and began to rub it onto the side of Andrew's face.

Nick couldn't resist the impulse to apologise.

'Sorry, I lost it for a moment.'

'No, I asked for that,' Andrew said. 'Get another bottle out of the fridge, why don't you?'

When Nick had found a glass for Nancy and they all had a full drink, he came to the point that he and Sarah had been pussyfooting around since they came to the house.

'Have you had any contact with Terence?' he asked Andrew.

'Not since before Christmas. He was planning to return to Jamaica. Didn't want to hang around to be deported for living off immoral earnings.'

'Do you know who his boss is?' Sarah asked.

'No, I never met him face to face or even heard a name.' He looked straight at Nick. 'I told you how these things work, on a need-to-know basis.'

'You also told me all that stuff about cells of three and how nobody knew who the other people were beyond their own cell. Only now you expect me to believe that your Nottingham business boils down to a cosy cell with you, Terence and an anonymous kingpin who's behind Chantelle's kidnapping.'

'It's not like that any more,' Andrew said. 'After you turned me down, I hooked up with one of the new Nottingham cartels. Terence was my contact, and, after a dodgy start, things worked smoothly. Terence's boss kept increasing his orders, even paid up front when he wanted a massive shipment. Then you asked me to help with Nancy. Only then I found out...' He stopped, pulled on his cigar and looked at Sarah. 'You told him, right?'

Sarah nodded. 'At first, I forgot I'd told Andrew about the undercover operation. I'd had a few that night. Then I started to put together that Chantelle had been taken soon after I spoke to him.'

'What's she on about?' Nancy asked.

Andrew explained. 'Nick's girlfriend, Chantelle, is an undercover cop. She was trying to get to me through him. After Terence got busted, he wanted to know who had sent the police in. The people Terence works for are very dangerous, when they choose to be. Not telling him wasn't an option.'

The confession was coming now. Nick had expected to feel angry. Instead he felt a cold, rational hardness descend upon him.

'Go on,' Sarah said.

'I needed them to trust me.' Andrew turned to Nick. 'But when I told Terence that Chantelle was due to be at that party, I knew she'd been ordered to chuck Nick before Christmas. There was no chance she'd be there. So I thought it was safe to tell Terence.'

Nick glanced at Sarah to see if she'd confirm what Andrew was saying. No reaction. He turned back to Andrew, leant in closer.

'You think she's dead, don't you?'

'I'm sure of it.'

Nick and Sarah looked at each other, trying to gauge whether the other thought Andrew was lying. Nancy spoke to Nick.

'Sounds to me like, if anyone's to blame for what happened to this spy girl, it's your ex here, spilling the beans. Not Andrew. He was only protecting his business.'

Before Nick could respond, his mobile rang. He checked the display. A Nottingham number. He didn't recognise it, but answered anyway.

'Nick, it's Eve.'

'I can't really talk just now.'

'Oh.'

'Are you OK?' She sounded upset. More than upset.

'Nick, I'm so sorry. It's all my fault. I've brought this on you.'

'What's happened?'

'I've just had the police round. They've taken Geoff in for questioning. My Geoff.'

'I don't understand. What for?'

'Abducting Chantelle.'

50

Sarah was too busy trying to piece everything together to pay attention to what Nick was saying on the phone. Then she saw his face freeze.

'Do you know how much evidence the police have?' he asked. 'I see. What about...? OK, I'll talk to you later.' He hung up.

'What is it?' Sarah asked.

'Eve's husband, Geoff, has been taken in for questioning on suspicion of involvement with Chantelle's disappearance.'

'Jesus,' Sarah said. 'But hold on. I thought Eve was single?

She'd seen the woman leave the New Year's Eve party with Tony Bax.

'She kicked him out not long before Christmas.'

'What would be this Geoff guy's motive?' Andrew asked.

'I mentioned him to you once. Eve, his wife, was with Chantelle when they saw him leaving the brothel. Eve dumped Geoff as a result of that.'

'This creep was one of your clients?' Andrew asked Nancy.

'He was a regular,' Nancy said. 'Once a week for half and half.'

'I don't understand how Geoff knew who Chantelle was,' Sarah said.

'Eve must have told him,' Nick said. 'Geoff would have known about the party. He was invited with Eve before they split up. He must have lain in wait outside the house. Could be he was waiting for Eve, then spotted Chantelle, saw red.'

'That's hardly a motive for murder,' Nancy said.

'Her meddling cost him his marriage, that's how he'd see it.'

'Does this mean there's more chance that Chantelle's still alive?' Sarah asked Nick.

'Eve says they haven't found a body.'

'At least we know it had nothing to do with Andrew,' Nancy said.

Her comment sounded forced, but Nick nodded. He was easily taken in by women, Sarah thought. Especially good looking ones.

Andrew went to the bathroom. On his return, there was a slight redness about the eyes and the beginnings of a bruise on the right side of his forehead. When he spoke, it was only to Nancy.

'I need to leave the country, for a few months at least. Will you come with me?'

'We hardly know each other,' Nancy said. 'I'm a mess. I'd only slow you down.'

'I want you to come, but you can stay here if you prefer, look after the place for me.'

Nancy gave a weak laugh. 'We're a stone's throw from Ladbroke Grove! I'd be back on crack before you got to the airport.'

'Nick would look out for you, wouldn't you, Nick?'

Nick gave an unconvincing nod. Nancy shook her head. 'Thing about Nick is, he's well-meaning, but he needs to look after number one first, and he's got a long way to go with that before he can help anybody else.'

Sarah could see some truth in this, but said nothing. Nancy turned to her. 'Also, now I've met you, seen the two of you together, it's obvious.'

'What's obvious?' Sarah asked.

'He's still in love with you, isn't he? You two ought to work that out.'

Sarah didn't dare look at Nick. Nancy stood, drained her glass of wine, and turned to Andrew. 'I'm coming with you. Let's go and decide where.'

Andrew followed her out of the room. Sarah had had a fair

bit of wine and nothing to eat. She wasn't in a fit state to talk about what Nancy had just said, so returned to the more urgent situation.

'Does Eve think Geoff killed Chantelle?'

'Eve wouldn't put it past him. Geoff has a temper, she says. He's an architect, has access to building sites. The police are searching a couple of them.'

'Chantelle's one of theirs,' Sarah pointed out. 'The police will be desperate for an arrest. It doesn't mean they're right about Geoff. Did you tell Andrew about him before?'

'Not by name.' Nick stared into space. He wasn't thinking about what Nancy had said about her and him, Sarah realised. He was thinking about Chantelle. Sarah looked away, to give him a moment, and saw that Andrew, unannounced, had returned to the room. He looked vulnerable, out of his depth. Then he spoke and the mask went back on.

'Nancy and I have come to an agreement. I'm taking her abroad, somewhere hot, with rehab facilities. The Bahamas, we thought.'

'Why do you need to go?' Nick asked him. 'They've got Geoff. The police haven't got anything on you or they'd have arrested you already.'

'You don't know that for sure,' Andrew said. 'Chantelle had the run of this house while we were both out of it. Who knows what evidence she found and passed to her bosses? Or what Terence will tell them if they catch him before he flees the country. I've dealt with this situation before. The only way out is to get somewhere the police can't extradite you *before* they have time to put a case together. Eventually files get closed, officers reassigned. Everything blows over.'

'I still don't see what the urgency is.'

'There's another problem,' Andrew said. 'Over Christmas, with the Nancy situation, I took my eye off the ball. Last time I saw Terence, he passed on an advance – a really big one – for the next shipment. But I was playing out of my league and got ripped off. Terence's boss would have sent heavies after me by now but for what's going on with Chantelle. Even so, I can't stall him much longer.'

Nick wasn't convinced by this.

'Why can't you tell Terence – or whoever – what happened and get them to deal with the people who ripped you off?'

'As far as they're concerned, it's my problem, not theirs.'

'You can't afford to pay them?'

'Nowhere near. Even if I sold this house, it wouldn't cover it. Since you gave Terence my address I've had people watching the house. I can't be too careful. Nancy's on the internet now, looking for flights. You're welcome to stay another night, but Nancy and I may be gone by morning.'

He left Sarah and Nick on their own.

'I no longer believe anything Andrew tells me,' Sarah said.

'The story about him being ripped off doesn't ring true,' Nick agreed. 'I believe him about being watched, though. There was a guy following Andrew in Nottingham, but that was long before the tensions began with Terence'.

Sarah wasn't ready to tell him the truth about this. 'I'm going to call a cab,' she said. 'Want me to drop you at the station? You can still make the last train to Nottingham.'

He went to get his stuff together. When the cab arrived, Sarah yelled for him. They left without saying goodbye.

The street was empty. Nobody was watching, thank God. She and Andrew weren't really friends, Sarah decided, and hadn't been for fifteen years. She wondered how Nick felt about him now. Nancy's words about them being in love still rang around her brain.

'Do you think there's any chance the police will find Chantelle alive?' she asked Nick, when they were sat in the back of the minicab.

'If she were still alive, I think Geoff would have let her go by now.'

'Did you think it was a little odd, the way Nancy spoke about her?'

'Odd in what way?'

'Like Andrew had told her what to say.'

'Nobody tells Nancy what to do,' Nick insisted.

At St Pancras, a building site these days, she gave him a peck on the cheek. 'Promise you'll phone if you get any news. Whatever the time.'

He promised. She watched him haul his heavy bag into the station's temporary entrance.

51

1983

Andy drove Nick and Sarah to East Midlands Airport in Sarah's Cortina. They couldn't afford a taxi. Driving themselves and leaving the car in the airport car park was even more expensive.

'This is really kind of you,' Sarah told Andy.

'My pleasure. Cool of you to lend me the flat and car while you're away.'

'Think you'll ever get your own place in Nottingham?'

'Nah. London's where the work is, what little there is of it.'

The recession showed no sign of ending and Andy didn't have a job. Nick's teacher-training course was nearly over, but he had yet to find a post. Sarah, because of her year out as president of the students' union, had only just taken her finals. They would return in time for her results. Her plans post-graduation were obscure – at least they were to Nick. She must have something in mind, for she didn't seem worried. Andy had spent the year since graduation doing manual jobs for an agency and had stepped up the dealing. Nick didn't let on to Sarah about the latter activity. Andy visited Nottingham regularly, to hang out with them and to see customers. The rest of his time he spent in his parents' Leeds home or at mates, in London.

The couple needed this holiday. On top of finals and coursework, both had been working for Labour at the General Election. To no avail. The Falklands conflict had turned around the Tories' unpopularity and Thatcher had hugely increased their vote. Labour beat the newly formed Social Democratic Party by just two percentage points. The candidate that Nick and Sarah had been working for, Ken Coates, had lost marginal Nottingham South.

Now the city had just one Labour MP, in Nottingham North.

At the airport Andy confirmed the time of their return flight and promised to pick them up.

'Don't worry, I won't be sticking around afterwards. In fact, I plan to do some travelling myself.'

'Somewhere interesting?' Sarah asked.

'I make everywhere interesting,' Andy told her, and she frowned. Nick was aware that Andy's arrogant side irritated Sarah. The two of them would never normally be friends. Nevertheless, she kissed him goodbye.

Nick and Sarah slept for most of the flight. In Palma, they treated themselves to a taxi for the short journey to the train station.

The city was bigger and greener than Nick was expecting. The driver took them along dusty roads to the seafront, passing old windmills and a huge cathedral. There were trees everywhere, not just the ubiquitous palms.

'Let's have a day or two in the city on the way back,' Sarah said. 'I'm not sure I can take Dad's company for a whole week.'

There were only three trains a day to Soller. The couple were just in time for the middle one. They boarded an antique set of wooden carriages that catered for tourists and a few locals. After trundling across countryside for half an hour, they stopped at a high vista. Nick and Sarah stepped outside to stare at the town below, which was framed by a low mountain range and surrounded by orchards of olive trees.

'This is a very beautiful island,' Nick said. 'I can see why your dad's stayed here so long.'

What he couldn't see was why Sarah had only visited Kevin here once before. Or why, the way Sarah told it, Kevin Bone hadn't left the island since he arrived here, thirteen years earlier.

In Soller, they had lunch at a tapas bar in the town square, sheltered from the sun by ancient, enormous trees. Then, as instructed, they boarded the tram down to the port of Soller, a steep, fifteen minute journey that took them to the heart of a wide, busy harbour. Sarah found a phone box. After a couple of attempts she managed to ring her father, who promised he'd be with them in less than fifteen minutes. They killed the time by shopping for hats. Nick found a magnificent Panama, one that had actually been made in Panama, and was tempted to buy it, until Sarah told him not to.

'Hats like that are for middle aged men. There are some nice fisherman's caps over there. Or you could try one of these. She held up a cap with a stiff flap at the front.

'What's that?'

'I think they're called baseball caps.'

He tried one on. 'Makes me look daft. What about a beret?'

She shook her head. 'You look like an old Frenchman. How do I look?'

She tried on a sombrero that had several corks attached to it and a bright pink ribbon round the brim.

'Perfect. Though it could do with *kiss me quick* written on the ribbon.'

'Kiss me, stupid,' she said. 'We're on holiday.'

He obliged. It was good to see her relax. At least her year as union president seemed to have cured her of politics. He'd been worried that, given the family she came from, Sarah might want to become an MP. Nothing wrong with that, but it was the kind of job that didn't leave much room for a personal life. For Nick, the big appeal of teaching was the long holidays. He wanted to travel the world with Sarah.

Back outside, the sun burnt their faces. Each of them soon regretted not having bought a hat.

52

Kevin Bone didn't behave like anyone's father. Or like a bloke in his mid-forties. He smoked dope all the time. The hash he had was stronger and fresher than the stuff that made it to the UK. Nick liked a smoke, but only in the evenings. Kevin's constant vagueness and wide-eyed stare were broken only by a forced bonhomie that got on Nick's nerves.

Happily, Kevin, assisted by Sergio, twenty years his junior, was a good cook. The four of them had long, al fresco meals, with a seemingly endless supply of excellent local red. Sarah was weird around her father, a different person to the one Nick knew at home: younger acting and straighter, with a barely concealed resentment that left Nick uncomfortable. Maybe her attitude contributed to Kevin smoking and drinking so heavily. The old man put away at least a bottle of wine a night, with beers and brandies on top.

Sergio was a tour guide, taking English and German speakers on boat trips from Soller harbour. He had to get up in the mornings, so was usually in bed by midnight. The exception was when they spent an evening at a cafe called Sa Fonda, in Deia. Kevin introduced them to a couple of English musicians, one of whom Nick had heard of. He was also called Kevin, and had recently moved to the island. Not much music was played, but a lot of dope was smoked, except by Sergio, who drove them home. Next day, while Kevin slept in, Sergio took Nick and Sarah to a hidden, private cove at Son Muleta. They swam in the sea and sunbathed for hours until Sergio returned to take them home, where Kevin seemed not to have noticed that they'd been gone.

Tonight, when Sergio announced that he was about to turn

in, Sarah did the same. Nick joined her in the kitchen and squeezed her waist.

'Want me to come too?'

'No need. Dad seems to enjoy your company more than mine. I don't mind him stoned, but I don't like him when he's very drunk, too. Do you think we can escape tomorrow, go to Palma a day early like we said?'

Nick thought about this for a moment. 'He'll be offended.'

'I know. Still, maybe you can persuade Dad to drive us there, have a late lunch, show us round a bit then go home. I want more time alone with you.'

'You can be alone with me now,' Nick said.

'I'm tired. But explain to Dad that we'd like to go a day early.'

Nick felt awkward. This was a situation that Sarah ought to handle, not him. If they went tomorrow, there'd be no opportunity to say goodbye to Sergio, which was rude when he'd been such a good host. Nick's powers of diplomacy weren't great at the best of times, but tonight he was quite drunk and decidedly stoned. Also, he'd seen how much black Kevin had crumbled into the joint that he was rolling at the moment. If Nick was going to do this, he'd best broach the subject straight away, before his thoughts trailed off.

The joint was already lit when Nick returned to the patio. A low moon hung over the rolling mountains beyond. From this angle, the pale disc was reflected in the small swimming pool. Nick stared at the moon in the water.

'Here, have some of this,' Kevin Bone passed Nick the joint.

Sarah's dad was going to fat, but he still had a full head of dark, thick hair. At a distance, when you couldn't see the bags beneath his eyes or the broken veins around his nose, he could still pass as a youthful hippy. Nick toked on the joint, the black hash clouding corners of his mind that had been operational mere moments ago. He had worked out what to say, but already forgotten how he was going to phrase it. Best just get it over with.

'Sarah wants to go to Palma tomorrow.'

'Fine. There's a train just after eleven. I can take you to it. You wouldn't get long, though. There's only one train back.'

'We were thinking of staying there an extra night.'

'Oh.' Kevin frowned. Nick handed back the joint.

'The idea was that you could take us, I think. Show us round a little, have lunch, help us find a place to stay. Then we'd have more time to explore before we fly home on Monday.' There, he'd got it out.

'Ah. Sergio will be sorry not to come. He'd planned to take Sunday off.'

'Yeah,' Nick said, awkwardly. 'That's a drag.'

'Fuck it,' Kevin said. 'I'm too stoned to decide anything now. We'll work it out in the morning, yeah? Time for a brandy.'

Before Nick could argue, Kevin had poured them both huge glasses of Metaxa. Nick wasn't keen on the stuff. Too sweet for him.

'Sarah mentioned that you met my dad. How is the old goat?'

'In good form, I think,' Nick said.

'Felicity looking after him?'

'She seems to spend a lot of time with him, yeah.'

'Always the way.'

Was there a hint of something there? Nick had wondered about the father and daughter-in-law relationship, but the only time he'd tried to broach it with Sarah, she'd freaked out.

Nick remembered a question he'd wanted to ask. 'I can understand you not wanting anything to do with Felicity, but Hugh's your dad. If you don't mind me asking, why do you never have any contact with him?'

Kevin took a big gulp of brandy. 'I don't mind you asking.'

Nick sucked on the spliff. He thought of handing it back to Kevin, but decided to wait until he answered. It was that time of the night, when everything slowed down and it was okay to bogart the joint. Where did that phrase come from? *Don't bogart that joint, my friend*? He knew it was a song. It was on the soundtrack to *Easy Rider,* performed by the Holy Modal Rounders, though he didn't remember it being in the film itself. But where did the phrase originate? Something to do with Humphrey Bogart, maybe?

'The thing about Hugh is, he's not what he seems.'

'Pardon?' For a moment, Nick had forgotten what question he'd asked.

'I'd go so far as to call him a traitor. To me, to Sarah, to his country. He's one of those people who always gets his way and doesn't give a damn about the people who get in his way. Are you going to hand that joint back?'

Nick passed the spliff. He didn't know how to respond to what Kevin had just said. Everyone resented their parents. It was the nature of the relationship: both sides made mistakes: you grew up and got over them.

'Maybe it had something to do with your being gay,' Nick suggested, gently. 'A lot of people of his generation just don't understand it.'

'Bollocks,' Kevin said. 'Dad was at Cambridge in the thirties. Half the guys he hung out with were queer. He didn't see my being gay as a problem, he saw it as an opportunity. I'm telling you, he's a calculating bastard.'

'You'd better not let Sarah hear you saying that. She idolises him.'

'There are things I could tell Sarah that'd change all that in a heartbeat. But she wouldn't take them from me, matey. Maybe from you. She's in love with you, I can see that. You're good with each other. And you're more like me than her precious grandad. So there's hope for her yet, though she's still got some of her mother's prissy, uptight small town snootiness. Do you want the dirt on Felicity?'

Kevin handed Nick the joint back. He took another slurp of the brandy, which Kevin topped up. His head was beginning to feel decidedly fuzzy.

'You'd better let me think about that for a minute,' Nick said. Did he want to know secrets about Sarah's mother? He could barely hold onto the smallest thought. He spoke without knowing what he was about to say.

'I don't... want to hurt Sarah,' he said. 'Do me a favour, and don't upset Sarah. She'll come round to you eventually. You're her dad, after all.'

'No, I'm not,' Kevin replied.

53

1999

Still no sense of time. Day or night, it was all the same. The gaps between his visits had grown longer, or maybe it just seemed that way. He could leave her here and nobody would find her. Deborah could starve to death. Her mouth was dry, and she felt cold. Not physical cold so much as a kind of numbness. She hoped he hadn't fled the country, leaving her here to starve to death.

Or maybe he'd been arrested. The police must have worked it out by now: who had her, and why. Could be he was hiding out upstairs here, wherever *here* was, and coming down to rape her when he felt like it. Could be the gaps between visits were getting longer because he was becoming bored with her. Or he was trying, in his perverted way, to make her dependent on him, make it so she looked forward to his visits.

Whatever. She would give him what he wanted.

Deborah lay on a mattress that smelt of him. Before his last two visits, she had arranged herself there, tried to look alluring, insofar as a woman with her hands tied behind her back could manage that. She had done her best to please him, to act pathetic. He had been a little surprised at first, then told her what he wanted her to do, became more excited when she complied. Last time, he had taken the gag off before he raped her. It was the hardest thing she had ever had to do. Rather than scream, she had let him ram his tongue between her lips, then gratefully given other favours with her dry, ulcerated mouth.

While waiting for him to return, Deborah exercised: stretches and sit-ups, as far as the ropes binding her arms and ankles would allow. She had to remain supple. When she rested, though, she stretched across the mattress with her legs apart. The defeated victim. The willing sexual slave. Next time, he would expect it to be like it had been before. He might give her a little more freedom. Or he might decide to kill her. Either way, she was prepared.

Eve phoned Nick while he was on the train home.

'They let Geoff go,' she said. 'He had an alibi.'

'Why did they pick him up in the first place?'

'An anonymous call.'

'When?'

'Late this afternoon.' Just before Nick arrived at Andrew's, then. 'Of course, Geoff thinks I made it. He phoned earlier, raging. Somebody had to have told the police about Chantelle and me seeing him leave the brothel. And since it wasn't her, it must have been me.'

'Are you OK?' he asked Eve. 'I mean, would Geoff try to hurt you?'

'He hasn't before, but there always has to be a first time. I'm worried he might turn up here. I should have changed the locks.'

'He's probably over it now,' Nick said. 'I'd come straight to yours but I'm on a train. It doesn't get in until around eleven.'

'I could pick you up,' Eve offered.

'Well...'

'School doesn't start until Thursday. I could stay at yours.'

Nick understood what this offer involved. Before Chantelle, he would have been more than tempted.

'Please, Nick,' she said.

'Of course,' he told her. 'I'll sleep on the sofa. Come stay at mine.'

He hung up and returned to the computer he'd stolen from Andrew.

'You like this now, don't you?' He'd undone himself and his stubby cock poked out between the buttons. Deborah nodded and tried to look grateful.

'They all learn to love it.' He tore off the gaffer tape that covered her mouth. 'Once you've had this, you're spoiled for anything else.'

'It's so...' Deborah tried to sound innocent and scared, but excited at the same time, '...fat. It fills me up.' She braced herself, then added, 'Let me lick it.'

Terence lifted her chin and looked into her eyes. This was the biggest test of her performance. 'Are you messing with me?' he said.

Deborah made herself sound even more vulnerable now, utterly beaten.

'I'll do anything you want.' She thought of adding 'just let me live', but didn't want to remind him that every aspect of her behaviour was governed by fear for her life. 'Why don't I stroke your balls while I suck? Nick taught me to do that. Would you like me to?'

Should she have mentioned Nick? It seemed to be OK. Terence was smiling. 'He might have taught you a few things,' he told Deborah. 'But I can teach you a few more. By the time I'd finished with her, that Nancy gave the best blow-job on the planet.'

Deborah put on her sweetest smile. 'If you untied me, I could hold you while we do it.' Was she laying it on too thick? 'Or hold myself up while you come in from behind,' she added. 'Whatever you want.'

Terence hesitated. He was thinking about it.

'Whatever you want,' Deborah repeated. 'Wherever you want.'

'You can have a little reward.'

He gave her some water from the bottle, then began to untie her hands.

'Try anything stupid and I break your neck. Understood?'

She nodded, lowering her eyes to denote fear, modesty, whatever would convince him to let her suck his cock without her hands tied behind her back. She remembered what she had learnt at college. The tip was the softest part of the penis, and the area with the most sensation. Hurt him there and he would be in too much agony to break her neck. She hoped.

He got out the sharp knife he kept in his jeans and cut her bonds. Deborah stretched. Her arms were stiff and her hands felt tingly, grubby. How many days had it been? Terence handed her the water bottle. She dropped it.

'Sorry,' she said. 'So sorry,' and found herself crying for real. Could she do this?

'It's OK, honey.' He handed her the bottle, then slid off his jeans and boxers. He was already more than half erect and she worried that he would want to fuck her straight away rather than let her fellate him.

'Why don't you undress for me?'

She did as he asked, slowly removing the sweatshirt and tracksuit bottoms he had provided her with. Beneath it was the silk dress that she had worn for New Year's Eve, badly torn now. Her bra and knickers had gone the first time he raped her. They were shoved in a corner by the mattress.

She felt very cold but tried not to show it. She peeled the dress from her body and stood proud, pushing out her plump breasts for him to admire. When his cock began to rise, she gave him a big smile. He smiled back.

'Kneel,' he told her.

She did as he asked, then began to lick. Terence sighed with pleasure. She pulled her wide lips over her teeth and sucked him. Although it made her want to gag, terribly, she sucked him deep into her, moving her head in and out, while he moaned with delight, lost in rapture.

'Yes,' he said, 'yes. That's right, keep doing that.'

She pushed him into her and pulled out three more times before she relaxed her lips, remembering how her last boss, the dentist, used to tell her she had the best teeth he'd ever seen. The strongest, too.

She used them.

54

The route to Nick's flat from the station side of town was complicated. When they got to Alfreton Road, Eve wanted to weave her way through side roads. He told her not to bother.

'Streets that way are a warren, lots of dead ends. Wait until Forest Road.'

'It'll be even more difficult once they start building the tram lines. They're going right outside your house, aren't they?'

Eve kept making small talk like this. Probably, it was good for him. She was keeping him distracted, but it got on his nerves.

'That's your old flat, isn't it? Above the locksmiths. It seems an age since Chantelle and I helped you move.'

It wasn't an age. August. Less than five months ago. The mention of Chantelle only served to remind both why they were here. He did not reply. They turned right onto Forest Road West and Eve started speaking again.

'The police told me her real name, when they thought they had Geoff for kidnapping her. Deborah. Deborah Bryce. Can I cut down here?'

She was indicating a right turn that led past All Saint's Church, onto Waverley Street.

'Sure.' These badly lit roads were still partially cobbled. Buildings full of bedsits rubbed shoulders with crack dens and the homes of large families, usually second or third generation immigrants who needed the space provided by tall terraces with deep basements. Until this moment, Nick had forgotten seeing Andrew go into one of these houses a few weeks ago. A property visit, he'd assumed. Andrew had been on about buying places close to the new tram route while they were cheap, making a killing.

Now that Nick was paying attention, he noticed something out of place. From behind, the woman running down the street looked like, but couldn't be, the woman they had just been talking about. She wore a donkey jacket, which was unusual. Eve saw what Nick was staring at and slowed down.

'Is that…?'

'It'll be a working girl. They don't usually come down here though.'

'What's she wearing? I think she's barefoot.'

Eve stopped the car. The woman who looked like the woman who was not called Chantelle but whom Nick could not yet think of as Deborah turned the corner. It was her. She was running to his flat. To him.

'It is, isn't it?' Eve said.

'Don't spook her,' Nick replied.

Eve turned onto Waverley Street and parked opposite his building.

'Let me go to her first,' Nick said and got out of the car.

Deborah was at his gate now. He saw that Eve was right, the cop was barefoot. Deborah raised her head. Her shoulders slumped when she realised that there were no lights on in his flat. Nick waited for a car to pass, then ran across the road. Hearing his rapid footsteps, Deborah half turned, her face filled with fear. Recognising him, she threw herself into his arms. Her body shook. Whether the tremors were from the cold or shock, he didn't know.

'It's OK,' he told her. 'It's OK. I'm here now.'

Eve joined them. Still holding Deborah, Nick fished in a pocket for the house keys and handed them to Eve, who opened the door. He led Deborah inside, up the stairs, into the cold flat, where he only stopped holding her for a moment, to switch the gas fire on. He turned to find her leaned against the sofa, bloody and dazed, then realised where he had seen the donkey jacket before. Terence wore it the day that he and two of his heavies threatened Chantelle.

'Would you like me to help you wash?' Eve asked Deborah.

Deborah shook her head and spoke for the first time.

'Forensics.' Her voice was surprisingly calm. 'There should be some clothes in the chest of drawers over there. Get me two sets. One to wear now, one for after the examination.'

'Do you want me to call the police?' Nick asked.

'No. I need to get my head together first. They'll have me in the rape suite for at least an hour.'

Her body was still shaking. Eve returned with the clothes. Nick helped her dress. He found it hard to look at her. She had been badly bruised. Strangely, there was blood smeared around her mouth.

'I'm not who you think I am,' she told him, after she had sat down on the sofa.

'I know what you are,' Nick said. 'Did Terence do this to you?'

She nodded.

'He grabbed you from outside the party on New Year's Eve?'

'Knocked me out with a baseball bat. Stupid thing was, my undercover had already been closed down. I didn't get enough evidence. But I wanted to see you one last time.'

'And you thought Andrew would be there.'

This time, when she looked at him, she was a stranger.

'He told Terence what I was.'

'Did Terence tell you that?'

'Not in so many words, but Andrew Saint is Terence's boss.'

'Are you sure?'

'There's nobody else it could be. I don't think he owns the brothel, but I'll bet he owns the building where I was being held. Terence was told where to find me and when. And he kept promising that, soon, he was going to kill me. He was waiting for the word.'

Nick remembered what Andrew had said earlier, about

dumping Chantelle's body on the steps of County Hall. Nick had taken it as a bad joke.

'There's something I need you to get rid of.'

She reached into the pocket of Terence's donkey jacket and flinched. Then her look changed to one of surprise. She pulled out a cheap phone.

'I didn't know this was in here. You'd better not touch it. Prints.'

It was switched on. She opened the messages. Nick read them over her shoulder. There were only a handful. Terence must be fastidious about deleting them. The most recent was sent at ten, while Nick was on the train.

Do it tonight, the message read.

'When did Terence come to you this evening?' Nick asked.

'An hour ago, maybe. After this was sent.' She began to shiver. Nick went and got the blanket from his bed to put around her.

'How about if I get you some sweet tea?' Eve offered.

'Yes. Yes, please. And you'd better call the police at once, now I think about it. He might send someone here, after me.'

Nick felt stupid that he hadn't thought of that himself. There were two locked doors and two flights of stairs between them and the outside world. He looked out of the window. Nobody on the street. He heard Eve on the phone.

'Police. And an ambulance. We have a woman here who's been raped.'

'Give me the jacket again,' Deborah said.

Nick did as she asked. She reached into the same pocket as before. 'Promise you'll get rid of this for me.'

'Of course,' Nick said. 'But what…?'

'I had to bite really hard,' she said. 'I thought he might stop me, but he was screaming with agony. Then I nearly swallowed it. Luckily, I choked.'

She handed him the bloody tip. 'I had to bring it with me,'

she told Nick. 'If they catch him, and the medics get hold of this, they might be able to sew it back on.'

Once again, Sarah found herself speaking in the House of Commons, even though parliament wasn't in session. She was giving her resignation speech.

'This is not about what my father was, or what he did. You can't choose your parents. But you can choose your friends.'

'You dated a drug dealer,' someone from her own side yelled. 'He'd spent five years inside. Don't pretend you didn't know what he's like.'

'That's true, but so what? He served his time.' Why not say this? She was standing down. There would be a by-election. Labour would lose. 'But the drug trafficker this house should be concerned about is a much bigger player, one who was also my friend, Andrew Saint. My continued friendship with Saint has been a gross error. For this reason, and for this reason alone...'

A phone began to ring. Sarah snapped awake and looked at her alarm clock. 1.30 AM. It could only be Nick.

'She's alive. She was being held two hundred yards up the road from me. She escaped earlier tonight, just before I got home, came straight to my flat.'

'That's wonderful,' Sarah said. 'You must be so relieved.'

'The police took her away a few minutes ago. I wanted to go with them, but wasn't allowed.'

'Did they get whoever was holding her?'

'Not yet. They've been combing the streets.'

'Was it that Geoff guy?'

'No. Terence had her. She thinks he was working for Andrew. So do I.'

'How did she escape?'

Nick told her. Sarah gasped. She'd read that it was possible for a woman to bite off a penis, but had never heard of it happening.

'He raped her, Sarah. Repeatedly. If anyone deserves it...'

'I'm sure he did. I'm just worried that he got away. With that kind of injury, however...'

'This time, the police asked me about Andrew.'

'What did you tell them?'

'I'd confronted Andrew and he claimed to have nothing to do with the kidnap. And I told them that he and Nancy were about to go on the run.'

'You gave him away?'

'I had to. You see, there was something else.' He told her about a text message that Deborah had shown him on Terence's phone.

'You think it was from Andrew?'

'Who else could it be? I told them where he was planning to go. I also gave them Andrew's laptop, which I took from his house. There might be something incriminating on there. I looked at it on the train, didn't find anything suspicious, but I expect the police will be more thorough than I was.'

'You did the right thing,' Sarah said. Now she understood why his bag looked so heavy when they left Notting Hill. Hopefully, there was nothing on the laptop about Dad's villa in Majorca. But if there was, so be it. She'd done nothing unethical where the villa was concerned.

They talked for several more minutes, getting their stories straight. Nick had not mentioned Sarah's being at Andrew's earlier. He'd told the police he went to confront Andrew about whether he was involved in the kidnap, but had not done so because Eve phoned to tell him of Geoff's arrest. He'd told them Andrew had worked out that Deborah was an undercover cop, but claimed not to know how he had worked it out. Nick had taken the laptop because he remained suspicious of his former friend and wasn't completely convinced that Geoff was responsible for Deborah's disappearance. The police appeared to have accepted all of these explanations at face value.

'Are you going to see Deborah again?' Sarah asked, when

they were done.

He didn't reply for a few seconds. 'I don't know Deborah. The woman I knew doesn't exist.'

'Maybe the person she made up for you was more real than the one who became a police officer. All those years ago, when I left you and joined the police, I felt that way. Like I was pretending to be someone I wasn't. Like my true self was a secret identity, and you were the only friend I'd trusted it to.'

Another long pause. Sarah regretted being so forthright. This wasn't the right time to talk about how and why they had broken up, all those years ago.

'You should have told me all that,' Nick said, finally. 'We could have talked it over. We might even...'

He didn't finish the sentence. They wished each other a good night.

55

Three months later

Nancy had something to tell him. Andrew had an idea what it might be. He distracted himself by opening a bottle of good Rioja. Then he took the shrink-wrap off a DVD he'd bought in Palma the week before, a film called *The Big Lebowski*. She'd seen it at the cinema and insisted that he'd like it, although stoner comedies weren't his thing. Nancy deserved a treat. She'd been clean for more than two months, using nothing stronger than red wine and cigarettes. Though she'd have to give those up if he was right about what her news was.

The external renovations were done. Andrew had sweetened the builder with two hundred euros to delay his informing Sarah, lest she decided on an early visit. He doubted that she'd be so inclined. Majorca in winter was no picnic: grey and cold. Not as cold as the UK, maybe, but the villa wasn't geared up for winter, with cold tile floors and no central heating. It had started to warm up recently, but the Easter parliamentary recess was three weeks away. By then, he and Nancy would be in South America.

Andrew had enough money to buy a new identity and live comfortably for a year or two. After that, if he didn't find a new income stream, he would need to sell the London house. Probably he would need to sell it anyway, to finance a new business. He'd had enough of moving drugs. Too much violence, too many sharks. The last time wasn't the first time he'd been ripped off. This time, though, it wasn't his money. Which made it so much worse.

The villa didn't have internet access, but Andrew bought

an occasional UK paper. He'd read how Chantelle Brown had escaped, and Terence Tailor had been captured. Good. For the time being, Tailor's boss would have bigger things to deal with than the million plus that Andrew owed him. Still, it made Andrew uneasy, ripping off people he hadn't met. Luckily, Tailor's boss – whoever he was – couldn't be all that competent. Chantelle had managed to get away, after all, while he couldn't even get Tailor out of the country undetected. He was unlikely to track Andrew down here, so far from the beaten track.

Nancy joined him in the living room, fresh and fragrant from a long bath. She let her gown fall open, so that he could see the sides of her plump breasts, her rounded belly and dark, soft pudenda.

'Think I'm putting on weight?' she asked, as he handed her a glass.

'A little, maybe. It suits you.'

'Liar!'

'I'd love you whatever size you were, my sweet.'

'That's good to hear,' she said, leaning over to tickle the beard on the underside of his chin. 'Because I'm about to get a lot bigger.'

'You're...'

'I think it happened the day we got here, but I only just took the test.'

He'd never asked her about birth control, had assumed, given her profession, that it was all sorted.

'It's so long since I had a period I didn't notice at first when I missed. But then I started to feel... something. So I bought a kit in Palma yesterday.'

He kissed her for a long time.

'You want me to keep it?' Nancy asked, gently, when he pulled away.

'Of course I do,' Andrew said. His head began to fill with vague visions of a family future. Not here, but in Brazil, or

Argentina, whichever suited best.

'Where will we go?'

'Somewhere wonderful, I promise. But right now, let's go to bed.'

Sunlight streamed through the blinds. Most men fell asleep after sex but Andrew rarely did. Instead, it was Nancy who dozed while he planned their joint future. The first thing he must do, he decided, was change his will. That might prove complicated, because his current will was at a solicitor's in London, where he dared not return. Now that Nancy was carrying his child, he needed to make her his sole beneficiary. And soon, in case Andrew's enemies caught up with him before the baby was born. Come to think of it, he didn't actually need access to the old will, provided he made a valid new one.

He heard a noise. Had he locked the front door? Almost certainly, but Nancy had been outside after him and she wasn't always so security conscious. Especially today. Footsteps. Oh shit, Andrew thought. It must be Sarah. She had a key for the place and it would be just his luck for her to show up so early in the season, ready to inspect her property. The builder must have sent his final bill after all. She'd want to check the place out before she paid him.

The footsteps sounded too heavy to be Sarah's. Of course, she'd brought Nick with her. That felt appropriate. Here were Andrew's oldest friends to hear his good news and see the happy couple off to a new life. He could brazen this out. Dust had had time to settle. Nick was bound to be over Chantelle by now. The cop had, after all, lived to tell the tale. And Nick was back with Sarah. The three of them could, perhaps, be friends again. Or, at least, part amicably. Surely they wouldn't try to hand him to the cops. Not that the cops had anything on Andrew, anyway, nothing substantial. It wasn't them that Andrew was worried about. There was no way the police even knew where Andrew was. Andrew had only taken one small risk. When he was leaving Notting Hill so hurriedly, he hadn't been able to find his laptop. And there might – probably not, but possibly – be some emails remaining in which he discussed the villa renovation project.

More footsteps. Doors opened and closed. Andrew sat up. Should he make himself known? Nick and Sarah would not be expecting to find him here. He needed to launch an immediate charm offensive, give them the full Saint bonhomie, insist they share in the celebration of his partner's pregnancy. He could fix this. Maybe he should wake Nancy so that she was forewarned.

Too late. The bedroom door opened. Andrew greeted the shadow in the hallway with a cheesy smile.

'Surprise!'

But the stranger in the doorway was not Nick, or Sarah. And he was holding a gun.

56

'Are you ready to return to duty?' The Chief Constable asked.

'I've been ready for weeks, sir.'

'No need to call me 'sir', Deborah. You're not seconded to my force any more. It's Eric.'

'Forgive me if I'm not comfortable using your first name, sir.'

Eric smiled sympathetically. Deborah was meant to appreciate that he'd come to her parents' home with a bouquet of lilies. Instead she worried that the Chief wanted to catch her off guard, that he was setting some kind of a trap.

'How have you been using your time, these last few weeks? I hope the counselling sessions have been useful?'

'They have, sir. But mainly I've been studying for my sergeant's exams.'

'I'm sure you'll do well. In the meantime, I've recommended you for the Queen's Gallantry Medal.'

Gallantry was a very odd word for what she had done, but Deborah kept this thought to herself. 'That's very good of you, sir.'

'It's the least you deserve.'

Deborah tried to imagine the citation. *Over a period of days, Constable Bryce succeeded in portraying herself as a defeated victim who had become a willing sexual slave, persuading her kidnapper to relax his guard until she was in a position to bite off his penis and make her escape.* So far, the sensational aspects of the case had been kept from the media, but people in the job were bound to have heard them. The story of Deborah's humiliation and violation would follow her for the rest of her career, no matter how successful she became. Were she to marry, change her name, move to the other side of the UK, it would do no good.

There weren't enough women of Afro-Caribbean origin on the force for her to become anonymous.

Her counsellor said that you had to turn your weaknesses into strengths. She must make this work for her. Already, when she encountered fellow officers, even the Chief, she could sense a new wariness: you didn't mess with a woman prepared to bite off a cock.

The Chief Constable still looked uncomfortable. She had no intention of making him feel comfortable, but decided to force his hand.

'I suppose you've come to see me about the court case.'

'You've been carefully prepared, I presume.'

'Yes, sir.' Terence Tailor had been caught at Dover, trying to leave the country on a fake passport. He would plead guilty to rape and kidnap and ask for the offence of living off the proceeds of immoral earnings to be taken into account. Deborah would give evidence in camera, so that she could not be identified. Neither prosecution nor defence thought that there was any use in making the case notorious by referring to Tailor's castration.

'Did you find out who he was working for?' she asked.

'He won't inform on any of his accomplices. There's insufficient evidence to bring any drug charges against Tailor. However, once he's facing twenty-odd years, he might want to earn remission and change his mind.'

'I still think his boss was Andrew Saint,' Deborah said. 'And I think Saint ordered him to kill me.'

'We never found Saint. He suggested to Nick Cane that he was going to the Bahamas, but there's no record of him or his mistress having arrived there. And there's no proof that Saint was behind the 'do it tonight' text. It was sent on a pay-as-you-go phone bought in Arnold under a fake name. It could just as easily have been Tailor's Nottingham boss, whoever that is. We do know that Saint made the call claiming Geoff Shipton was behind your kidnapping.'

'Surely that proves something?'

'Only that he knew we were closing in on him. You may be right about Saint's involvement in distribution, but there was only a brief interruption in the city's drug supplies when Tailor was arrested and Saint vanished. Which suggests that we didn't take down the kingpin Tailor was working for.'

'What about the laptop that Nick Cane gave you?'

'It had an interesting internet history, but there was nothing directly incriminating on it.'

'What was interesting about the history?'

'I'm afraid I can't tell you that.'

Which meant what? Deborah knew that Saint was tied up with Sarah Bone, who was a close friend of the Chief. Saint also had a bigwig Tory MP in his pocket. The idea that Eric knew all this and still came to see her, that he expected Deborah to play along, that kind of hypocrisy made her sick to the stomach.

'Did you find out who owned the house where I was being held?'

'A drug dealer called Frank Davis. He's serving a long prison sentence. Presumably Tailor knew that it was empty and took advantage of this.'

'Or Andrew Saint did. Did you find out who owned the brothel?'

'The brothels were bought with mortgages that were immediately defaulted. It takes building societies up to a year to repossess, by which time the brothel has moved on. The names on the mortgages led nowhere.'

Now that Deborah had all the details, it was time for the big questions.

'Do you know how Tailor found out I was undercover?'

'No, but some procedures were lax. Lessons have been learnt. In future, we'll leave this kind of operation to Special Branch, who have the expertise to create more substantial legends for officers in your position, genuine birth certificates, the works.'

While he waited for her to respond, his left eye twitched, a sign of stress. She wasn't going to let him off the hook.

'Did Sarah Bone know that I was an undercover cop?' Deborah asked.

Eric ignored the question, but the corner of his left eye twitched again, which was answer enough.

'It was very good of you to bring me up to speed,' she told the Chief Constable, her tone polite but formal, a dismissal. 'Thank you for the flowers.'

She let him shake her hand before he left. It was the game. Deborah was twenty-five years old and planned to be an inspector by the time she was thirty. A superintendent at forty, if she held her nerve. She'd been promised a transfer to Traffic after she passed her sergeant's exams. Modern policing didn't get more prestigious than that. The last few months would turn out to have been worth all the pain.

That was what she kept telling herself. One day, she might believe it.

57

Three weeks later

Nick and Sarah took a flight to Majorca from East Midlands Airport, just as they had nearly fifteen years earlier. They hadn't spent this much time together since 1984. It was early in the season and the flight was only half full, so they had a free seat between them and the aisle. While they were waiting to take off, Nick told Sarah about his new computer course, which he had been talked into by a young woman called Jerry, who Sarah suspected he was seeing, although he insisted he was merely helping her study for A-levels.

It was an early flight. The day's newspapers had only arrived at WH Smith's minutes before they boarded. Sarah didn't look at her *Independent* until they were in the air. She found a short account of the Terence Tailor trial. Tailor was portrayed as a violent pimp. Deborah Bryce was given the anonymity due to rape victims. Her role as an undercover police officer was not revealed. Tailor had been sentenced to fifteen years imprisonment. After serving his time, he would be deported to Jamaica.

Sarah showed the report to Nick.

'I went to the first day of Tailor's trial,' Nick told her. 'It was strange to be in a courtroom again, on the other side.'

'Did you know any of the other spectators?'

'No, but Terence recognised me from the dock. He stared me down. I realised it was a mistake, giving in to my curiosity. I didn't go back after lunch.'

'You wouldn't have been able to see Deborah's evidence anyway. They held it in camera.'

'I glimpsed her when I was leaving. I didn't recognise her at first. She'd lost weight and her hair was pulled back. She had on these narrow glasses, made her look like a university lecturer, maybe, or an accountant.'

'Did she see you?'

'For a second. The expression on her face was like I'd stepped out of a bad dream. Then she lowered her eyes, stared at the floor until I was gone.'

'And that hurt?'

Nick hesitated. 'Sort of. It underlined that what went on between us wasn't real.' He gave a grudging laugh. 'Since you and I split up, I've had a poor track record with women. Every single one has lied to me then left me.'

'You're exaggerating.'

'Only a little. But Chantelle's lies were in a different league.'

'It's the liar who hurts themself, not the person who's been deceived.'

'Says the MP. Don't politicians have to lie all the time?'

'And we hurt ourselves every time we do.' She changed the subject, but only a little. 'Have you heard from Andrew, or Nancy?'

'Not a thing.'

'Still think he was behind it all?'

'The police didn't find any evidence on that laptop.'

'Or if they did, it didn't suit them to use it.'

'What do you mean?' Nick gave her a sharp glance.

'I used to be in the police, Nick. There are plenty of bent coppers. Some are in the Drugs Squad. Whoever was behind Terence must have had a tame detective or two in their pocket.'

'Maybe. There was somebody following Andrew and he was very paranoid about it. I assumed it was the Drugs Squad, or CID.'

'You assumed wrong.' Sarah decided that it was time to tell him about Gill's 'due diligence'.

'How long did her investigation last?' Nick asked, when she was done.

'She decided to resign from Saint Holdings before Christmas.'

'Then who was outside Andrew's the last day we saw him?'

'I don't know. But it wasn't necessarily the police Andrew was running from. That night, in the restaurant, he was on edge, certainly not the guy I used to know. He'd become reckless. Maybe he was telling the truth when he said that he had to leave the country because he owed money.'

'There's something else I've been trying to figure out,' Nick said. 'When the police raided the brothel, they brought out five people. Four of them were in the news, including Andrew. But there was a fifth.'

'What did he look like?'

'All I know is he was white. The guy covered his head with his coat as he was being led away. It was an expensive looking coat.'

'Must have been somebody who could pull a few strings with the police, but that doesn't mean he was there for any reason other than to get laid.'

'Thing is, what if Andrew wasn't Terence's boss?' Nick said, thinking aloud. 'Which is more than possible, given the difficulty Andrew had tracking Terence down. Suppose Terence's boss was the other guy they arrested, and Andrew was there to meet him? On the day of the brothel bust, Andrew told me the police had nothing on him because the money man hadn't turned up. Suppose the guy he was meant to meet was the one who covered his head...'

'And he's well enough connected to have his name kept out of it.'

'Then who is he?'

'If he's that well connected, we'll never find out.'

They hired a car at Palma airport. Nick offered to drive. The island hadn't changed much. Sarah had never been so early in the year before. The valleys were even greener that she remembered. The steep, verdant terraces thronged with wild flowers. Once they joined the winding, narrow roads that took them past Deia, towards Soller, the traffic got hairy. Sarah was glad she wasn't behind the wheel. It took an hour to reach the port of Soller, where a lawyer was due to hand over the keys to the villa. On the harbour front, Nick insisted on buying Sarah a straw sun-hat. She bought him a baseball cap advertising the Brooklyn Dodgers.

Sarah had sent money for the necessary refurbishments and the house was now up to code. Or so she'd been told, in a fax from the local lawyer. He was on his lunch break, but the keys had been left at his office. Sarah asked what state the villa was in. The secretary didn't understand the question.

'Is there somewhere comfortable for us to sleep?' Sarah asked.

The villa had three bedrooms. Sarah sort of hoped that only one of them would be fit for use, as this would speed along the inevitable.

'I think, yes. Housekeeper looks after.'

'No housekeeper,' Sarah began to say, then thought better of it. Probably a mistranslation. The lawyer would have arranged for a cleaner to come in after the builders were done.

The villa – or *finca*, as Kevin sometimes called it – was off a side road, halfway between Soller and Deia, halfway down a single track road that ran towards the coast, but did not go all the way to the cliffs. They used to be able to reach a cove near Muleta by following a wild path from near their back door. Sarah hoped that this area hadn't been developed. Building there was difficult, with so many steep, narrow terraces between the house and the coast.

'Once you've seen the place again do you think you might change your mind about selling?' Nick asked, once they were back on the road.

'Too much history. But I'm looking forward to a week when nobody has any idea where I am.'

'Nobody?'

'Well, Mum. She doesn't have the address, though. The only other people I told about this place are you, the Spanish lawyer, Gill and Andrew.'

And Eric, but she decided not to remind Nick of the chief constable's part in her romantic history.

'The police will have the address, if they had a good look at Andrew's email,' Nick pointed out. 'When I went through the stuff on his laptop on the train that night I found some deleted emails to his Spanish lawyer about the builders there. It would have looked too suspicious if I'd double deleted them.'

'Eric didn't say anything.' So much for not mentioning him.

'Do you still see him?'

'He rang me up to invite me to his retirement do this summer.'

'I knew he was old. I didn't think he was that old.'

'He's 54. That's ancient in police terms. He was really phoning to tell me that he's got engaged, to a solicitor younger than me. And good luck to him.'

58

Nick felt reassured that Sarah had no romantic interest in the police boss. Since they started planning this trip, she'd been giving him signals that she wanted to get back together. That was why, three days ago, he'd broken things off with Eve. They'd been… comforting each other, he supposed you'd call it, since the middle of January. There was an inevitability about their reunion. They were good for each other. But they weren't cut out to be a long term couple. Eve was only three years younger than the Chief Constable. Nick wanted to be with someone he could have children with. Eve already had kids at university, was too old to have more even if she wanted to.

This holiday had been the catalyst for their split.

'I think we should take a break,' Nick had told her, in bed, in the dark.

Eve didn't answer straight away. He thought she'd fallen asleep. Then: 'You want to sleep with Sarah in Majorca. It's OK. One gets more broadminded as one gets older. I'm fine with this being an open relationship.'

'I'm not. I can't work that way. Tried it once, felt guilty whichever one I was seeing.'

'Oh.' Eve sounded surprised. Maybe they didn't know each other as well as he thought. Or maybe…

'Are you sleeping with someone else?' Nick asked, catching on.

'I've been seeing Martin once a week since that party and things are… progressing.'

Which meant she was.

'Does he know that you and I…?'

'God, no.'

'That's not how you define an open relationship.'

'I suppose not. You won't tell him, will you?'

'He knows that we had a thing, once?'

'He knows that.'

'We'll leave it there, then.'

Another secret Nick was forced to keep. Martin was an old mate. They had been out for a drink a fortnight ago. Neither man had mentioned Eve. They would go for another drink in a couple of weeks' time, when Nick returned from Majorca. Her name probably wouldn't pop up then, either.

'Did you say something about the lawyers providing a housekeeper?' he asked, as he slowed down to look for the narrow lane that led to the villa.

'The secretary said something about a housekeeper, but I never said I'd pay for one. I expect that whatever she meant was lost in translation.'

They turned into the tree-lined driveway, which reminded Nick of the road into Sarah's grandad's old pile, near Chesterfield, if on a smaller scale.

'Stop!' Sarah said, although the house was still round the next bend.

When they got out, Nick saw what she had spotted. Two marble gravestones, one lightly weathered, the other new: *Kevin Bone, 1939-1986* and *Sergio Mantelo 1951-1998.* Both men had died at the same age, Nick realised, 47, only ten years older than he was now: two generations ravaged by AIDS. Sarah crouched by the stones and took a tissue from her pocket. Silently, she wiped away the grime that had settled around her father's name and dates.

'Let's walk from here,' she suggested when she was done.

The pool had been filled, but not recently cleaned. The patio outside was dusty. Sarah went to unlock the door and it swung open.

'Wait!' Nick told her.

There was a crack in the doorjamb and the lock casing was twisted. The door had been kicked in.

'Stay back,' he ordered. 'Have your phone ready, just in case.'

'I don't think there's a signal,' she said, but he went in anyway. Whoever had done this would be long gone, or there would have been footprints in the dust. Still, best to make sure. He walked through the kitchen. There was food by the sink. A packet of corn flakes, half a loaf that, when he felt it, was rock hard. Two desiccated apples in a bowl on the shelf. A shrivelled peach.

There was a short corridor off the kitchen. It led to three bedrooms, a living room and bathroom. It was nearly sixteen years since Nick had been in the house, and he couldn't remember which room was which. The first bedroom he came to was empty, with only a stripped mattress on the single bed. The second was tiny, and stuffed with boxes. It would need clearing.

The room opposite, Nick remembered now, was the living room, where they used to retreat when it was too hot to sit outside. He opened the door. The room he found might have been abandoned the day before. There were magazines and two empty glasses on the coffee table. An open bottle of wine, half full, sat on the tiled floor, by the large TV. Only a thin layer of dust betrayed the owners' long absence. That, and the framed Miro print propped against the wall, which Nick remembered from his previous visit. It sat beneath the wall safe that it used to conceal.

'Nick?' Sarah called. 'Where are you? Is everything OK?'

'I'm in the living room,' Nick called. 'There's been a burglary.'

She joined him. 'What have they taken?'

He pointed to the hole in the safe's door mechanism. 'Looks like they helped themselves to some wine while they took turns to drill into the safe.'

'I doubt there was much of value in it. The lawyers didn't mention a safe, but whoever did this has saved me the trouble of having it opened.'

Nick reached into the safe and pulled out a few papers. He spread them out on the coffee table. Miscellaneous documents in Spanish. Kevin Bone's birth certificate and passport, presumably kept for sentimental reasons. Sarah took her father's passport and flicked through the pages. It had last been stamped in 1970, the year Kevin came to Majorca. A photograph fell out. Nick picked it up from the floor. The candid image could have been from a *Carry On* farce or a McGill postcard, were it not so explicit. He took a closer look.

'Oh.' The naked couple were Sarah's mother and grandfather, caught in flagrante, their embarrassment evident in their shocked faces. Sarah stared.

'You probably didn't want to see that. How come..?'

'I have no idea. And I don't think my mum's likely to tell me, do you?'

She put the photograph in her bag without another word. Nick opened a window. The room was suffused with a rancid smell that was starting to get to him. Warm air was better than the stench.

'These magazines,' Sarah said, holding up a copy of *Hello* magazine, 'they're only a few weeks old. What would Spanish builders be doing with British gossip rags?'

Nick felt a terrible foreboding.

'Stay here,' he said. 'There are two rooms I haven't checked yet.'

The next room along was the bathroom, which had a short bath as well as a shower. Towels were draped over it. The shelf above the sink was filled with bottles. Nick recognised some of the brands: for hair styling and make-up removal. He knew who they belonged to. Maybe, he told himself, maybe they heard the men coming and had time to run for it. Maybe Nancy, at least, escaped. He opened the final door, to the master bedroom.

The bodies were naked and bloated, but still recognisable. They had both been shot in the head. Nick closed the door and returned to the bathroom, where he vomited in the sink. Sarah hurried in behind him.

'What is it?' she asked. 'What's wrong?'

He told her.

59

Six weeks later

'This is my treat. To make up for missing your retirement do.'

'No need to apologise,' Eric told Sarah. 'You've had a lot on your plate.'

The former Chief Constable flicked through the rich dishes on the Rules menu, made decisions. First thoughts, best thoughts, in his experience. He suggested they share a bottle of Châteauneuf du Pape.

'I'll only have a glass,' Sarah said. 'I hardly drink at lunchtimes.'

Women always said that, and never kept to it. Eric gave Sarah his most unctuous, admiring smile. She had worn a dress for him: light green, which wasn't really her colour, but the neckline showed off plenty of cleavage, and that he appreciated. He liked how the MP, so keen to seem worldly, remained a little awkward when it came to men she fancied.

Eric hadn't given up on bedding her. They had come close, more than once, but Sarah wasn't another of his eager to please, anxious for promotion police women. At first, he'd thought it was his being married that put her off. Then he'd become single, which seemed to put her off even more. She'd kept him at a distance and had an affair with Paul Morris, who was very married. Once Eric had remarried, to a woman younger than Sarah, the MP might become interested again, be flattered that he still wanted her, and finally succumb. He would bide his time.

The waiter arrived. Sarah finished looking at the menu.

'I'll have the monkfish,' she said.

Eric ordered his steak rare. Sarah got down to the real reason she had invited him to lunch.

'Have there been any developments in the Andrew Saint case?'

'The Spanish police had very little to go on. They checked the lists of people who visited the island during the relevant period, but found nobody suspicious. Officially, it remains a violent burglary. Saint was known to have a great deal of money. Presumably much of it was in that safe, in cash.'

The killing of Andrew Saint and Nancy Tull had had one unexpected benefit: it scuppered Sarah's reunion with Nick Cane, who had long been a thorn in Eric's side. Cane had taken control in Majorca, sent Sarah straight home, dealt with the authorities, and closed up the house before he returned to the UK. He had also made sure that the Spanish lawyer didn't mention Sarah's name to anyone. Since her return, Sarah had asked Eric to help keep the story out of the press. However, he'd had nothing to do. Cane had already done it all.

The wine arrived. Eric insisted that Sarah be the one to sample the bottle. She took a deep gulp.

'You didn't go to the funerals?' Eric asked.

'I took your advice and steered well clear. Haven't seen Nick since he came back. We spoke on the phone just the once, after the story died down. He said he hadn't had any press enquiries at all, so thanks again for that.'

Eric gave a modest half-nod. 'Do you recall the laptop Nick Cane took from Saint's house in Notting Hill? You'll be pleased to know that it was lost. So there's no trace of your connection with Saint in our files.'

The disappearance of that laptop had been convenient for other reasons. There was evidence on its hard drive that could, had a conscientious copper investigated it thoroughly, have implicated Eric and his chief associate. It may also have suggested that Saint had misappropriated a large sum of money from Eric's associate, and this led to his elimination. But Eric had loyal officers on the enquiry squad, ones with their own secrets to protect. The computer had been smashed to pieces and dropped into a deep section of the Trent.

'I felt bad,' Sarah said, 'not going to Andrew's funeral. We went back a long way. Nick said only a handful of people were there. Just family and him.'

'Not just family. We had an officer present, in case anyone of interest showed up. At Nancy Tull's, too. That was rather better attended. People like to forgive a fallen woman. There is one thing I should say about Nick Cane.'

Sarah put down her glass, which she was already halfway through.

'I've already told Nick – I can't stay in touch with him any more. I care about him, but he does have this tendency to drag me into awkward situations.'

'And you'll no longer have me to drag you out of them, I'm afraid.'

She reached over and squeezed his hand. 'Don't think I don't appreciate it, Eric. I really do. I sometimes wonder why we never quite...'

He gave her his sincerest smile. 'Part of the reason that I never pressed you was your close involvement with Cane. It's still not clear how deep his association with Saint ran. He was in Saint's will, I'm told. I had to be careful who I associated with, even by proxy. Of course, none of that matters now.'

Sarah smiled gratefully, accepting that it was he who had held back, even though it had always been her. How easy it was to rewrite the past. If only the future were so straightforward.

'You're getting married soon,' she said. 'Life's all about timing, isn't it? Do promise me that we'll stay good friends, trusted friends. I need somebody outside politics that I can rely on to be straight with me. Believe it or not, you're my best friend.'

Eric reached beneath the table and squeezed her knee.

'I promise,' he said.

60

1984

The Lords wasn't sitting, so Hugh went to Ashley Gardens first. When he visited the flat, he was told that the former Prime Minister had gone for a walk.

Since leaving the Commons, the ex PM had become Baron Wilson of Rievaulx of Kirklees in the County of West Yorkshire, but Harold never went back to Yorkshire. These days, he rarely strayed far from his stately London flat. He was fond of St James' Park, so Hugh tried there. Sure enough, after five minutes, Hugh found the baron sat at a wooden bench, watching the ducks. Harold seemed unaware of the alky who occupied the other end of the bench; an unappetising figure who lacked both front teeth.

Hugh approached them. Harold stared into space. The alky recked of piss. Hugh fished in his wallet for a pound note and offered it to him.

'Take this and leave us alone, will you? I want a word with my friend.'

The drunk departed with alacrity. This got Harold's attention. His hair had thinned and he looked old. Hugh, his senior by several years, was looking old himself. And ill. The doctors said he'd be dead by Christmas. Pancreatic cancer. This would be his last chance to have a long talk with an old friend.

Hugh had, at least, enjoyed five good years of retirement. Quality time with Flic. He'd stood down from parliament at the 1979 General Election, the one where the Tories first got back in. Harold had hung on for another four, useless years at the Commons, only retiring last May. He'd spent seven years in parliamentary limbo, for he had resigned as Prime Minister not long after his last formal meeting with Hugh.

That evening, in 1976, Harold had hinted to Hugh that he was about to go, but Hugh had misinterpreted him. He'd thought he was being offered a job, not being warned that he was about to lose his protector. No complaints: Harold's successor, Jim Callaghan, had sacked Hugh in the friendliest possible way.

Hugh sat next to the man who had won Labour four out of five General Elections.

'Harold, how are you? It's Hugh. Hugh Bone.'

'I know who you are.' Bit of a twinkle in the eye. 'Hugh. It's been years. Very good to see you. How's that lovely daughter of yours? Sarah, wasn't it?'

'Sarah's well, thanks. Have you heard the latest? She's only joined the police force.'

'Better than MI5. She'd have had to chase her own brother.'

Hugh smiled. Kevin was still in Spain, out of harm's way.

'I've always wanted to thank you,' Hugh said, 'for keeping my secret all those years.'

Harold chuckled. 'About your secretary having your baby? I've kept much bigger secrets than that. Marrying her off to your son so you could keep her close, that was shabby behaviour. It's why I didn't promote you for years.'

Harold sounded sharp as a new pin. Hugh was relieved to find him on one of his clear days. He'd had a long operation for bowel cancer in 1980. Since then, his memory had deteriorated badly. Alzheimer's, some said.

'Kevin and Felicity were happy with the arrangement at the time. She kept her small town respectability. He was rewarded with a well-paid job that gave him a reason to live in London. Even so, deep down, I always knew that was the reason you took so long to have me in the cabinet.'

A benign smile. 'Is that why you came, to tell me that you knew I knew but couldn't say so before?'

'Partly. Mainly because there's something I need to apologise for,' Hugh said. 'Confess, you might say. About MI5.'

'Never apologise unless you're cornered.' Harold looked Hugh straight in the eye: a familiar, no-nonsense gaze. 'About MI5? It was you who first told me the full extent of the plots against me. I didn't believe you at the time, but it was worse than you said. They were all after me. So it's I who should apologise.'

'One of my oldest friends in MI5 was one of your biggest enemies,' Hugh told him. 'Peter Wright. Used to be the Chief Scientific Officer.'

Harold frowned. 'I don't remember that name. Was he important? Was he the fifth man they're always talking about?'

Hugh shook his head. 'No, he wasn't. Actually, Harold, that's what I wanted to confess. You see, I was the fifth man.' He paused. 'Or the fiftieth, or the five hundredth. There were so many of us.'

'You.' Harold stared at Hugh, with no recrimination in his eyes.

'Yes. I joined the Communist party when I was a teenager, at Cambridge. Never left. Sometimes it seems like more of my generation were working for Moscow than for their country.'

'It does. I was never one of them, though. I expect you were told that.'

'I didn't know for sure.'

Harold thought for a moment, as though considering his verdict. 'Did you do much damage? To the country, I mean.'

'I don't think so.' Hugh hesitated. 'One doesn't get told. Betrayal is betrayal, but I never had the names of agents in the field. Budgets, decisions about weapon systems, how much we knew about the Soviet operation, those were the sorts of thing I passed on. I must have done some harm, I'm afraid.'

Harold frowned. 'And this happened while you were working for me?'

'Before, mostly. I all but stopped passing intelligence on once

I got into parliament. Never completely. I needed money, you see.'

Harold mused on this for a moment. 'So it was for the money as well?'

'At first, not at all. But, after the stroke, there was Edith to look after. Then Sarah came along and I had to keep Kevin sweet. It got complicated.'

The warmth went out of Harold's voice. 'Life always gets complicated,' he said. 'Yet I find it hard to understand how a man can carry on for so long, living a lie.'

'You learn to lie to yourself, I suppose.'

'Yes, I expect that's it. Why are you telling me all this?'

'To make amends. You did right by me, but I tried to manipulate you. I so badly wanted to be in the cabinet. I fed your most paranoid fears.'

Harold shook his head emphatically. 'I had to be paranoid. They really were out to get me. You weren't though, were you? I never got the sense that you were a rival. As for what you just told me, well, you were only trying to protect your son.'

'No, I was a spy long before Kevin was born. I...' Hugh stopped. There was no point in repeating himself. 'What I'm saying is that the pathetic bit of spying that Kevin did was the result of his carrying on a family tradition. It was in the genes. Either that, or I instilled it in him when he was very young.'

'Instilled what in him?' Harold asked.

'The art of the double life. Treachery.'

'Treachery's a hard word. Still, I'm glad neither of mine followed me into politics.'

'I don't think Sarah got the bad seed. She's always seemed more innocent, more passionate than Kevin or I. More intelligent, too.'

Harold thought for a moment. 'We all want the next generation to outshine us, don't we? But it can't always be the way. Especially with people like us who...' He paused, then picked up the sentence again. 'People who...'

The former Prime Minister turned to look at a pigeon that had decided to perch on a nearby litter bin. Hugh waited patiently. You never knew how long the clear spells were going to last. It had been this way last month, and the month before. Harold turned back. His eyes lit up again.

'Hugh! It's been years. Very good to see you. How's that lovely daughter of yours?'

The old man stared at the lake, willing himself to remember. 'Sarah, wasn't it?'

A note from the author

Wherever practical, the historical details concerning public figures who appear in the preceding pages stick to the known facts. Of those who appear, George Brown died in 1985; Peter Wright and Harold Wilson died in the same year; 1995; James Callaghan and Edward Heath both died in 2005. With this novel I am particularly indebted to the late Ben Pimlott, for his fine biography *Harold Wilson* (1992). I also made some use of Peter Wright's *Spycatcher* (1987).

Thanks to my old friends Georgina, Paddy and Martin for reading drafts of this novel. Also to my intrepid new editor, Russel, and my indefatigable agent, Al. Another old friend was my premier source of parliamentary research on this novel and its predecessor. Meg Munn stood down as MP for Sheffield Heeley at the May 2015 general election. Therefore I can, for the first time, publicly credit her helpful, ongoing assistance, while pointing out that Sarah Bone is not in any way based upon her. Thanks, Meg.

Biography

David Belbin is the author of more than thirty novels for teenagers and has been translated into twenty-five languages. These include the bestsellers *Love Lessons* (1998), *Festival* (2002) and *The Last Virgin* (2003). In 2004 David established Turning Point, the UK's first conference on Young Adult fiction. He was born in Sheffield but has lived in Nottingham since going to university there. He now teaches Creative Writing at Nottingham Trent University. *Bone and Cane* (Tindal Street, 2011), the first in Belbin's crime series, was an Amazon bestseller. The second in the series is *What You Don't Know* (Tindal Street, 2012).